A SHOT AT LOVE

Taylor LaVonne

WINTON PUBLISHING
TL PUBLISHING

TL PUBLISHING
An imprint of Winton Publishing
Wintonpublishing.com

ISBN 9798218742553 (paperback)

Printed in the United States of America
1st Printing

This is a work of fiction. The likenesses of famous or public figures have been used fictitiously. The author does not speak for or represent these people. The opinions expressed in this book are those of the characters and should not be confused with the author's or with those of the actual persons mentioned.

*To all the women who broke the glass
ceiling and came away bleeding,
this love story is for you.*

Author's Note

I began writing this book in 2021, before Caitlin Clark, before Angel Reese, before the WNBA playoffs were entirely televised on ESPN, before the NCAA even *allowed* women to use the title "March Madness" for their end-of-season basketball tournament. I was frustrated with the lack of equality in women's sports and wanted to subvert the sports romance stereotype by having the main athlete of my romance novel be a woman instead of a man. I wanted to write about the joy sports bring me, the joy the WNBA brings me, but also include some of the harsh realities of being a woman athlete.

Don't worry—this is still a romance novel with a gooey and sweet relationship at its core! But the subplots relating to gender inequality, the pay gap between the NBA and WNBA, and the media coverage women receive are also important. I am delighted to report that there have been great strides made in the realm of women's sports in the last few years, but there are still some glaring issues (looking at you, WNBA salaries!).

So, while this novel might not be a perfect representation of the WNBA today, it is an amalgamation of many decades of ups and downs.

A *Shot at Love* follows an entirely fictional WNBA team called the St. Louis Arrows. However, many of the opponents and athletes my fictional girls play against are *real* teams and *real* people. The reason for this was that I wanted to celebrate the women athletes who inspired this book, particularly all the players in the WNBA. However, it's worth noting that I know none of them personally. I tried to only include them in a celebratory and positive light, but please do not make assumptions about them or their character based on my writing. Also, I tried my absolute hardest to put players on the correct teams and update rosters as they changed, but publication moves slowly, and the WNBA moves lightning fast. If you notice a player on the wrong team or a fictional injury, it was for plot purposes only.

I hope you give the women of the WNBA, or other women in sports, a chance. They are the reason I even picked up the pen this time around.

And if you're just here for an epic love story, I don't think you'll be disappointed.

Taylor LaVonne

Chapter 1

I can tell something is wrong the moment I'm ushered over to the post-game interview.

Jadea is usually the one interviewed after a game, and she is a consummate professional. She mentions every possible teammate, Coach Rembert, the rush of the game. She's humble, she's bright, she flashes that fierce smile, and the media eats it up. Me? With my red frizzy hair falling out of its braids, freckles overshadowed by red splotches and a sweaty brow, stuttering and nervous as the mic hovers nearby—no, just no.

I rack my brain as I walk over to the scorer's table. My stats tonight were decent, and we beat Phoenix easily, both points in my favor if I was the only one on the court. However, Jadea had a triumphant 24 points and 11 rebounds. Allyson, our center, had four blocks. *Those* are interview-worthy stats. My 13 points and eight assists are slightly above average, especially for a point guard, but it's nothing to shout about. I'm not the star you usually see on ESPN2 after the game.

If we even make it on ESPN2.

I see Misty Haverford waiting for me, exchanging whispers with her crew and gesturing at her cameraman. The more I look at them, the more nervous I become, a cold sensation lingering in the pit of my stomach. A post-game interview should be exciting, but I've never been one for making speeches or being thrust into the spotlight. That's why Jadea and I are the perfect team. I dish and she swishes.

Was there something important about the day? An anniversary? A holiday to commemorate? Did I reach a statistical milestone? I rack my brain, trying to put the pieces together.

The day started just like any other St. Louis Arrows' game day. Arch Arena was in full swing for our evening rout against the Phoenix Mercury. Jadea came out of the locker room early as usual, and I followed her, her phone clutched in my hand. Clint, the arena manager, hustled over when he saw us cross the court.

"Are you sure this is a good idea, Miss?" He looked at Jadea nervously, then behind her as a crew set up a trampoline beneath one of the baskets.

Jadea grinned at him, taking the microphone he offered. "Clint, women hear every day that their version of sports is less entertaining. Less competitive." Her smile did not waver as she surveyed the crowd. The arena was still filling up with the scarlet and white decked out fans. She turned back to Clint, in full Jadea Jones superstar mode. "This ensures that we stay on the map. That they *see* us."

Clint gave her an admiring look and bowed his head, ceding center court to her. Some fans noticed our early arrival, giving a shout of recognition. I waved shyly, stepping behind Jadea's shoulder as she gave the crowd what they wanted.

"What's good, St. Louis?" she roared into the mic, and they screamed back. The arena wasn't even full, which is common on weekday games, but it made my heart flutter to see them engage with her so passionately. I could see our moms sitting together a few rows up, waving scarlet and white pom poms. "Who's ready to see me play MY GAME?" The fans went crazy, and Jadea smirked, passing the mic off to Clint once again. I can't imagine pumping the fans up, saying the right words to make them cheer, but Jadea has that talent fizzing through her blood.

I held her phone at the ready, stepping back as she approached the basket. One of our assistants passed her a basketball.

And it began.

Overhead, the scoreboard showed a pre-recorded video of Jadea. I gave it the same curious look I always did. Pre-recorded Jadea looked just like the Jadea in front of me. Wide, happy smile, dozens of thin braids pulled back from her face, some of them dyed our beloved scarlet, St. Louis Arrows' white uniform gracing her muscled body.

Video screen Jadea pointed at the crowd. "People say women can't dunk!" I swiveled back to the Jadea in front of me and watched as she dunked the ball into the basket that didn't have the trampoline set up beneath it. She leaped in the air, right hand arcing up, feet spread wide. She looked like Michael Jordan's fire-spitting niece. The ball jammed through the hoop, and the crowd roared. I let myself smile, glad to see Jadea unhurt and grinning again. I kept the phone's camera trained on her, live streaming her routine for her million-plus Instagram followers.

When the crowd quieted again, Jadea put a hand to her ear and lifted her other into the air, pumping them back up again. She pointed at the scoreboard. Her pre-recorded self continued. "People say women can't compete in a dunk contest!" Jadea dribbled up to the trampoline this time, effortlessly passing the ball back and forth between her legs. The crowd noise built in anticipation. When she finally hit the trampoline and took flight, a hush fell. She had an incredible hang-time, passing the ball in between her legs and then stuffing it into the hoop.

The eruption from the crowd shook the arena. Jadea hung on the rim and pumped her fist, and I saw a little girl in the first section with her hands on her cheeks, eyes comically wide. I couldn't help but laugh a little at Jadea's audacity. No one in the NBA would ever dare put on a show at every home game, too worried that they might injure themselves. Their agent, their coach, *their team* would kill them. I know Coach Rembert felt that way about Jadea's little show. Our agent, Jermaine, certainly did. But to Jadea, it was worth it. She was doing this for the WNBA, for her peers, for all women athletes. She wanted to refute any complaints people had about women's basketball. It must have felt like being a show pony sometimes, which she didn't deserve, but she wore it well. She never complained. She didn't even wince when people mentioned that the NBA would never force their athletes to put on a show.

Pre-recorded Jadea finished with her last plea. "People say women CAN'T HOOP! Who's ready to watch your St. Louis Arrows play today and prove them wrong?" The response was as deafening as our crowd could manage.

Jadea ran in for the finale. She sprinted up to the trampoline, the ball clutched in both hands. I didn't recognize the approach. Jadea and I have worked on her dunks since we were kids, playing on her driveway court. But this one was unfamiliar, and I steadied the camera to make sure its glory was captured for her Instagram audience.

I wondered if my gasp was audible on the livestream as Jadea front flipped once and dunked the ball. There was sharp silence and then a cacophony of screams and shouts of disbelief. Jadea grinned as she dropped back to the ground. I ended the livestream with shaking fingers. How long had she been working on that one? What if she had hurt herself? Coach was going to kill her.

This was confirmed when I saw the rest of my team coming out for warm-ups. Coach Rembert stood at the edge of the court, arms crossed. Olabisi, one of our shooting guards, shook her head in disapproval. Jadea approached center court and waved to the crowd, bowing and saying thank you.

The trampoline was hurriedly dragged away, and I walked over to Coach Rembert. "Annie," she looked at me sharply, "did you come up with that one?"

I tugged nervously on one of my braids. "No, Coach." I couldn't help but try to defend Jadea, my best friend of two decades. "You know why she does it. She thinks she can help create change." I didn't need to explain what I meant by change. Even as the NBA hurtled ahead with $250-million-dollar contracts, cutting-edge sponsorship deals, and every one of their games televised in some capacity, the WNBA played for sloppy seconds. We got some TV time, but usually on smaller networks, and some games were lost completely to the average viewer. A rookie's salary never touched the million-dollar price tag, and most of us have to play year-round overseas to make enough to live.

Coach Rembert considered me and then Jadea, who was finally heading towards us. "If she breaks her arm, her leg, even her *thumb*, our season is over. She might want to think about *that*."

I opened my mouth to respond, but Coach turned away. I nibbled my lip, torn. I understood Coach's worries, but that smaller, angry part of me was glad Jadea was turning herself into something unforgettable. Women deserve glory, too. However, was she losing that glory by doing something professional men players would never lower themselves to? That's how I felt when she first started doing it. What was the right call for a professional woman in sports?

I snap back to the present, realizing I'm steps away from only my second post-game interview this season. And the first one was because I had a season-high 18 points and 14 assists. That was understandable. This? Not so much. Thinking of Jadea's dunk show before the game, I try to reassure myself. Maybe they want to talk about her. Or us. We are the WNBA's favorite come-up story. Both born and raised by single mothers in St. Louis, both attended Stanford University a year apart, both randomly drafted to their hometown team, a team that had been created by owner Jack Smith and his family's billions only *two years* before Jadea's draft class. The NBA's St. Louis Archers and the WNBA's St. Louis Arrows, established in 2019.

It sounds like a dream, a fantasy, complete make-believe. I still pinch myself when I wake up in the morning and lace up my custom scarlet Jordans.

I give Misty a smile, covertly wiping some of the post-game sweat off my upper lip. Hopefully, the red splotches have begun to recede. I'm standing in frame now, Misty only a few feet away. She's our local sideline reporter, as this game is not being nationally televised. Her assistant hands me a mic. The cameraman adjusts his position, and I try not to look his way, unnerved by the way the camera lens looks like a big, unblinking eye.

Misty doesn't return my smile, and I shift nervously. If *I* seem nervous, Misty seems even more so. The alarm bells begin to go off in my head. "Hello, Annie," Misty says, glancing between the camera and my face. "Great win today." Usually, Misty is genuinely excited to talk to us about the game, as she is a huge proponent of women's sports, but now she seems almost stiff. She shifts from one leg to the other, tucking her hair behind her ear.

I tilt my head and try to sound at ease, like Jadea would. Or Lynn. Or almost any of the other badass women on my team. "Hi, Misty. Yes, it was a tough win today against Phoenix, like it always is. I respect them and their style of play so much. Fortunately for us, we were playing our best basketball."

I mentally high-five myself. Mike, our team's PR guy, would be delighted by my answer. I notice Misty's fingers unclench and clench around her mic. I'm not even sure if she heard my response. "Annie, I apologize in advance if you find this next line of questioning too personal, but we would like to give you a chance to respond to new allegations."

I instantly stiffen, reacting to her pointed choice of words. Apologize? Personal? *Allegations*? These interviews are essentially fluff, a few questions about the game and the season, maybe a joke or two. Hard-hitting journalism it was not. I steel myself, but even then, I'm wildly unprepared for what she says next. "Would you like to respond to a report that came out today about your father?"

Your...*father*?

Immediately, my eyes begin to fill with tears. A knee-jerk reaction to stress, one I haven't been able to kick since I was a kid. I blink several times and manage to croak out, "My father?"

Misty presses on, but the look in her eye is apologetic. "An anonymous source came forward this afternoon saying businessman Jack Smith, owner of the St. Louis Archers and Arrows, is your father. Care to respond?"

The tears become nearly blinding, and I can hardly think of a response; I'm trying so hard to keep them from falling. Jack Smith? *My father?* He's in his seventies. He's a billionaire. I've only met him in passing a few times, and there was zero indication that we had any hidden father-daughter bond. Misty is waiting, and now some of the crowd, who had been filing out, are also waiting, and I can see Jadea and Coach Rembert's worried faces in my peripheral vision, and I finally blurt out the truth. It comes out husky and broken, not clear, not easy. Not sounding like the confident woman I want to be.

"I don't know who my father is."

There is a sudden flurry of activity. Jadea and Coach come into frame, Coach stepping in front of me, Jadea ripping the mic out of my hand and dropping it. She hooks my arm with hers as the tears fall down my face, and pushes me across the court, towards the locker room.

I can hear Coach Rembert's cold voice behind me. "That was uncalled for, Misty."

As Jadea ushers me off the court, I can't feel my fingers, and a chill has once again settled in the pit of my stomach. Just as we enter the tunnel, I look up to where I know my mom is sitting in the 100 section. I can see her frozen figure for just a moment, decked out in my jersey, sitting next to Jadea's mom who is whispering in her ear and clutching her arm. I wish I could see her expression, but they're too far away. My eyes drift up to the VIP boxes, and I imagine that Jack Smith is up there, looking down at the chaos.

It's not possible. It can't be.

That's not why Mom wouldn't talk about him growing up. It's not because my mysterious, absentee father was a *billionaire*. A billionaire who owns me. My team.

My dream.

As soon as the crowd can't see me, the tears really start flowing. Jadea pulls me towards the safety of the locker room. "Are you alright?" She sounds worried, a tone I rarely hear from her.

"I don't know." I try to wipe a few tears away with trembling fingers. "It must be a big misunderstanding, right? Jack Smith is married. He has a son who's older than we are. Why would he know my mom?" I'm stumbling over my words, unsure what to think. I can't shake the cold, nerveless feeling sweeping through my body. "It has to be a mistake, right?" I look at Jadea, ready to feel comforted by her dismissive attitude towards the report, but she still looks worried.

I sit down by my locker room stall and wait for my mom to come down like she always does after a home game. Wait for her to tell me it's crazy, that Jack Smith, the owner of my team, is *not* my father.

But she never comes down. And the cold feeling never leaves.

Chapter 2

I decide the only strategy against a scandal of this magnitude is to hide in my apartment indefinitely. The night of the game, I stumble home and head straight for bed. When I wake up, this will all be gone, I reassure myself. My mom and Jadea will figure it out, and my life will go back to the way it was. Point guard of the number one team in the league. Best friend to a megastar. Daughter of a kind, hardworking social worker.

Instead, I wake up the next morning to someone pounding on the front door. I know without checking that it's Jadea. She lives in the nicer building across the street, a perk that comes with being the first pick of the WNBA draft, but that short walk never deters her from coming over. What I don't expect when I open the door is to see our shared agent, Jermaine Flowers, standing with her. He and Jadea met at a gay bar they both frequented at Stanford where he impressed her with his knowledge of women's basketball and business acumen. She waited for him to finish graduate school and then plucked him to be our agent.

Seeing the two of them with their game faces on already exhausts me, and I fight the urge to shut the door. Jermaine and I have never clicked the same way he and

Jadea have. They're both confident, brash, and bold. He admires her no-holds-barred style of play, and she admires his similar style as an agent. However, my subtler style of play grew on him, and he bluntly told me as I entered the draft, "It never hurts to have a straight, white girl on my roster."

"We're coming in," Jadea announces. Jermaine follows behind her. I glance around the apartment, hoping there isn't anything too embarrassing that Jermaine might comment on. My books are shelved nicely, my gray sectional clear for sitting, no visible garbage or laundry in the living room. My kitchen also looks clear, except for the Twizzlers package that I demolished last night as a stress-induced 2 AM snack.

Jermaine gives the Twizzlers a cursory look, which is his way of being kind. We all headed to the living room in silence. Jadea considers me as we sit down. "How are you doing, Annie?" I know I look like a mess. My braids from last night's game are still in, frizzier than ever—a clear sign I never hit the showers—my eyes are puffy from numerous bouts of crying, and I'm wearing my most worn-in Stanford sweat set, which I've never stepped out of the house in.

"My mom texted." My lip trembles, but I viciously blink back the tears. I pull my phone out of my pocket. "This is all she said."

I pass the phone to Jadea, who reads it with Jermaine peeking over her shoulder. "Please, honey, let me explain. There's more to the story." Jadea's eyes widen as she hands the phone back to me. "So, she's basically admitting it's true."

I nod glumly. "I haven't responded. What is there to say? I've been on the Arrows for *three seasons* now. It seems like she could have mentioned that the owner is my mysterious absentee father before I got ambushed with it."

Jermaine sighs, leaning forward to look me in the eye. "Even without your mom's texts, the feelers I put out confirmed the report. They were unable to find the source who leaked it to the press, but the word on the street is that it's someone close to Jack Smith. No one seems very worried about the validity of the story." My head is already spinning, wondering who would spill Jack's secret. Why now? The affair between Jack and my mom would have happened decades ago. Did someone just find out about it?

"Has Jack released a statement?" Jadea asks.

Jermaine and I both nod at the same time. I haven't been able to stay away from social media, watching masochistically as people report and react to the news. Jermaine is the one who answers first. "His publicist basically said that it was a personal family matter and asked for privacy from the media."

I snort. Jadea looks aghast. "He's not denying it either?" She gets up, nervous energy oozing out of her. I watch her custom rainbow pride Jordans pace across my living room. "I mean, this isn't bad for Annie, right? Jack and her mom had an affair, which sucks, but it's not that unusual. Especially for a billionaire, right?" Jadea cuts straight to the point.

She looks at Jermaine. He sighs again, and my heart sinks. "If he were just *any* billionaire, sure. Annie might deal with some light heckling or added press, but it would fade quickly. However, Jack Smith *owns* the St. Louis Arrows. It seems damning that Annie plays for his team."

I press my trembling hands in between my knees, trying to hold them still. "I saw the stuff on social media. I know what you mean."

Jadea looks between the two of us. "What stuff?" I can already feel her growing indignation on my behalf. It shows just how worried she's been about me that she hasn't been on her socials.

I remember scrolling through Twitter (my brain still actively resists calling it X) last night, seeing the reactions to the situation.

"Annie Larger's daddy bought her spot in the league, it's obvious."

"The WNBA claims to be progressive and ready to rise above men's sports and yet they attract a billionaire scandal. Who's talking now, WNBA?"

"Anyone remember how surprised they were that Annie got drafted at all? Her stock was so low people were shocked when she was taken early in the second round."

"How much of Annie Larger's success has to do with her daddy pulling strings behind the scenes?"

"Crying real tears because she's upset or crocodile tears because she wants to look sympathetic?"

"Annie   Larger   is   just   another   example   of #billionairenepotism."

When Jadea hears Jermaine rattle off a few, she grows furious. "This is bullshit. Annie fought harder than anyone to get into this league. The Arrows saw her for who she really was, and now she's second in the league in assists and fifth in steals. She is the starting point guard on *my* team. No one can doubt her talent!"

I reach out and squeeze Jadea's hand. I appreciate her support, but every woman athlete knows how difficult it is to get respect in the world of sports. I essentially lost all of mine in one fell swoop.

I focus on Jermaine's stoicism. "What's the plan? Lay low?"

Jadea makes a sound of protest, but Jermaine nods. "Unfortunately, Jack's statement is the best avenue to take. We deny any mismanagement regarding the team and reframe this as a personal, family issue. We try to make it no one's business. Refocus on basketball."

Jadea opens her mouth to argue, but I squeeze her hand again, and she goes quiet. "I think that makes sense. I've never been good at articulating myself and that video of me crying is *not* helping my case. I'll just keep my head down and play. That's it."

Jermaine nods sharply. "I'll post something to that effect on your socials." He stands up to leave, and I surprise him with a hug.

"Thanks, Jermaine."

He holds my gaze, resolute. "We'll figure this out, Annie. I won't let them tear away all your hard work."

Once he's gone, I sag against the couch, closing my eyes. Jadea comes to sit with me. Her voice is softer now, her anger over the situation temporarily shoved down. "How are you, really?"

I don't open my eyes, trying to breathe evenly and not let any more tears fall. "You know how we were raised, Jadea. We didn't need our dads because we had the best moms in the world. They're best friends. So are we. I might have had some questions about my dad during my teens, but I understood my mom not wanting to indulge my curiosity. How would knowing who he was soften the blow that he never gave us the time of day? It would only hurt more."

My face crumples. "And it *does* hurt. It hurts so much. Not only does my biological father have the power to destroy everything I care about, but my mom never clued me in to that very possibility. How could she keep this a secret from me? And how could he ignore me after being in such close quarters for years? None of it makes any sense."

Jadea loops her arms around me, leaning our heads together. I sniffle, feeling a little relief that she's here and she's on my side.

"Thanks for being here," I finally say, voice wobbling.

She squeezes me gently. "Nowhere else I'd rather be."

We sit in silence for a while longer, clinging to each other.

*

I'm not surprised when I hear the key turning in the lock. Jadea left an hour ago, promising that she'd be by later with my favorite Thai take-out and more tissues.

I'm sitting on the couch scrolling mindlessly on my phone when my mom walks in. She looks almost as rough as I do. Her scorching red hair, a shade brighter than mine, is pulled into a sagging topknot, and she's wearing a very old pair of jeans with a hoodie. Not her typical fashion-forward, colorful style. We both look like faded photographs of ourselves.

I don't have an immediate reaction as she comes into the living room. There are so many ways I could go. Anger that she kept Jack a secret and let me be ambushed. Sadness that my life has been upended, and she hasn't forced herself into the mess until now. Relief that my mom is here, and she won't leave until this is fixed. Everything is so jumbled; I can't pluck out one emotion.

When she sits down, I notice she's already crying. I get those trigger-ready tears from her. Whether it's a sad commercial for ASPCA, a colleague's breakup, or a failing grade on an exam, they're hard to squash. I've spent years trying to curtail them, at least in public.

I wait for my mom to say something, but I know she's doing the same thing. As a school social worker, she knows how to let that silence bleed until you cave. "Mom." I swallow some of my own tears down and try to focus. "Why didn't you tell me about Jack?"

Her watery green eyes train on me. "Well—"

I hold up a hand. "No. Not when I was a kid. Not in college. I understand that. I imagine he was some smooth-talking, charming one-night stand who was very uninterested in having a kid. He already had one. But when I got drafted, Mom." Here, my voice cracks, and she places a shaky hand on her forehead. My words turn pleading. "He owns the team. Me, essentially. And I never knew. Do you know what I could be accused of? What he could be? And because I didn't know about him, about this situation, I have no defense! No plan!"

"Defense?" My mom looks bewildered. The words surge out of her, jumbled and quick. "Against what? We had a brief affair. I was drowning in grad schoolwork, catering on the side for extra cash. We met at one of his foundation dinners. He was exciting and said he was separated from his wife, and he helped distract me—"

I cut her off. "I would never accuse you of breaking up a marriage. If he lied or went back to his wife, that's in the past. We've made it 25 years without him, and personally, I believe we could go a hundred more." I lean forward and grab her hands, holding fast. "But I love basketball, Mom. I love it more than breathing. I breathe *better* when I play." There's some anger now in my words. I'm probably gripping her hands too hard. "And now there's a real chance I could lose it. All I can think is—do I deserve to be on the Arrows? Was he involved in drafting me? Did he insist upon it? Do you know *anything*?"

The understanding that floods my mom's face is both a relief and a blow. If she doesn't know anything, she isn't complicit in anything that goes against league regulations or good sportsmanship. However, I'm still in the dark about Jack. How to defend myself when I don't know the truth?

My mom shakes her head, her top knot bouncing precariously. "When I told him I was pregnant, he explained that he had decided to stay with his wife. We had only been together a couple months, and I think a part of me expected him to back out. He was in his forties and had been with Tiffany for decades. To rip that apart—I understood. I was a fling. A billionaire's fling." I flinch at her harsh words. "When he said he didn't want to be in your life, I was almost relieved. I felt very sure about you, Annie Bananie." My childhood nickname falls easily out of her mouth as she squeezes my hand. "He offered to make a child support agreement, but I didn't want his money. I told him to leave you to me." She takes a shaky breath. "And he did. I sent him a picture of you each year growing up, and he sent a thank you card. That's it."

The flood of information is overwhelming. My mom has always been a free spirit. She has a few tattoos from her youth she regrets, a propensity towards wearing overalls, a delightful habit of singing every morning to wake you up, a few boyfriends, but nothing that stuck—the best mom. To imagine her standing up to a billionaire at twenty-four is shocking. I knew I had a biological father out there who hadn't wanted to be in our lives, but besides a few moody years as a teen, I never let that fact bother me. I had Elaine Larger, the mom who refereed my childhood one-on-one games with a bright orange whistle around her neck.

I try to gather more information. "But what about when I was drafted? You knew he owned the Arrows. When they were first founded, he was always on the news."

I remembered when Jack announced it. St. Louis hadn't had a basketball team in decades and when he announced not only an NBA team, but also a WNBA team, my heart started pounding. I was just beginning college and suddenly playing for my hometown was possible. The WNBA was gaining traction, albeit very slowly. Maybe women could become household names—just like Steph, MJ, and LeBron are. I overlooked Jack Smith's silver spoon money, made in the 1800s from his family's Arch Railways, and instead saw a man who was willing to bet a tiny bit of his money on women. On *our* success.

My mom lets go of my hands guiltily. "I knew I should say something. When you were drafted...higher than you thought, I wondered if he was trying to be a parent. Just that one little blip. And I...understood." My jaw drops. "He's not your father. I don't consider him to be. But maybe when he saw that you might lose your dream, he couldn't resist. I didn't want to tell you, because...I don't know. It could have just been a coincidence."

I feel a flash of cold, then an even brighter one of hot anger. I stand up. "Mom, this wasn't just *my* dream. It was hundreds, maybe thousands of women's dreams! Getting drafted into the league is almost impossible. There are only fourteen teams, and each year, they have only one or two spots available. Even if you're drafted, you could be cut soon afterwards! What if I took someone's spot?" The tears flood back in, and they feel scorching as they race down my hot cheeks. I angrily wipe a few away.

Mom shrinks a bit under my glare but fights back. "You are a starter in this league, Annie! You've proved your worth. You run that offense; you have more assists than almost anyone in the league. You average over two steals a game. That's proof!"

I laugh bitterly. "We got lucky, Mom. I worked hard. I glowed under the idea that the Arrows believed me to be something more than I was. I got to be on the same team as Jadea, the best player under thirty in the *entire league* and my best friend in the world. I managed to slap myself together and become a good player." I take a deep breath to stop the flow of tears, letting some of my disgust slip into my words. "And now that hard work and growth might be taken away or diminished because I'm some nepo baby. And who knows what else? We're completely in the dark about what Jack has done behind the scenes."

I almost feel bad when I see my mom's eyes watering again. If anyone understands that feeling of overflowing emotion, it's me. She manages to croak out, "He might have done nothing. You know owners."

She means that all owners are different. And though Jack is the majority owner, he's not the only one involved in deciding which players to draft. There's Coach Rembert, our GM and head coach, and tons of other front office staff. Any of them could have suggested drafting me, and if it *were* someone else, that might make this situation less murky. Maybe I'm just a philanderer's love child and not the eye of a WNBA shitstorm.

I stiffen my spine, resolved. "I'll talk to Coach tomorrow. See if she can shed any light on my draft. I'll text you when I hear." It's as good as a dismissal because I can't look at her yet. I can't reconcile the memory of her blowing that orange whistle while Jadea and I played pick-up basketball on the driveway with the beaten-down image before me. She nods once and gets up from the couch.

"Annie, I'm sorry." She looks at me, eyes glimmering with tears. "I just didn't know how to tell you."

I close my eyes. Take a sharp breath through my nose. "We'll talk later. I need some space." It feels impossible that she would keep something so important from me, yet here we are. "Don't talk to the press," I add sharply as she opens the door to leave. She nods again and shuts it behind her.

I let my emotions truly go then. I collapse on the couch, spreading out and letting those final, silent tears out. I have a plan. Coach Rembert. Laying low. Ignoring Jack Smith and his family. Staying away from the scandal. All of these are doable. Best-case scenario, this is just personal and has nothing to do with the draft or the team or the WNBA.

Worst-case scenario? Jack has been pulling strings without me knowing it for years. I'm a fraud that he created.

I want to scream into a pillow, but instead I just lie and cry.

Stupid tears.

Chapter 3

That night, I lay in bed, scrolling through social media even though I know it's a poisonous stream. The latest tweets say more of the same, and I angrily punch the numerous decorative pillows behind my head. The one that takes the brunt of my anger is a pink sequin one that Jadea bought me for my last birthday.

I think of her, and despite her own social media addiction, I know she would tell me to turn it off. Go back to the kitchen and eat more of our Thai leftovers from earlier. Better yet, more Twizzlers. Watch more sports clips that make me cry, like Suni Lee on the balance beam and a brave Simone Biles cheering for her. Or Michael Phelps reaching up into the stands to kiss his baby after winning his 28th Olympic medal. Or Candace Parker crying as she hoists up the Chicago Sky's championship trophy. All of those things would be better than wallowing before I have all the facts.

I'm about to close the app and go to bed when a tweet catches my eye.

I almost drop the phone on my face when I see who wrote it.

5 minutes ago

@DanielChan: Funny how mainstream media all but ignores the WNBA until they make a misstep. Is it that mainstream media and most men don't want women in sports to succeed? Seems that way to me. Maybe you should give these amazing players a chance before just reaching for any opportunity to tear them down.

#OurWorldThroughSportswithDanielChan.

My heart pounds in my ears. Daniel Chan, the premier sports analyst for HBO, is tweeting about me. HBO launched his show two years ago after seeing him do a low-budget version on his wildly successful YouTube channel. He's an Asian American version of John Oliver, except he largely focuses on where real-world issues and sports intersect. I was watching a clip of him a couple days ago where he was analyzing the ramifications of younger men and women being considered "professional athletes" before they're even eighteen. He pokes holes in sports, and he lifts them up.

He also happens to be my ex-boyfriend.

Daniel and I dated for a little over five months during my senior year at Stanford. He was my first serious boyfriend and the first person I really felt connected to romantically. The only other boyfriend I've had was a friend of Olabisi who was gentle and easy to be with. We broke up amicably last year after admitting there weren't any fireworks in our relationship.

On the other side of the spectrum, Daniel was my whole world. He was a track star at Stanford, with a good chance of going to the Olympics. A mutual friend introduced us at a party. We spent every minute together, as Jadea had graduated the year before me and was already playing for the Arrows. We went on runs together, lifted weights together, watched WNBA games together. We loved each other, and it was explosive, glittering, so sweet, and comfortable.

Right before his outdoor track season and our graduation, a car hit him while he was running, and his track career was effectively finished. He had several broken ribs, a fractured femur, and a collapsed lung. His family flew in from New York and stayed with him while he had numerous surgeries. I visited him a few times, dropping off the numerous gifts and cards from our Stanford classmates. I was hopeful that soon he would heal, and we could start our life together, even if he couldn't run competitively again. Then, one day, I showed up at the hospital, and the nurses told me he had been discharged. I thought he'd be back at Stanford, but it was as if he had disappeared without a trace. I called and called, and he wouldn't answer. I assume he went back to his parents' house in New York. We haven't spoken in the nearly five years since.

But I see him everywhere. A poster for the new season of his show on the train. A viral clip of him interviewing Shaq on Twitter. A cute Instagram pic of his dog (he's a public figure; I *do not* follow him). I watch every episode of his show, masochistically wondering why he's smiling and why he left and how he transitioned from running track to sports media. He's wildly popular online because of his active social media presence and numerous affiliate podcasts. He has about five million Instagram followers and two million Twitter followers. No matter our history, he wields an impressive amount of power for someone his age in the world of sports. I feel a strange prickle on the back of my neck. Daniel covers sports, and I play them, so he must be aware of me, but this is a direct acknowledgment. I almost feel naked.

I try to focus on the actual content of the tweet and ignore the tidal wave of feelings that are building in my chest. Should I favorite the tweet? I certainly agree with what he's saying. The WNBA isn't a perfect place, but we deserve a chance. Daniel is right. We can't let this scandal take away from everything we can give.

And a small part of me wants to like it, so he knows I see him, too. To maybe shake him up and force him to relive some uncomfortable memories, assuming he even feels that way about leaving me. Finally, I click favorite and then practically throw my phone onto my nightstand. Like I need Daniel Chan involved in my life again. There's nothing that could complicate it more. The father I never knew and the boy I thought was the love of my life.

I drift off to sleep feeling confused and restless.

Daniel. Chan.

*

When I get to practice the next day, it feels like everyone is waiting for me. Maybe because they are. Lynn, our shooting guard, rounds on me first. I cringe in suspense, waiting for accusations and angry questions. If anyone will tell it to me straight, it's Lynn.

Instead, she leads me to the bench, as though I need to sit down. "Are you alright, baby?" Her voice is soft, but there's a touch of menace. "Anyone giving you a hard time?"

I try not to look as surprised as I feel. "No one besides some bored internet trolls. Thanks, Lynn." Lynn is our team veteran at 32. She has been an All-Star three times and was one of the players traded to St. Louis when the team was first formed. She and I always battle it out for top defender. She always wins.

Olabisi and Allyson, the other two starters, huddle around us. Soon, Taherah, Jasmine, and Flo are there too. Their voices all overlap with concern and kind words. I haven't seen Jadea yet, but that's no surprise—our superstar always runs a few minutes late. Allyson's sweet Australian accent filters through the noise first. "We don't believe it, Annie. It's all a misunderstanding. Maybe someone who wants to make Jack look bad." She tightens her long blond ponytail angrily.

The words take a moment to process. I look at their kind faces and something clicks. They believe the story is a lie, that Jack isn't my father. I'm almost afraid to tell them. I take a deep breath. "Some of it's true. I talked to my mom, and Jack *is* my biological father."

All their chatter stops. Taherah's eyes widen in shock, and her hands drop from where they were fidgeting with her Nike hijab. Olabisi swears softly. Jas' mouth opens and closes several times.

I finally look at Lynn. Jadea is our star, our energy, our non-stop thrill ride. But Lynn is our calming force, our voice of reason. She nods twice, resolute. "That doesn't mean anything yet. That's your business, not ours. Whatever people might say—this is your team. We stand with you."

You'd think all the tears would have left my system, but a few glimmer on my lashes at her kind words. "Thank you so much." My voice pitches, and a few of my teammates smile that knowing Annie-be-crying-again smile. "Let's practice." I'm resolved to have the ball in my hand and feel normal before I confront Coach Rembert about my draft status. She stands a few paces away with some of the assistants, pretending she's not listening to our conversation.

Just as we head to the ball racks, Jadea comes running from the locker room. "Arrows!" She yells to get our attention. "Annie!" She almost runs into me in her excitement. I can't see Coach Rembert over Jadea's head, but I imagine her folding her arms and pursing her lips. "Did you see this?"

To my immediate panic, she shows us the Daniel Chan tweet I saw last night. "Wow!" Taherah finishes reading first, her brain moving faster than the rest of ours, per usual. "Finally, he's saying what we were all thinking."

"Exactly!" Jadea waves the phone around emphatically. "I already retweeted him and posted it on my Instagram story." I don't say anything, shifting on the balls of my feet. I never told Jadea about Daniel, for reasons I can hardly explain. She had already graduated from Stanford when we got together. Every time we talked on FaceTime or the phone, she spoke excitedly about her first year in the WNBA and asked me about Stanford, but never about my love life. She assumed I didn't have one, and I didn't correct her. And then I just didn't know how to start the conversation after so long of not saying anything. I imagine my mom saying with tears in her eyes, "I just didn't know how to tell you." Guilt squirms in my gut, but I push it down.

"It's great," I say, but the words sound hollow to my own ears. Fortunately, no one seems to hear it. And his words *are* great. Daniel was always a feminist, raised by his mother who is a surgeon and a badass. I had the pleasure of bonding with her at the hospital. Before he disappeared forever, obviously.

Jadea looks at us like we're missing the point. "Yes, yes, finally a man who understands us, blah blah! Who cares? Look at the favorites? The retweets."

She shoves the phone screen closer to show me his original tweet. I squint and then gasp. "There are over 100K likes. 12K retweets. In like twelve hours." I knew Daniel was wildly popular, but as his jaded ex it seemed appropriate to try to ignore him as much as possible. Even as I fell down a YouTube rabbit hole of clips from his show. Only a few brought tears to my eyes.

Jadea bounces on her heels, gesturing to the phone wildly. "This is what we need. Something to cancel out all the trolls. Something that proves this is not what people should be talking about." With Jadea's two million Instagram followers and nearly a million TikTok followers, I know she, too, can feel the rush of social media's unique brand of justice. My piddling 20K makes me more cautious, though.

Plus, the Daniel of it all.

"Jermaine said to lay low," I remind her evenly. Does she hear my secrets in my words?

Coach Rembert calls practice to order behind us, and our little huddle disperses. Taherah shoots me a look as she passes by. "Lay low? Jadea doesn't have it in her."

I try to ignore that small part of me that fully agrees with Taherah. Jadea *can* lie low, right? Maybe if she really tries. Daniel tweeted his support of us, as he should, and that will be our new relationship. Internet acquaintances. That's better than a jaded ex-girlfriend who was ghosted by a boyfriend with a broken femur, right?

The circling drain of my thoughts is interrupted by Coach Rembert directing us to do a screen passing drill. It's a little out of order for our usual practice, since, like any pro team, we tend to start slow with shooting and rebounding drills. That's also after we each come in and work on smaller individual workouts. Despite my concerns that

Coach Rembert is possibly keeping secrets from me, I allow a little warmth to bloom in my chest. Coach knows this is my favorite drill. It's no secret that I'll never be the shooter Jadea is, or Taherah, whose lights-out three-point shooting won her the sixth woman of the year award last year. But— I see the floor. I see my teammates. I see them cut without really looking. I can pass the ball anywhere on the court, and I swear it magically ends up in their hands. I just *know*.

When I start at the top of the key, where point guards bring up the ball, Taherah behind me to sub in, I feel like myself for the first time since the news broke. Assistant Coach Zak tosses me the ball, and everyone begins their motions. A blur of scarlet and white. Jadea's brown and red braids. Olabisi's green and white sneakers, in honor of her home country of Nigeria. Lynn playing defense, brown eyes narrowed as she streaks towards the bright red fingernails at the end of Allyson's outstretched arms. Seeing my split-second opportunity, I whip the ball through the gap created by the screen. Allyson snatches it and goes for the easy lay-up.

What follows is routine. Lynn clucks her tongue and shakes her head. Allyson double pumps her fists and laughs. Jadea points at me. Olabisi rolls her eyes, like, *let's run it again*. I step back for Tahereh and let the second team run it.

I dare Jack Smith and the naysayers to take this away from me.

*

"That was kind of you." I approach Coach Rembert after practice ends, and most of the facility has emptied. Our entire practice was upended, and I suspect I was the reason. Passing drills are rare at this level, but Coach knows

I love them. It was an obvious act of mercy on my obviously frayed nerves.

Coach Rembert straightens at my approach, turning away from the bag she was packing up. "Annie." At first, her voice sounds resigned, as though she knows what I want to talk about, but when she finally faces me, her face is the usual cool mask of analysis. "I don't know what you mean." She folds her arms, showing off the patches on her varsity jacket. We got it for her after her first year here, the same year I was drafted. We add a patch for every incredible thing she accomplishes. A winning record in her first season here. Three playoff berths in a row. And just this year, she was named one of the All-Star game coaches. All she's missing is the Championship patch. Jadea and I bought one last year when we made it to the finals. We had to put it back into retirement when we lost to the Las Vegas Aces in overtime.

"Coach." I quirk my lips in a wry smile. "There's no use pretending you don't care about me. I'm your favorite, right?"

I mean to sound light, bright, as if my world isn't on the verge of crumbling. Instead, I sound sad, like I'm saying goodbye. Coach Rembert collapses her firm stance and rubs a tired hand over her face. "I don't have the answers you need, Annie. I'm sorry."

I stubbornly refuse to believe her. "You were hired the same year I was drafted. A few months *before* the draft. You had to be involved. You're the coach and the general manager for god's sake!" I anxiously rub my sweaty palms on my shorts. I lower my voice. "You've seen what they're saying online. That the only reason I made the league is because Jack requested it. Because I'm his..." I stumble and finally spit out, "Daughter."

Coach Rembert shakes her head quickly in dissent. "I *was* here, but it wasn't my idea to draft you. Unfortunately, you weren't on my radar. I wish I could say it was my idea, but the whole front office would know I was lying. I might be the general manager, but it takes a lot of staff to run this team and even more executives and minority owners." She's right, of course. Jack Smith owns the Arrows, and their NBA counterpart, the Archers, but he's just the *majority* owner. The founder. Numerous people invested in the team and became minority owners. While the Arrows and Archers are two separate teams, they intersect in a lot of ways. As you go further up the corporate ladder, there are more and more people working on behalf of both teams. The Archers do get more money, support, and attention, but I know this isn't just Coach Rembert's team. As great as that would be.

"But when did you first hear about me?" I ask desperately. "Who wanted to draft me? Do you know?"

She shifts her feet, thoughtful. "It could have been your fath—Jack." She almost stumbles but quickly regains her composure. I let her, not ready to give him power over me with that title. "But it could have been anyone. Most likely, it was a random scout who was hired to find the best fit for the team. They come and go, but I could see if any of the organization's current scouts went to see you play at Stanford. If they brought you up as a potential draft pick, that means it wasn't Jack's idea."

"Thank you." I tug nervously on my braid. "Coach...what if I am a nepo baby? What if he demanded, come hell or high water, that I be drafted to this team? The trolls are right that my draft analysis shows it was unlikely I would be drafted at all, let alone early second round."

Coach Rembert fixes me with one of her unflinching looks. "Personally, I won't care." Her light brown eyes are piercing. "It's not like you were raised by a billionaire. You were born here, with your mother to raise you right. I can already see that your teammates will defend you. The draft is a game of luck anyway. We got very lucky when we picked you." My eyes start to water again, but I know Coach won't appreciate an emotional display, so I blink them back.

Before I can get too happy, crying into the collar of her varsity jacket, she raises a hand in caution. "However, I want to prepare you, Annie. This could be very bad for your career. The WNBA has tried to present itself as something above scandal. And while neither you nor Jack is a criminal, this is something people will get stuck on. They will like you, Jack, and possibly the team, less." I flinch a little at that one. Coach spreads her hands helplessly. "And that's just based on rumors. If anything more is revealed about Jack's conduct, our reputation as a team, league, and as players could plummet. Women's sports always need wins. We need to show ourselves as flawless, competitive, and entertaining. Mainstream media and a patriarchal society are looking for any excuse to take us down. We need to tread carefully here." She picks up her stylish leather tote and begins to head out. She hesitates right before she leaves the court, turning to see me standing there limply.

Her voice is softer when she speaks again. "I'm sorry, Annie." She hesitates, as though thinking over what she wants to say. "Sorry that your father isn't who you wanted him to be."

A shiver of cool anxiety runs down my spine. It feels too real to call him that, but I know what she means. I'd rather my biological father was anyone else, yet I'm stuck with

Jack Smith. I try to smile for her. "Thanks, Coach." She nods again and heads out, leather varsity jacket gleaming in the fluorescent lights.

I swallow down my jumbled feelings and grab a ball off the rack. I shoot until I feel hot again. Until sweat drips down my cheek, beads on my upper lip, slides down my spine. I shoot until I've missed as many as I've made.

I shoot to remember that I can't surrender. I won't.

Chapter 4

Our next game is against the Chicago Sky at their home arena. They're basically our rivals because of the proximity, but I love playing against them. If there's a team that is even more cohesive than ours is, it's the Sky. Their coach, Tyler Marsh, is well known for creating a team with a lot of grit and offensive pressure. Courtney Vandersloot plays point guard the way I aspire to one day. Like she has eyes in the back of her head and always with a hand on the trigger. Angel Reese flies almost as high as Jadea for rebounds and isn't afraid of anything. Kamilla Cardoso has great touch around the basket and incredible blocks. We play them, and we burn with the desire to win. That's how sports are. How competition is. But I've always loved stepping back, too. If you step back, the Sky were a team everyone expected to suffer after losing league MVP Candace Parker. Instead, they're a team with will and determination.

A team we have to beat.

The game is the battle I expected, and it's tied up with 22 seconds left in our single overtime period. I'm bringing up the ball with some urgency, switching from hand to hand. Vandersloot is pushing on me, not giving me any room. I whirl, bringing the ball with me. She's a step behind now. I cross over the half-court line, surging towards my waiting teammates.

The clock is down to 18 seconds. I pass it off to Olabisi, who has Angel Reese breathing down her neck. I break off a screen from Lynn, shoving around defenders in black and blue. I can see Jadea and Cardoso pushing underneath the basket, and I get the ball again near the right sideline. I'm close to the stands, reading the play. Jadea runs up to the free throw line and then cuts towards the basket. I know the exact moment I need to pass it to her, she'll run right through to the basket, and knowing her, dunk it in spectacular fashion. I'm about to thread the needle and help us win the game when the man sitting courtside, a Chicago fan, yells out, "Is it Annie Larger? Or Annie *Smith*?"

I freeze. Just for a second. I let that old panic flush through me. A young girl who feels unsure about who she is, a slightly older version who finds herself in basketball, an even older version that feels that identity being torn away.

I miss Jadea's cut to the basket.

My opening for the easy win is over. The clock is down to six seconds. If I was some incredible shooter, I might go for it. Shoot it right in front of this heckler's face and walk off with a buzzer-beater sizzling in my blood.

Instead, because I'm just Annie, I find Jadea again at the top of the key. She dribbles for a moment, creating space until she feels confident enough to cut to the basket. She Euro steps right into the lane, shoving through three defenders, and kisses it off the glass. We win the game with 0.4 seconds left. I didn't even contribute an assist on the play.

My team cheers and cheers, thumping Jadea on the back. This win cements us as the top team in the East. Instead of the usual rush, I feel strangely hollow. Is Jack Smith invading even these moments? My love of the game?

I push it down, even as everything in me is screaming yes.

Yes, he is.

*

Back at Arch Arena the next day, I try to create a calming practice environment. I work on the mechanics of my free throws, which are the easiest baskets to make. I talk with Coach Zak about one of our new plays. I do some extra stretches with our trainers. There have been no updates regarding Jack, my draft, or the rest of it. No more confusing tweets from Daniel. It's possible that the media is going to let this be the "personal, family issue" that Jack's publicist says it is. An ironic label considering I refuse to even call the man my father. But if it stops the barrage of doubts and head-spinning rumors, I'll take it.

However, this calming reprieve is ruined by my apprehension about Jadea. She's been avoiding me at practice. We're still high-fiving and passing to each other but not talking. I would be worried about her, but she looks almost excited. As though she's trying to hold on to a tantalizing secret.

Practice wraps up after a few hours. The assistants and practice players begin breaking down the court, gathering towels, water bottles, and balls. We all start to disperse, ready to gather our things and head to the garage. We have a game in three days, but my afternoon is clear, and I intend to lie on my couch and eat my weight in Twizzlers.

35

Before we can truly go our separate ways, Jadea calls us to attention. "Arrows." She beckons us back to center court. She has her phone pressed to her ear, listening intently. Whatever she hears makes her happy because she grins widely, twirling one of her red braids around her finger. We all exchange the usual worried glances and head to her side. She's just hanging up the phone when I reach her.

"Who was that?" I ask, arching a brow. "Secret paramour?"

She rolls her eyes. "Like I could keep any paramour a secret."

Oh, sweet irony. I put my hands up in surrender. "Alright, sorry. What's going on?"

Even Coach Rembert and Assistant Coach Zak come closer, sucked into the sparkle and pizzazz of the Jadea show. She spreads her hands, a pastor ready to give a sermon. "We all agree this stuff with Annie is BS, right?"

I shift awkwardly. "I'm not sure *BS* is quite the right term, Jadea. Jack Smith *is* my biological father."

She waves her hand dismissively, not distracted from her goal. "While that might be true, you had no idea. He had no hand in raising you or making you into the fantastic player you are. If he's been doing things behind the scenes that are underhanded, that also has nothing to do with you. You never asked him to do anything."

Lynn and Taherah are nodding in agreement, but I'm unsure. If someone does something morally wrong, and you unknowingly benefit from it, does the lack of knowledge even matter? The ethical dilemma makes my head spin. Jadea plows forward. "And, Annie the worrier, we don't know if Jack even *did* anything. It could all be a coincidence you were drafted to his team. Everything on Twitter is rumors."

More nods from my teammates. I allow myself to be dragged into Jadea's soapbox fairytale, like I always do. Maybe she's right. Maybe I'm worrying over nothing. It wouldn't be the first time. "Our best play is *not* to lie low." She claps her hands for emphasis. I snap to attention, immediately wondering what scheme she's pulling behind Jermaine's back. "We need to create positive press for the WNBA and for this team." She falls back on her heels, her skin practically buzzing with excitement. "So, I called Daniel Chan."

Everything erupts into a cacophony of noise. I'm just blinking, unsure if I've heard Jadea right.

"Daniel Chan? As in *Our World Through Sports* with Daniel Chan?" My voice sounds wrong, too high-pitched. As in *my* Daniel Chan? Light of my life? Ghost of my dreams? An ex I haven't seen in nearly five years?

An ex my best friend knows nothing about.

My bickering teammates turn my way. Olabisi's eyes light up at my crazed expression. "Isn't he, like, your celebrity crush, Annie?"

A flush creeps up my neck, not helping my case. "No!" I protest feebly. Over the years, they might have noticed my interest in his show and my light internet stalking. When they assumed he was my celebrity crush, I didn't correct them with the more complicated story. "No, I just respect his show. And how he tries to better our industry. That's all." There, I think, that's a very diplomatic response. Not at all suspicious.

It's as if I didn't open my mouth in the first place. "That is brilliant, Jadea!" Taherah claps her hands in excitement. "Is he going to profile the team?"

"Yes, he and his production team will be at practice tomorrow. They'll follow us around and interview us. Being on his show is the perfect opportunity to get some good press. I heard the new women's softball league had a surge in ticket sales after he profiled them a few months ago. He'll tell *our* story, and he won't focus on stupid Jack Smith and the rest of his boys' club." Jadea folds her arms smugly. I'm about to launch into a panicked tirade about how ridiculous this is when Coach Rembert cuts through with her own perspective.

"Jadea Jones, are you telling me that you invited a camera crew to our practices without my approval?" She sounds dangerous, and even Jadea has the good grace to look chagrined. I almost start cheering. Maybe Coach can save me from this awkward mess.

"Sorry, Coach, but I had to look out for Annie. And our team. This could boost our reputation. Put our names out there in a positive way!" She fixes Coach with a pleading look.

There is a brief standoff where Jadea's enthusiasm is matched with Coach's severity. Eventually, Coach relents. "Fine." She spins away, calling over her shoulder, "But they will follow *my* rules."

The team officially begins to disperse, almost all of them talking excitedly about Daniel Chan and the show. Jadea stays with me and pantomimes wiping sweat off her brow. "Whew. I wasn't sure Coach would go for it. Thank God she has a soft spot for you."

I do a double-take. "Wait, really?" I had been joking about that yesterday; it's Jadea and Coach Rembert who engage in all the witty banter. Jadea even texts Coach Rembert on off days—a brave action I'm never willing to try. Jadea is hardly listening to me, already typing away on her phone. Probably texting Daniel Chan for all I know. I tuck that comment aside for later and focus on my actual concern. "Jadea, what were you thinking?"

I must sound as freaked out as I am inside because Jadea immediately looks up. "What do you mean? You love Daniel Chan. A couple of weeks ago, you talked about how great he looked in his new glasses for literally fifteen minutes."

Now my cheeks are officially burning. "They were a better shape for his face, that's all!" I struggle to overcome how flustered I sound. I, maybe, mentioned those glasses to Jadea, but only because he used to wear these tiny wire ones back in college. The old Daniel could hardly be bothered to go shopping, but the new, famous Daniel has unearthed a sense of style. "But that's not the point! If you thought this would help me, you're crazy!"

My voice rises at least three octaves. Jadea puts her hands on my shoulders, leaning towards me so we're eye to eye. "Annie, I can't follow your panicky thoughts. Try again, please."

I should tell her. I should tell her that we went out and that we exchanged I-love-yous and that I went to his track meets and that he went to our games and that when Jadea visited me that spring he was out of town, and I couldn't voice what had happened up until that point. When Jadea left Stanford, some of the sparkle of my life was sucked out. I didn't have a lot outside of basketball, and Daniel was a happy accident. I hadn't dated much before him, and our relationship felt weirdly sacred, like as soon as I told Jadea, I would burst the bubble of safety around our new love.

When I see the enthusiasm on her face, the love and faith she has in me, I know I won't tell her. Daniel and my secrets are all in the past. I don't need to hurt Jadea now; I need to get out of this twisted situation.

I take a few deep breaths and try to focus on the other issues involved, Daniel aside. "Jadea, I can barely do a two-minute post-game interview. I don't like talking in front of people or being on camera. That's why I'm always *your* camerawoman."

Jadea keeps her warm brown gaze on me. "You can do this, Annie. You're smart, you're accomplished, you're beautiful. If you let people see you that way, it can only help your case. And they can see you hoop, where you *truly* shine. Who cares if you can hardly string two words together when you play like a ginger Sue Bird?"

I nod like a puppet. My voice is still squeaky. "Right, right. Except you also picked..." I flounder to describe him. "Daniel!" Jadea pulls back from our personal huddle, a laugh bursting from her. "This is not funny, Jadea! This is my worst nightmare!"

She blows me a kiss, heading across the court and towards the locker room. "You're welcome, Annie! Who knows? Maybe Daniel will be a welcome distraction?"

"No, he won't!" I shout at her like a crazy person. She waves over her shoulder as I try desperately not to think about Daniel's extremely attractive face and his very nice new glasses and the fact that I'll be seeing him for the first time in five years tomorrow.

Deep breaths.

Chapter 5

I stand in front of the mirror the next morning, trying to get ready for practice. This process typically requires five minutes of face washing, ChapSticking, and French braiding. However, this morning all I can think about is Daniel sitting behind his fancy TV desk wearing his fancy TV suit. Will he be wearing a suit today? I was lucky if I saw Daniel out of his running shorts, track pants, and a reliable Stanford red zip-up back in the day. This new polished version of him with five million followers is intimidating.

I survey my freckled face critically. Should I do my hair differently? Put on some mascara and tinted lip balm? How much deodorant is too much deodorant? Despite my affection for vintage fashion, something I get from my mom, I usually wear sweats to practice. We change into practice clothes when we get there, so there's no purpose in wasting good outfits on practice. But what about today? Will they film us as we enter the garage? Will the cameras be on us the entire time? Not only will Daniel be watching me, analyzing how I've changed, but there will also be film crews, directors, and interviews—an endless nightmare for an introvert with a low social threshold.

Paralyzed with indecision, I shoot Jadea a text to come over before she leaves. We used to carpool to practice anyway, but her tardiness gave me anxiety, so I drive on my own now. Today is different; I *need* backup. I'm about to put my phone down when I see a slew of notifications, including a few texts from my mom, which I guiltily ignore. The idea of having a conversation about all her lies makes my stomach churn. We've never gotten into a fight that lasted over 24 minutes, let alone 24 hours.

There are also three missed calls from a number I don't recognize. They left a voicemail. I press play to listen to it and immediately drop the phone when I hear, "I didn't know how to do this, Annie...but it's me, Jack. I felt like I should reach out so we can...talk. Call me back at this number."

I'm still staring at the phone when Jadea knocks. I go to let her in with numb fingers. "I knew you'd be freaking out!" She's still brimming with the victory of booking Daniel's show. "What fabulous outfit are you going to randomly show up in today? Your vintage leather jacket? That burgundy corset that snatches your waist? Your velvet green boots?" Jadea is about to continue crowing about my absurdist fashion finds but stops when she sees my face. "What's wrong? Did you hear more news?"

"He called. Jack," I say finally, rubbing my arms to dispel the goosebumps. "He called a couple of times and left me a voicemail."

Jadea looks as shocked as I feel. "I thought your mom insisted he stay out of your life. That was the agreement."

I sigh at my reflection before swiping my keys off the kitchen counter. A Scarlet Arrows sweat suit, it is. It seems almost worse to dress up for Daniel and try to impress him. "I figure that agreement is now void. Even ESPN knows about our relationship."

We leave the apartment together, heading down the stairwell. "I wonder how it's going with his wife," Jadea muses, hoisting her practice bag higher up her shoulder. "I assume she never knew about you. That would be a tough thing to hear on SportsCenter."

We spill out into the lower level of the parking garage, making a beeline towards my sensible red Prius. The lights in the garage flicker ominously, matching my mood. "He has a son, too," I remember aloud, swallowing nervously. "My b-brother. Trenton or something? He's in his forties."

"Oh, yeah," Jadea says, getting into the passenger seat. She won't be late today. "We met them both at some charity event, right? The son was blonde, blue-eyed, wearing an expensive watch. Exactly what you'd expect."

Blue-eyed. Just like me?

I pull out of the garage, feeling a light sweat break out on my brow. Between Daniel coming back into my life with a full-on camera crew, and my new twisted family life, my body is freaking out. "Oh my God!" Jadea suddenly shouts. I nearly hit my head on the roof in surprise.

"Shit, Jadea! You scared me!"

Jadea ignores me, tapping a perfectly manicured finger to her lip. "Do you think you'll be a part of Jack's will? Are you going to inherit any of his fortune?"

Now I'm full-on sweating. My voice gets squeaky. "What? No! I'm not his daughter."

Once Jadea sees my reaction, she tries to calm herself down. We've always been good at the give-and-take. Jadea is usually fast, loud, and sure of herself, whereas I'm more measured, slow, and precise. The only time Jadea takes on that role is when she thinks I need it. Another alarming sign. "Annie." She speaks softly. I try to focus on my breathing and not swerving off the road. "He is and he isn't.

When he calls, you don't have to answer. When he tries to be a father after twenty-five years, you don't have to let him. But he isn't going anywhere. These questions aren't going anywhere. We both know that." I can only gape at her, pulling into our practice facility's garage.

Our practice court is adjacent to Arch Arena, so our commute is only a few minutes. We're lucky to be coupled with an NBA team because we get to use their facilities. I know some of the WNBA teams don't have that luxury and practice in smaller, inconvenient practice facilities, like local YMCAs. Of course, it also means that people don't see value in us, but in our NBA counterpart. I'm jealous of teams like the Las Vegas Aces, who built a multi-million-dollar practice facility just for *them*. Not a single men's team in sight.

Once we're safely in my parking spot, I press my forehead against the steering wheel, absorbing Jadea's words dejectedly. "Was it too much to hope that things could just stay the same?"

Jadea has never been one to soften the blow. "Yes."

I breathe out a long sigh and then straighten resolutely. "I'll think about it. I just have to decide what I want." A seemingly impossible task when I feel so confused.

"And you'll call your mom." I already updated Jadea on our argument, and I know she wants us to make up already. She loves my mom.

I want to make up with her, too, despite all the secrets she kept from me. I'm just avoiding the hard conversation I know we'll have to have. I sigh again. "And my mom."

"Good." Jadea breaks out into one of her beautiful smiles, one dimple popping in her left cheek. "Now, let's go get you some Daniel Chan!"

I groan as we exit the car, slinging our practice bags over our shoulders. "Please stop with that! You're just encouraging the others." God, what if Jadea mentions to Daniel that I have a crush on him? Is it even possible to get out of this situation unscathed?

Jadea doesn't miss a step. "That's my intention."

I groan in response. "Of course, it is." I pray I can make it through today without embarrassing myself too much. I will be cool, calm, and collected. Polite. Distant. Professional. How many adjectives can I recite before seeing Daniel again feels almost mundane?

We weave our way up the garage and into the atrium of our practice facility. Jadea heads to the locker room with a spring in her step, chirping a hello to every security guard and facility staff member we pass.

After changing into reversible practice jerseys and our basketball shoes, we walk out onto the court. I see most of my teammates also showed up early today, with Jadea and me the last two to arrive. The atmosphere feels charged, almost electric, and inside, I ruefully admit that Jadea has accomplished at least one of her goals. Instead of worrying endlessly about a scandal that may or may not explode, now the girls are just excited about our Daniel Chan piece. Even Coach Rembert seems to be fighting a smile.

"Coach?" Taherah asks. "Should we start practicing, or do you want us to wait for Daniel Chan?" It's as if no one can say his first name without his last. It just rolls off the tongue. Daniel Chan, Daniel Chan, Daniel Chan. I'm so mesmerized with the ridiculous circle of my thoughts I almost miss her answer.

"After talking with Jadea, Daniel's producer, Iris Langley, contacted me. She was very respectful of our time. We agreed that it would be best to hold a meeting and make introductions before practice today. They'll also go over expectations for the next two weeks. Besides a few extra interviews here and there, they will not be disrupting our practices." She slowly scans our loose huddle, catching our eyes. "We are still the number one team in this league. And I will not let us be distracted, even if it is for good reason."

We all nod solemnly, even Jadea. This piece may be a good fit for the team, and it may help with the possible Jack Smith repercussions, but winning a championship is still our first priority. We had a taste of winning last year but ended up making enough small errors that we lost in the championship game.

I mentally wind myself up. New social situations are always stressful for me, but it feels a million times worse with Daniel because it's not exactly new. I know him intimately; he's also a stranger. He works in New York. He's a TV star. He probably has a beautiful girlfriend. I just need to ignore the past and focus on basketball. Lying low. Fortunately, the spotlight isn't just on me, it's on the team and how we navigate the world of women's sports. No matter how personally difficult this is for me, Daniel is amazing at what he does. Sports broadcasting was his major in college, though I know he always thought of it as something he would do after he retired from track. A small part of me wants to tell him that he's a natural at it, just like running. And even though I'm furious at him for disappearing, there are so many things I could say that aren't fueled by anger.

Should I mention how much I love his show? Should I mention that he's changed my perspective on sports? That I cried the other day watching his piece on Paralympians and how they are shortchanged in terms of Olympic coverage?

No, definitely not. I need to act professional but ultimately keep it short and sweet. If we start a conversation, who knows what Daniel will say. I need to corner him sometime later today, so we can privately agree to never mention our past. When he introduces himself, I'll do the same and then say, "I'm a big fan." And then I'll smile. Short and sweet. That's a polite response. A true one. It makes me the bigger person and reveals nothing to my teammates, who just think Daniel is my celebrity crush.

Just as my pulse begins to lower in response to my internal planning, I hear Allyson giggling. "Do you think he'll say, 'It's Daniel Chan and this is Our World through Sports.' That would be *so hot*."

Olabisi rolls her eyes. "Why on earth would he say that?"

Jadea leans over from where she's seated on the bench, retying her shoe. "Allyson, you don't even like men."

Allyson looks at Jadea with bewilderment. "So?"

I'm still laughing when he walks in. Surprisingly, he's not wearing a suit. Instead, he dressed more casually, his lean, muscled body clad in a Gotham FC jersey and black sweats. His black hair is curling a bit on top, and when he smiles, it lifts up crookedly. He's still wearing the black framed glasses I supposedly (definitely) waxed poetic about to Jadea. He looks better than I remember him. Better than he has on my TV screen. My breath stutters a bit in my chest, and I cover it with a cough. Jadea shoots me a smug look that I return with venom.

Daniel is walking with a woman in her forties carrying a clipboard. She must be Iris Langley. They pan to her sometimes on his show. She was the one who saw potential in his YouTube channel three years ago and pitched it to HBO. At least, that's what it says on his Wikipedia page.

Daniel stops a few paces away from us to introduce himself to Coach. They shake hands, and Iris begins animatedly talking to Coach Rembert and pointing to her clipboard. For a second, they look like exact mirrors of each other. Two driven women with big goals in mind and a protective energy.

Though we're all straining to hear what they're saying, we act like we're not by straightening our things or whispering to each other. Lynn says something in my ear, and I can't hear it over my elevated pulse. It must be the stress of the week that's making my body go haywire. It can't possibly be seeing Daniel. I'm over him. Fully.

Finally, Iris, Daniel, and Coach Rembert finish their little conference. Coach turns our way, immediately keying in on our attempts at listening. She waves her hand at us, and we all scramble to create a semi-organized line so we can introduce ourselves.

Daniel smiles easily as he approaches. Up close, I can see the small mole on his square jaw and the faint scar above his right eye. I remember the stitches he had there from where the car smashed his glasses into his face. My hand twitches unconsciously as though to touch it. "Sorry for the formality, everyone. I know some of you…" his eyes trace over us, and I swear they linger on me for a moment, "…from watching your games, but I'm a New York Liberty fan first, so introductions seemed appropriate." That earns him a few chuckles and an eye roll from Olabisi. He launches in with, "My name is Daniel Chan, and I'm here to put a voice to this team. I know you've recently been grappling with some negative media attention and want to use this piece to combat that. While I think that is an admirable goal, I also want to show people what the WNBA can do. I want them to see your talent, your grit, and the utter lack of equality you deal with on a daily basis."

I think my teammates' metaphorical jaws drop. He says it like it's obvious. He doesn't equivocate or quibble with the details. He just says we aren't treated equally to men in this sport. A fact many men refuse to face. "If you've seen my show, you know I take this seriously. Sports can be fun and exciting, but they have an impact. I don't intend for this to be a puff piece. This will be real. Real interviews. Real practice clips. My show and this story are very important to me, just as I assume it's very important to all of you. Right?"

He looks at each of us in turn, and I give a firm nod. No matter our history, on this, Daniel and I agree. Sports are a facet of society, and unfortunately, they are not equitable. He's trying to create change with his show, and I have to respect him for that. Jadea speaks up for us. "Absolutely. We're ready."

The business-like expression melts off his face. He smiles again, and I feel a little starstruck. *A lot* starstruck. Allyson lets loose a nervous giggle beside me. Daniel steps forward and offers a hand to Jadea. "Jadea Jones, right? An honor."

She winks. "Me too, Chan."

He chuckles a little. "I saw you play a bit at Stanford. You and Annie." I'm basically hiding behind Allyson at the end, but even I hear the warmth when he says my name. What does it mean? Does he feel guilty for the abrupt ending to our relationship? Is he just trying to move on and be polite?

He shakes everyone's hand as he walks down the line, sincerely responding with a "nice to meet you" or "it's an honor". He sounds professional, but kind. As he gets closer,

I feel a little relieved. I can manage a conversation with the tone he's setting. He recognizes Lynn, too, as she's a veteran of the league, but otherwise, he practices saying everyone's names, repeating them each time.

When he steps up to me, I open my mouth, ready to repeat the script I created in my head. Ready to pretend. Instead, Daniel's warm, familiar hand engulfs mine. I look at him, startled at the intimate contact. We're basically eye-to-eye, both of us being six feet tall. "Annie Larger." I must look like a deer in headlights. What will he say? Will he spill our secret history? Will he say the reason he left me? Definitely not that last one. His eyes are sparkling dangerously, long lashes surrounding his dark gaze. "I'm a big fan."

He's trying to shake my hand, but I'm of no help. He said he was a big fan. Of me. His ex.

He stole my line.

Someone starts snickering, probably Olabisi or Jadea, and I realize I'm still holding his hand. I haven't said anything in response either, totally frozen. How long have we been standing this way?

He's leaning in a bit towards me, as though waiting for a response. I drop his hand quickly, taking a half step back. My heartbeat is too loud in my ears, but I manage a shaky smile. "Thank you. It's so nice to *meet you*." I wonder if he hears the spark of defiance in my voice, the warning. For a brief moment, I think I see disappointment flash across his face, but it's gone so quickly I blame my paranoid brain.

He thanks all of us, smiling again, and gestures to Iris. Our line relaxes, everyone sitting down or leaning against the table as we listen to her go over our schedule for the next two weeks. I can barely hear what she's saying as I try desperately not to look at Daniel. He stands a few paces away, next to Iris.

Jadea covertly comes to stand by me, nudging me with her elbow.

I raise a brow in question.

"Oh my God!" she mouths, tilting her head toward Daniel.

"I don't know what you're referring to," I whisper, turning my head stubbornly.

Jadea continues to look at me as if it's the first time she's ever seen me. "Sure. Sure, you don't."

I try to focus on Iris again, but eventually I give in and peek at Daniel. I almost fall out of my chair when I find his dark gaze already on me. There's one electric second where we stare at each other, and the roaring in my ears gets louder. I find myself wishing I could go over and talk to him, hear more of his passion and intensity, watch that mole on his chin move as he smiles.

Instead, I snap my gaze away, flushed. Daniel left me. He's acting like his old self—kind, and hardworking, and intense—but that doesn't mean we should fall into our old habits. I'll be the one who ends up hurt and alone. From my peripheral vision, I notice Daniel's lips settle into a firm line. Fortunately, Jadea didn't seem to notice our exchange.

This will be a long two weeks.

Chapter 6

Daniel sticks to his word when it comes to Coach Rembert's rule. He's unobtrusive, always on the outskirts, a flash I see hovering just beyond reach. He watches our individual workouts, frequently typing on his phone or talking to Iris. He always has a slight smile on his face, a kindness to his expression. He has no camera crew with him, and if I remember anything from Iris' speech, it's that today is only observational for them. Maybe sniffing out a story or an angle or building their plan for the next week. There's been no subtle way to pull him aside and clear the air, so I've just ignored him instead.

When it's time for my individual workout, I'm focusing on passing drills. As the team's starting point guard, it's my job to get the play started and keep the ball moving. Today, Coach Zak whips out the giant tire, rolling it towards me. One of our practice players, Patrick, stands in front of me to act as a fake defender. I have to keep passing the ball through the hole of the rolling tire while Patrick is all in my face. It's designed to improve my passing accuracy under pressure from my defender.

I nervously peek around just as we're about to start the drill, but to my relief, I don't see Daniel. I'd like to say I'm cool enough to do this drill perfectly with him watching, but it's more likely I would embarrass myself. Putting his handsome face firmly out of my mind, I perform the drill. I keep pushing Patrick back, shoving him with my shoulder and throwing the ball through the tire pushed along by Zak. The first ball hits the side of the tire and bounces off. Patrick, who shoots me an apologetic glance, blocks the second ball. I grit my teeth and catch the third ball. Zak nods at me encouragingly, and I focus past Patrick's bulky shoulder and towards the moving target. The next ball rockets through. And the next. And the next.

By the end of my individual workout, I'm sweating and grinning. Basketball has so much rhythm and getting in the groove made my body hum happily in response. I turn to the bench, looking for Jadea. Instead, I see my entire team huddled around Daniel and something he's showing them on his phone.

Daniel and Jadea both look up at me at the same time. Jadea is clearly furious, her lips set in a grimace. Daniel's expression is softer and unsure.

Surprisingly, Daniel speaks first. "Annie? I think you should come take a look at this." How do they not hear the familiarity in his words? The easy way he says my name?

Now Taherah, Lynn, Olabisi, and Allyson are looking at me too. Everyone is, even Coach Rembert and Iris Langley. The heaviness of their gazes weighs me down, making the walk over to them seem slow and painful. When I finally reach their huddle, Allyson steps aside so I can stand next to Daniel and see the video he's playing on his phone.

His volume is turned all the way up, and I catch the ESPN analyst's words mid-sentence. "...information about the Jack Smith and Annie Larger controversy. Inside sources at the Archers/Arrows front office say that Jack Smith has been tracking Annie's trajectory ever since she went to Stanford. The source says Jack Smith paid several journalists in the Stanford area to write articles about Annie when she was in season. The source also confirms the suspected mismanagement surrounding the draft, saying there was an explosive argument between executives over Annie being picked early in the second round by the Arrows. Many other executives on the team disagreed with Smith's choice, and the source says many felt Jack was able to sneak Annie in because of the change in coaches from Jim Stance to Candace Rembert."

"Besides the anonymous source, this story has been corroborated by the Arrows' old GM and three of its board members. They confirm the mismanagement and admit their part in looking the other way. A lesser investigation will be opened on them as well..."

Every part of me that felt like it was singing moments ago has now gone icy cold. My breath is tight as I listen to the analyst finish their report. "The NBA and WNBA are launching a full investigation into Jack Smith and his front office. While there are no current legal issues surrounding the case, the NBA and WNBA would like to guarantee Mr. Smith did not break or bend any rules relating to league policy. Even if he managed to work through loopholes, the nepotism and manipulation of the draft will not go unnoticed by the world of sports. Moving on to the world of NASCAR..."

Daniel closes the video, quiet. So are the rest of my teammates, watching me carefully. Jadea reacts first. "This is bullshit!" She paces violently, breaking up the huddle that surrounded the phone. I watch her meltdown numbly. "Annie got coverage at Stanford because she was great! She was drafted because she was great! Who is this source they keep referring to? Has anyone even verified their accusations?"

I find my voice, trying to speak calmly. "They said the statements were verified by some of the board and our old GM. It can't all be lies." Jadea stops her pacing, looking at me with a furrowed brow. It feels like every word that comes out of my mouth is being said by a stranger, far away from me. "Excuse me, everyone, I need a minute."

I don't know how I walk away so calmly when it feels like my skin has been plunged into an ice bath. "Shit." Jadea swears. "Annie, I'm sorry. Come back!"

I walk faster, feeling the tears threaten. I don't want to cry in front of Iris Langley and the newly reformed Daniel. They probably deal with this level of risk and reporting all the time. They won't understand why I'm acting like my life is ripping apart.

I slam through the door to our locker room, feeling blindly for a bench to sit down on. I press the heels of my hands to my eyes, trying to force the tears away. Instead, I let out a small sob.

Do I even deserve to be out there? To stand with Jadea and Lynn? Sometimes it feels like I do, when I'm passing that ball through the tire and my blood is on fire, but right now it feels like I'm the only player in the league who bought her way onto a team. I might have taken a girl's spot who had more talent than me. A girl who needed no help from her billionaire, manipulative father.

I'm surprised when I hear a knock at the door. I expect Jadea to burst in, full of blistering swear words and apologies for me. Instead, a wry voice asks, "Are you decent?"

Daniel Chan.

"What?" I squeak, voice full of even more cracks from crying. "Of course, I am!"

He opens the door a few inches, peeking in at me. I must look a picture. Two fiery braids trailing down my back, tears drying on my cheeks, fists clenched, and an indignant look on my face at basically being asked by my ex if I'm sitting naked in the locker room. He slips in, hesitating by the door. "I told Jadea I would talk to you, but as soon as I got to the locker room door, I had this paralyzing fear that I was entering a space I shouldn't."

I snort, rubbing some tears off my cheeks. "I guess that's fair. Most men would probably love an excuse to push in."

Daniel makes a brief disgusted face before coming to sit next to me. His thigh brushes mine as he sits, and I hope he can't see the blush through my tears and splotchy cheeks. Neither of us says anything, but my tears slow. I feel almost rational. I abruptly turn to face him on the bench, bringing one knee up so I can lean in. "Daniel, what the hell are you doing here?"

The words fly from my mouth, and for once, I'm proud of myself for just saying what I'm feeling. For better or worse, I always had an easy time talking to Daniel. We understood each other.

He finally looks as guilty as I'd expected, ducking his head. "I wanted to make things right."

A crazed laugh burst out of me. "And so, you came back into my life right when it's going to pieces? After we haven't spoken to each other in *five years*?"

Daniel looks at me intensely. There's a flash of us a few weeks before the accident, the first day after we said I love you. Daniel kept looking at me, and when I would ask what he was doing, he'd just laugh and say he loved me again. It was such a fizzy, deliriously happy feeling to be with him those months. All those memories feel strangely tainted now, like I'm seeing them through warped glass.

Daniel clasps and unclasps his hands. I wonder if he's as nervous as I am. "Annie, I ruined our relationship. I know that, and I don't expect your forgiveness. But...Jadea's right. You desperately need some good press, and my show could do that for you. If there is some small way I can help, let me do it. I owe you."

I'm silent for a moment. It's strange, talking to Daniel again. Our relationship is broken into stages in my brain. Falling in love. Being in love. Sitting in the hospital and reading at his bedside. Me excitedly driving to the hospital to visit him but finding his bed empty. I had a lot of time to wonder endlessly what I did wrong. And then even more time to be angry at how he treated me, no matter what he felt about our relationship. However, I never really fought *with* Daniel. All our actual, in-person interactions were before his disappearance and were *good*. He sounds like that now. Still good. Smart. Kind. Extremely driven.

It's making my head spin.

"We need rules," I blurt out. Daniel nods patiently, waiting for me to gather my thoughts. "I never told Jadea about us."

Now, it's Daniel's turn to be surprised. "Never?" I hear his unspoken questions. All that texting, FaceTiming, and calling she and I did during my and Daniel's relationship, but we never talked about him? When he left me randomly, I didn't complain to her?

I refuse to explain myself to him. Partially because I can barely understand it myself. "No, I didn't. No one really knew except my mom. Maybe some of our old Stanford teammates who paid enough attention. That's it. We can keep it professional, and no one will be any the wiser."

Daniel takes it in stride, nodding. "I want to help, Annie, I promise. I'll do whatever makes you comfortable."

His words calm me somewhat, and I wipe away a few more tears. Daniel stands up as if he might leave, following the rules I set for us, but I don't let him. I grab his hand at the last second, pulling his dark gaze back towards me. "Daniel, do you think I deserve to be in the WNBA? After hearing that report?"

I don't take my eyes off his face, bouncing between his sparkling eyes and that stubborn mole marking his strong chin. Daniel has always been a kind, moral person, the ghosting he did to me notwithstanding. However, he's also intense and honest. It's what made him a world-class athlete and competitor. It probably makes him a good reporter, too. I know that he'll tell me the truth, no matter how things have changed between the two of us.

Our haphazard handhold tightens as he leans towards me. For once, I'm looking up at him. The moment lingers, both strangely awful and strangely wonderful. I can't imagine what he sees in my face—*how* he feels when he sees my face.

"Annie." My heart skips at the way he says my name, just like before. His voice is deep, but quiet. "I know you. I know you grew up in St. Louis with a single mom. I know you met Jadea on the first day of fourth grade when she moved here from Kansas City. You became fast friends because you were both the tallest girls in your grade." I picture Jadea the first day I saw her, wiry and lean, bare ankles on display because her pants were too short. I remember us shooting her first dunk video in ninth grade. When she finally made it in the hoop, we both screamed. "I know that it was your dream to go to Stanford together. When you joined her your freshman year, you averaged 5.4 points and 6.6 assists. By the time you were a senior, without Jadea, you were averaging 13.1 points and 8.4 assists. You got better each year and that had nothing to do with the press you received, which, despite ESPN's report, we both know was minimal at best."

I'm speechless at the way he rattles off my college stats. I only knew him during my final semester at Stanford. He doesn't stop there. "I know that in your first press conference with Jadea she talked endlessly, and when a reporter asked you if that bothered you, you scrunched up your face and said, 'Why would it? I don't like talking to people'."

I let out a surprised laugh, and Daniel grins at me. So, he *has* been watching me, just as I've been following him. Something crackles in the air between us. That synchronicity, familiarity. I feel a little warmer, my chest loosening. Daniel grows serious one last time. "Annie, society looks for labels every day. They want to label you and these women incorrectly. All of this is Jack's fault, not yours. I *know* you deserve to be out there, which means you have to fight for yourself. Jadea believes in you. Your coach does. All your teammates. None of them even considered that you were in league with Jack. You need to punch back. Let me help you do that."

He sounds like he's on my TV screen, inspiring people to think about sports differently. To think about myself differently. Being the tallest girl in school who didn't know her dad meant that nothing ever seemed to fit. Friends. Boys. Cliques. My clothes. When I found basketball and Jadea, I truly saw myself, and I liked what I saw. If I let Jack damage that, he'll damage my whole life.

"I won't quit," I promise Daniel and myself. "I love playing too much."

Daniel smiles easily and drops my hand. "That's what first drew me to you. Every practice, every game, every teammate—they all mattered to you. When I saw you play that first time, I *felt* it. I knew I had to talk to you." Daniel presses a hand to his sternum, over his heart.

My brow crinkles, sifting through my memories. "What do you mean? Your friend introduced us at that party senior year. You never came to one of my games until we were together." He was friends with one of the men's basketball players, Justin, and asked him to introduce us.

He nods, swallowing nervously. "Right. Well, that's not really the whole story. I actually noticed you for the first time junior year. For one of my broadcasting classes, we had to write an op-ed about a sport on campus and argue why it was the best one. As a diehard runner, I intended to write about track. However, one of my friends told me I'd be an idiot not to write about the women's basketball team, which was undefeated and just starting March Madness. He told me Jadea Jones was the future of basketball." Weirdly, my heart begins pounding, imagining a younger Daniel, *my* Daniel, tentatively entering our packed college stadium. "When I went to see you guys, you were playing Gonzaga. I came in late to the game, rushing from practice. I missed the team's introduction, but it didn't matter. You were on fire that game. You had..."

"Twenty-one points and twelve assists," I fill in without thinking. That Gonzaga game was the best in my collegiate career. It was the second round of March Madness and Jadea had been dealing with a hamstring strain and unexpectedly had to sit out the game. Feeling the pressure,

I pushed my team to try to find a way without her. We did, winning by a basket.

"You stood out so much, with your red hair and red uniform. I thought you were Jadea the first few plays. To my surprise, it was your name they said each time you scored or stole the ball away. I've never seen a more exciting basketball game, to this day." My leg twitches, as if to stand up and reach for him again. I resist the impulse, keeping my eyes on him instead. "You were lightning in a bottle that game. I think about it whenever sports get me down. I remember you scoring at the buzzer and your teammates piling on top of you. The clip they showed on the jumbotron of Jadea tearing up on the sidelines. It was a perfect game, and it was you I couldn't stop staring at. I *asked* Justin to introduce us. I guess I never told you because it seemed a little embarrassing."

He shrugged bashfully. "So, that's how I became a big fan. I've watched a few of your WNBA games when I can catch them. Even after our relationship...ended, I never stopped rooting for you. You're still one of my favorite athletes."

"Daniel..." I trail off, off-kilter. "You never told me that story before." He shrugs a little, avoiding my gaze. There's a little color on his cheeks. To imagine that I played some small part in his passion for sports is mind-boggling. That he thought I was Jadea. That he remembers that buzzer-beater jump shot I took. That he remembers the celebration afterwards and Jadea hugging me with tears in her eyes.

That game motivated him to talk to me senior year.

Even as I resent Daniel and want to rail at him for the way he lit our relationship on fire, I agree with him. That game was one of the best days of my life. Every word he says, that's how I feel about those moments too. It's basketball to me. It captures everything I love about sports.

I look at him, dry-eyed, but a lump in my throat. "Thank you."

He reaches down to help me up, pulling me so we're only a foot apart. I'm still just a hair taller than he is, my eyes roving over that tiny, white scar above his eye. He doesn't let go of my hand, and for a moment, I have a flashback of him wrapping his hands around my waist and pulling me closer.

The door to the locker room bursts opens and bursts the memory. I blink twice and step away from Daniel, dropping his hand. "Daniel!" Jadea swings into the room. "You said five minutes, and it's been close to ten!"

She pauses a moment, taking us in, but Daniel only salutes her and backs out of the room. Jadea reaches for me immediately, engulfing me in a hug. She smells of sweat and her jasmine perfume. When she pulls back, she puts both hands on my cheeks. "Have you been crying?"

I'm surprised at the strength in my voice when I say, "No, no I haven't been." While I haven't been crying, I do feel a little strange. This Daniel seems like the old one I loved so much. Our conversation felt so inspiring, so invigorating.

Yet, somewhere in him is that version of Daniel that left me on a whim. That broke my heart and didn't come back for five years. If I'm not careful, I'll let him swoop back into my life and rip it apart. Again.

Lightning in a bottle, he said. He doesn't lie.

Or he didn't, back when I really knew him.

Chapter 7

The next morning's practice is surprisingly normal. Considering my propensity for crying, something that is now immortalized on the internet forever, I've been trying to toughen up a bit. Straighten my spine, grit my teeth, maybe act like Jadea or Olabisi. Badass women who take no shit. It's not my natural disposition, but it seems worth attempting.

That attitude works well most of the morning. Jadea and I practice some cutting and dunking plays that have us both excited. We don't have a game until Thursday, two days from now, so we have a nice mid-week break. I do have to field several calls from reporters, answering with a meek, "No comment." I also declined two more calls from Jack and four more from my mom. I promised Jadea we'd make up, but the idea that she was keeping more potential secrets for Jack, or at least hiding suspicions she had, makes me furious. She might have thought she was protecting me, but what about now? It would have been nice to know about this potential disaster ahead of time. Jermaine calls again before I leave for practice and reassures me that lying low is still the best strategy. Angry women are frequently ridiculed. Crying women are even worse.

Daniel has his whole film crew with him this time, and I watch them out of the corner of my eye. Most of the filming doesn't feature Daniel; it's just footage for him to cut to during his on-air discussion. I wonder what parts of practice have any merit. What complaints will people have? Will this piece make any impact at all, or will people just see another women's team that they find less interesting than the men's?

Jadea must see the anger and frustration through my steel-spine facade because she tries to distract me. We stand on the sideline, hydrating after our last scrimmage. I did well, sinking two threes and assisting Jadea on two dunks. Allyson, Lynn, and Olabisi cheered, and the reserves grumbled good-naturedly. Lots of men, and some women, believe women's basketball isn't as fast paced or athletic. Dunking is their number one example. Women can't dunk, so naturally, the whole game suffers in comparison (gag me). And while many incredible WNBA players could dunk, such as Brittany Griner, Jadea forced it into her gameplay. She throws it in the misogynistic pundits' faces, and everyone on the team loves it. Mostly.

Jadea's face lights up with what promises to be a troubling idea. "I know! We should go dancing tonight! We only have film tomorrow, and then we're on the road." Our next game is a day game against Indiana, which is two days away. We rarely do a full practice on the same day we're traveling.

I groan immediately, but several of my teammates perk up. Olabisi throws her hands up in the air. "Yes, thank God! It has been a *drag* around here recently."

I toss her a look, and she blows me a kiss. I roll my eyes. "I hate going out." I look at Jadea pathetically, hoping it will work. As someone who prefers to linger in the shadows and sip on a beer all night, clubbing has never really been my scene. It's difficult to fade into the background when you and your friends are all over six feet tall.

Jadea puts her hands on her hips, eyeing me sternly. "Oh, stop pouting, Annie. You need to blow off some steam, and preferably in a place where you can't hear yourself think." Allyson nods enthusiastically, high-fiving Jadea. I'm about to open my mouth and complain that Jermaine said to "lay low" not "blow off some steam", when she says the few magic words that usually convince me to leave my apartment. "You can get dressed up."

I try not to let my face show any excitement, but it's difficult. Jadea knows just what to say. Throughout middle school and high school, I struggled to find clothes that I liked and that fit me. I was six feet tall and not without a little curve and had bright red hair. Just going to Target wasn't going to cut it. Fortunately, my mom loved vintage fashion and DIY. We would go shopping together, hunting for that magical item that fit perfectly or just needed a little editing. I was always attracted to the different eras of fashion, the patterns and cuts and how they changed over time. It helped that my mom always wore whatever she wanted. A necklace made of pearls and soda tabs. A jean jacket with a mouth embroidered on the back. Overalls with rainbow paint splatters.

When I'm not playing basketball, I'm shopping online or in vintage stores. I can even sew and design a bit, thanks to my independent study major at Stanford that emphasized fashion design and renewable fashion business models.

I must not have a good poker face because Jadea claps and shouts, "We're going out tonight, Arrows!"

I have to laugh at her antics and catch Daniel looking at me curiously. He and his crew are packing up for the day. Jadea notices too and gets a scheming expression on her face. Ever since she caught me and Daniel talking in the locker room, she's been obsessed with pushing us together. If only she wanted to pull us apart. I widen my eyes at her, shaking my head.

She chooses to ignore me and calls in Daniel's direction. The curiosity grows on his face as he walks over. He looks between Jadea and me. "What's up?"

I refuse to speak, narrowing my eyes at Jadea.

"Well," Jadea draws out the word, "the team is thinking of going out tonight, and we were wondering if you would like to join us. We're going to a club called Fire Town." I nearly groan aloud at her choice. A club that takes itself too literally, keeping the room at a dripping-sweat 80 degrees. It's swanky, expensive, and sexy. The only reason we can get in is because Jadea's ex-girlfriend manages it, and they're on good terms.

"Fire Town?" Daniel raises a brow. "Sounds intense."

Jadea approves of his response. "It is! They play 'Hot in Here' every hour." She grins cheekily, slanting a look my way. "And I'm sure Annie would love for you to join us."

"What? No, I wouldn't!" Realizing they're both looking at me as if I'm crazy, I try to reroute. "I mean—not me, specifically. *Everyone* would be happy, I'm sure!" I told Daniel I didn't want everyone to know we're exes, but now I'm wondering if I made a mistake. I can hardly keep up the lie for one small conversation.

Jadea cuts off my embarrassed stuttering. She doesn't even look at Daniel, like we're having a private conversation. "But, Annie, you're obsessed with *Our World*

Through Sports. I'm sure you'd love the chance to talk with him about it. You're practically his biggest fan."

If looks could melt, Jadea would be a puddle on the floor. I huff a breath, glancing at Daniel apologetically. "She's joking." How embarrassing to be your ex's biggest fan! If Jadea knew the context, she would realize I was just keeping tabs on him. It was the only way I knew he was alive.

He grins at me. "So, you're not my biggest fan?" He leans closer to me, puts a hand to his heart. "I'm wounded. I told you that I was a big fan of yours, and yet you don't return the favor?"

I think back to the locker room when he said I was still one of his favorite athletes. Athletes...but not girlfriends?

My face is hot, and every fiber of me wants to curse at Daniel for playing his part a little too well. "I do...do care, obviously..." I stumble over my words, noticing the playful twinkle in his eye.

"So, you want me to come out tonight?" He reaches out a hand, clasping mine and pulling me closer to him. I bump into his chest, our hands trapped between us. "You'll even *dance* with me?"

His words break through the hypnosis of his presence. I jerk back and narrow my eyes at the two of them. Jadea watches the whole thing with a gleeful expression. Daniel looks pleased too, eyes still on me. I point my finger between them. "Did you two plan this? An elaborate scheme to get me to go out and go dancing? I don't dance. Clubs are hot, dark, and most people are too drunk to form a sentence. I'd rather stay home and eat Twizzlers in bed."

"You guys can do that tomorrow," Jadea says cheerfully.

Daniel chooses to ignore her, which is wise. I'm thinking about ways to not ruin her beautiful braids and yet pull every hair out of her head. While I'm plotting, Daniel looks at me hopefully. "I've hardly seen the city, Annie. It would be nice to go out and do something. Is it really so hard to be around me?"

There it is, the challenge. Is it really so difficult to be around an ex? Obviously, it is. But no one wants to admit that, so I just sigh.

"Fine. But *no* dancing."

I head to the locker room, dread swirling through me. I should tell Jadea about Daniel and me, but I know she'll just be hurt that I kept it a secret in the first place. Daniel will only be here two weeks, just long enough for us to keep up our lie. If I can stay away from him and his smile, I should be fine. Then, our past will repeat; Daniel will disappear, and we won't speak for at least another five years.

That's the only way this works.

*

Hours later, Jadea and I are playing dress-up. Typically, it's my favorite part of going out, but tonight every outfit I try on feels wrong. Even Jadea, who usually relishes the opportunity to give my clothes a review, is getting frustrated.

"Annie!" Jadea groans from my living room, waiting for me to come out with my next option. "I've eaten all of your Twizzlers, even the sour-filled ones that I hate. Let's go! I'll be dead before we leave at this rate."

I roll my eyes, stepping out of my bedroom. "That seems unlikely."

She's lying upside down on my couch, her red and brown braids skimming the hardwood floor. Her eyes are closed in dramatic fashion. "Maybe it's my boredom. Makes me want to gnaw off my own arm."

I huff a laugh. "I'm out with the next one."

She opens her eyes, squinting up at me. "Outfit eleven, thank God!" She rights herself on the couch, eyeing me critically. I'm alarmed when her mouth falls open. "What are you wearing?"

Considering this is never what you want to hear, I look down at myself. I'm wearing a leather red mini skirt that I thrifted and lengthened to fit my long legs, and a black crop top. Black cropped boots, too. "What's wrong with it?" After my first ten looks, this seemed a safe choice. "It fits the theme of Fire Town!"

Jadea crosses her arms over her favorite outfit—black ripped jeans and a graphic tee with Sheryl Swoopes' face on it, as well as her red and black Jordans. She looks effortlessly herself, with just a little extra winged eyeliner. "That's too tame. You never wear anything boring unless we're at practice. You even dress nicely for flights."

I join Jadea on the couch, slumping dejectedly. "I know. It's just not working. I think I'll have to stay home."

I'm whining, and I hope she notices. My world is in turmoil, so you'd think she'd let me live my antisocial lifestyle. Even if she doesn't know about Daniel being my ex, I have recently learned that my biological father might have been manipulating the system on my behalf and sabotaging my dream job. It is *a lot*.

"Don't even try that on me, Annie." She narrows her eyes. "You live for this part of going out. Okay, yes, maybe the club or bar scene isn't for you, but you love dressing up. Taking pictures with your friends. Sipping on an overpriced beer and taking an Uber home after an hour. This is not outside the norm. What's the issue?"

"Nothing." What a lie. There are so many things wrong with my life that it's hard to keep track of them.

"Is it Daniel?" she presses.

"No!" I protest, gut reaction. After a moment of her silent skepticism, I sigh and rub my eyes. "Maybe a little. We had this moment in the locker room. He was so kind and handsome, and he shared this memory..." I drift off, remembering his warm hand on mine. His story about my game versus Gonzaga. "But it's utterly ridiculous for me to think about him that way." I need to stop that thought train right in its tracks. Daniel left me. Without a word. He was perfect and kind and intense *before* he disappeared. Even if he's the same way now, that means he could disappear again. I *cannot* let him back into my life.

Jadea practically jumps off the couch at my confession. "I knew it! You do like him. More than just some dumb celebrity crush!" She reaches down and yanks me off the couch. I almost tumble across the rug. "We need to find you the right outfit!"

I laugh a little, mostly out of guilt, as she pulls me into my room. My closet looks like it vomited a sequined rainbow. "I thought you hate clothes!"

"But you don't!" She begins tearing through the pile of clothes. "And you have to show him your best self."

"Jadea!" I pull her attention back to me. I'm starting to feel the icy talons of panic in my chest. "I don't like Daniel. I swear. I don't want to go out with him." The more time I spend with him, the more likely it is that he'll somehow pull me back in. I have enough problems without him.

Her brow furrows. "What's wrong? I thought you just said you had *a moment*." She emphasizes the last two words, the way all best friends do during girl talk.

There's a moment where I waver, looking at Jadea. We've always told each other everything. When she graduated from Stanford, I felt a quiet sense of abandonment. I was always close with my teammates and some of the people in my classes, but it felt like Jadea and I were a set. I hardly went anywhere without her. At the beginning of my senior year, I struggled to figure out my personality with her gone. It was horrible, until it wasn't. I started to lead my team in a silent but steady sort of way. I met Daniel, my first love. Really, my only love. I've never been predisposed to being boy crazy or having lots of crushes or one-night stands. Evan and I dated for six months last year and were pretty serious, but it didn't feel like Daniel and I did. And because it was so confusing and wonderful to be with Daniel, I never could explain it to Jadea. She knows that dating and love are not something I can just jump into, and she's always thought Evan was my first boyfriend, beyond the one I had in the sophomore year of high school, whose greatest passion was baseball trading cards.

I push through my fear. I need to explain Daniel now, when it still feels like I'm not caught in a web of lies. I could maybe explain the secrecy during college, since hundreds of miles separated us. But now, the longer I wait to tell her, the worse the lying gets. "Jadea, the thing is…I already know Daniel."

She looks at me like I have two heads. "How? You mean *in real life?*" She makes it sound like maybe I'm just a delusional fan girl who feels like she "knows" a celebrity.

I sigh. "Yes, real life. We knew each other at Stanford."

Curiosity and excitement flash across her expressive face. "How could you not have told me? That is so cool." She jumps up from sitting on the bed and paces, trying not to step on my avalanche of clothes. "You mean we've been talking about him all this time, and you *actually know* him? Were you in a class together? I can't believe you didn't tell me, considering we talk about his show all the time." Her expression morphs a bit, confusion reaching her eyes. "Was he a big jerk or something? I always thought you liked him, so why keep him a secret?"

She's talking so much; I begin to shrink a little. Her assumption that we only knew each other *in passing* feels like a stake in my heart. If this is how she reacts to that, how will she react to our secret five-month relationship?

So, the words fly out of my mouth before I can stop them. "We *were* in a class together!" I wonder if my voice sounds as hollow to my ears as it does to hers. "And we were doing this huge group project and he..." I search for a reason not to like Daniel and what comes out is shockingly close to the truth. "Abandoned me! We got a C, and I had to do extra credit to maintain my GPA." It all sounds silly to my ears, but it might explain the weird tension between us. "We argued after I accused him of wanting me to do all the work and then we didn't see each other again. Now it's a bit awkward."

"Huh." Jadea ponders this. "He seems like such a nice guy. I guess he's grown up a lot." She says it so easily; I wonder if it's true. Has Daniel grown up? Should I forgive him, just like that?

Fortunately, Jadea has moved on from interrogating me to worrying about my love life. "He really seems to like you, Annie. He always has this soft look on his face when he sees you, and he practically begged to be the one to chase after you the other day. Maybe you intimidated him at Stanford! You *were* a big basketball star." She waggles her eyebrows at me.

I snort. "Yeah, because my quiet girl routine is so intimidating."

"Seriously, give him a chance." Jadea clasps her hands in a pleading gesture. "You two really seem to connect, no matter how stupid he was in the past."

I swallow at the truth in her statement. *Lightning in a bottle. Biggest fan.* "Right." Say Daniel did grow up. Say he had a legitimate reason for leaving without a trace, which I'm not sure even exists. Being with Daniel would still be a mistake. We don't even live in the same city. I'm currently involved in his work and a massive league scandal. My paternal family is potentially full of toxic manipulators, and I'm currently giving my mom the silent treatment.

Yet, my heart still lurches every time I see his smile.

Jadea watches as all the conflicting emotions play out on my face. "No matter your beef in the past, he can bring you and this team some good press. We'll show him a good time tonight, and if he's really so bad, he'll be gone soon."

I take a deep breath. "Right."

She looks at the clock on my nightstand. "Olabisi and the other girls are meeting us downstairs in twenty minutes. We need to figure out your look *now*." We survey the mess we've created. "Let's take a step back." She reasons, "If we took the pressure off, if you were just going out and wearing whatever the hell you wanted, what would it be?"

I mentally race through the possibilities and an epiphany strikes. I smile at Jadea. "Give me ten minutes."

I step out of my bedroom to show her after the promised ten minutes, give or take a few. I put my hands on my hips. "What do you think?"

I'm wearing an unbuttoned, oversized plain white baseball jersey with painted flames running around the hem and sleeves. I created it in college. Underneath, I'm wearing a white body con dress. My shoes are red Converse high-tops decked out with the same flames as the jersey. For the finishing touch, a backwards red Stanford baseball hat and glitter stripes on my cheeks like the eye black players sometimes wear. My hair is loose and falling in waves, half of them stuffed in the cap and the others arranged loosely around my face.

Jadea looks me up and down, a slow grin spreading across her face. "Perfect. You look amazing."

I'm grinning, too. "Let's go."

*

Fire Town is as hot and crowded as expected. We also attract just as much attention as I thought we would.

It's not because we're WNBA players, though a couple gazes latch onto Jadea as if she looks familiar. It's because out of our group—me, Jadea, Olabisi, Allyson, and Taherah—Taherah is the only one under six feet tall. Jadea is a staggering 6'4" and Allyson's lanky Australian frame comes in at 6'5". They're two of the tallest people here, gender notwithstanding.

The other girls make a beeline for the bar, with Taherah already shouting about some new craft root beer she wants to try, but Jadea loops an arm through mine and shouts in my ear, "Let's try to find Daniel."

I must give her a slightly panicked look because she smiles too brightly in response. Fire Town is my least favorite of our usual haunts for several reasons. It's the hottest: the thermostat is set at 80 degrees, and a huge fire feature in the middle of the room keeps the dance floor scorching. It's the loudest: a mammoth DJ stage sits in the back, and the bass is pounding at all times. It's swanky:

drinks here are well past twenty dollars, and my unrefined palate wants one light beer the entire night.

Jadea pulls me around the fire feature, which makes me immediately erupt into my first sweat of the evening, and towards the outskirts of the dance floor. There are small booths there for people who are not into dancing or who need a cooler reprieve. They're very dark, with just a small fake flame candle sitting in the center. I'm scanning the booths for Daniel, but Jadea finds him first. "Over there." She's still shouting in my ear, though I can barely hear her. She gestures to a booth in the corner, a very distinguished spot in Fire Town. Though it frequently slips my mind that Daniel is somewhat famous, I bet the hostess at Fire Town was not so forgetful.

As we get closer, I notice he's not alone. He's with another guy and they're talking quietly as they sip their drinks. He's Indian American, and I'm pretty sure his name is Jeff. He's a part of Daniel's production team. A writer, maybe? We've hardly spoken, though I know he's friendly with some of my teammates.

Daniel looks ridiculously handsome, wearing what is the official hot-guy uniform of Fire Town. A black button-down with the sleeves rolled up and the collar unbuttoned, showing off his smooth chest. He's paired it with black jeans and—to my secret delight—black high-top sneakers that match my own.

I wish I could see the back heel of the left shoe. Daniel always loved my wacky clothes, but he hardly ever wore anything besides track clothes or sweats. If he had to dress up, he wore black. However, some wave of nostalgia made him unusually attached to his black high tops. I once doodled a tiny basketball and track cleat on the white part of the sole, right on the heel, and though I know they're probably a new pair, that rebellious part of me is obsessed with the idea that he might have kept the pair I personalized.

We arrive at the edge of the booth, and I smile, trying not to look nervous. That he's dressed so well. That his curls are already slightly damp with sweat. I don't know if it's the smile or if he just wasn't really looking at first, but he does a full double-take, and the two cut off their conversation. His eyes trace me up and down, and I suppress a shiver. Stupid, rebellious body.

Perusal over, Daniel's gaze turns. "Jadea! Great to see you!" It's a little quieter over here, but he's still almost shouting. "Do you want to dance?"

I feel like I'm having whiplash. Did he just ask Jadea to dance? He knows I don't dance, because I *can't* dance, but he also knows Jadea is my best friend. I used to talk about her all the time. My horror only continues to grow as Daniel tugs an equally stunned Jadea onto the dance floor. Has this all been in my head? He says he owes me, but maybe he also wanted to do this job to meet Jadea. She's beautiful, confident, and speaks her mind. Suddenly, it seems like she has everything in common with this famous version of Daniel, and I'm just the college girlfriend he wishes he could forget.

Daniel's friend Jeff doesn't seem too perturbed, watching them curiously. I suddenly can't stand the sight of them talking as they bop along to the music. "I'm going to get a drink!" I shout at Jeff, who I just barely see nod before I'm heading away to the bar.

I don't see Olabisi, Allyson, and Taherah at first, leaning against the bar, waiting for the bartender to grab my beer. Then I notice them holding down the dance floor near the fire feature. Olabisi's braids are whipping around,

Allyson's cheeks are bright red, and the edge of Taherah's hijab is darker with sweat tonight than it is at practice. They're jumping around and screaming to the music, grabbing hands and pulling new partners in and out of their little circle. They look like they're having the time of their lives.

I grit my teeth with determination. Every part of me hates the idea of dancing in front of other people. I already stick out like a sore thumb with the hair and the height, so making a fool of myself seems likely. However, as I watch everyone on the dance floor, I have to admit that few of them look sexy and suave. Maybe I'm overthinking this.

I throw back the rest of my beer and march determinedly towards Olabisi and the girls. When I stop next to them, a brief feeling of fear overcomes me. Is everyone looking at me? How can they not be? I'm dressed like an overgrown little league player. Before I can spiral too much, the girls grab me and pull me into their circle. Taherah grins up at me, her scarlet Nike Dri-FIT long sleeve plastered to her body. She's wearing matching scarlet cargo pants and the coolest red leather creeper sneakers I've ever seen. She begins jumping up and down to the beat, gesturing for me to do the same. Olabisi and Allyson are already doing it, hardly looking at me. I don't know how Olabisi is managing it in her four-inch hot pink heels.

I rise on my toes a little, trying not to feel too self-conscious. I want to copy everyone else, but my body is too stiff. What should I do with my arms? Taherah sort of punches them in front of her, Olabisi keeps hers on her hips, and Allyson flails around mindlessly. I try to let them sort of sway with me, but it doesn't quite match the beat of the song.

Even as my hesitation continues, I don't quit. I keep dancing, letting the music wash over me. There are even a few seconds where it feels nice, freeing, before the anxiety creeps back in. Fortunately, my friends seem to know just what I need, dancing next to me like I'm not an ice sculpture in comparison. Allyson even spins me around once, making me giggle and more hair falls out of my baseball cap.

When the DJ's beat finally fades a bit to transition to the next song, I hear a familiar voice up on the DJ stage. "Annie, baby, this one's for you!"

My whole group whips around to face the stage, and there's Jadea, alight with joy and a little sparkle of sweat. Her red braids are pulled up into a massive bun, and she's tucked half of her t-shirt into her bra. Most of the bar has turned her way, watching her. That's her magnetism.

She points at me from the stage. "To trying new things!" she shouts into the mic the DJ has clearly surrendered to her, and the crowd goes wild. My girls are screaming next to me, but I'm just standing in awe. When I hear the song, my mouth falls open.

"It's Jock Jams!" I'm screaming then too, looking at my teammates in delight. They're already jumping up and down. When Jadea and I were growing up and making shoddy dunk videos on her camcorder, we frequently played Jock Jams in the background. The first practice I had with the Arrows, Jadea put this mix on, and we played as if we had wings on our shoes.

I start jumping, surprised that the crowd seems really into it. Though considering their age of mostly twenty and thirty-somethings, it hits just the right nostalgia spot. With C+C Music Factory's "Gonna Make You Sweat (Everybody Dance Now)" blaring, I feel that final bit of anxiety lift.

We've only been dancing for about thirty seconds when someone pushes through the crowd towards our group. My heartbeat gets louder when I see that it's Daniel. He's grinning, that sparkle back in his eye.

"You liar!" he yells at me.

I stop dancing, leaning in towards him. "I am not!" But I'm smiling like maybe I am.

"You're dancing! You told me for months and months that you didn't dance!" He grabs both of my hands, pulling me a step or two out of my dance circle. His hands feel like fire in mine. "I told Jadea all you needed was the right song."

It's so loud in there I wonder if I've heard him wrong. "You told Jadea?"

"We were brainstorming ways to get you out here, and this was our big idea. Though it seems you ventured out on your own without our help." The chorus restarts, and the crowd is yelling "Everybody dance now!" so loudly I can't think.

I try to clarify. "That's why you were dancing with Jadea?" Jealousy, meet irony.

He swings our clasped hands, his smile still firmly in place. "Partially. We mostly talked about you, which was a little awkward considering that I already know you so well." He gives me a look, and I cringe a little.

"Working on it," I mutter.

He continues as if I haven't spoken. "It was mostly because of Jeff. He wanted me to ask her if she's open to dating shorter guys."

I let out a delighted, shocked laugh. "What did she say?"

"She just rolled her eyes and went over to talk to him herself. He looked scared when she dragged him onto the dance floor."

"No way!" I put my hands on Daniel's shoulders and push up onto my tiptoes, peeking behind him. I can just see Jadea trying to dance battle Jeff and his absolutely bewildered and delighted expression. "He's not even that short!" I protest, about to lower myself back down. Instead, Daniel turns partway to look back at them too, nudging my leg with his. I rock back on my heels, losing my grip on his shoulders slightly. I think I'm about to crash into the couple dancing behind us when Daniel's firm grip grabs my waist.

The breath flees my lungs and when I meet his gaze, we're only inches apart. "You okay?" he asks, also sounding slightly out of breath.

"Yeah," I whisper, my brain feeling short-circuited. Our sticky bodies are pressed together, his hands hot on my waist. With shaking hands, I loop my arms behind his head. "Daniel, will you dance with me?" I'm still whispering, perhaps unwilling to admit what his touch still does to me after all these years.

He leans in fully, so our foreheads touch. "I was waiting for the most beautiful girl in the room to ask me to dance." I snort a laugh, and we begin to slowly sway, which is totally at odds with C+C Factory's 90's sporty hip-hop fusion. "Did you dress that way for me?" he murmurs, that telltale smile twitching on his lips.

I pull away, about to launch into a feminist rant about dressing for yourself and how he wasn't even in my thoughts when I designed the outfit, but he continues before I can. "Because I work in sports, right?" He swivels my baseball cap around, so he can see the Stanford logo. At the sight, he lets out a low whistle. "And the beloved

Stanford tree? You know how to make a guy weak in the knees."

I laugh again. "Next time I'll wear full football pads."

He's laughing then, too, and I grab his hands, spinning us both. I'm surprised to see that Daniel is actually a good dancer. I never really gave him the chance when we went out at Stanford. Once the shock at my extremely risky spin move has passed, he starts spinning me around more and more. I step on his feet at least twice, but he doesn't flinch. He even tries to dip me, but I keep tensing up like a board and that leads to him demonstrating the proper technique by having me dip *him*. A woman next to us takes a video, and I don't even mind. Three songs come and go, with us laughing and hardly keeping our hands off each other.

Some of the glitter on my cheek has transferred onto his cheek and when I try to wipe it away, it just smears into his skin even worse. "What?" He rubs his cheek. "Don't tell me you think men can't wear glitter."

I laugh and spin him around again, my gaze snagging on the back of his shoe.

And there it is, the Sharpie-drawn basketball and track cleat. Representatives of Daniel and me. I grow even warmer at the sight. Daniel left me, and I don't know why. Maybe that car accident made him realize he wanted someone better. Or that he needed a fresh start. Both terrible excuses to ghost your girlfriend of five months, but Jadea might be right. He could have grown up since then. Shaken off the accident. Maybe we can be friends. It would make things easier these next two weeks.

I'm still dancing foolishly when my phone vibrates in my dress pocket. I ignore it at first, sure that it's my mom. I'll call her back tomorrow. Considering it's after midnight, it seems unlikely that it's the press. After the first call, it rings two more times. When I still ignore those, I feel the quick buzzes of numerous text messages coming in.

Maybe there's an emergency? "One sec," I promise Daniel, taking a step back from him apologetically. He shrugs good-naturedly as I pull out my phone.

There's a split-second of relief when I see it isn't my mom calling. Instead, my heart starts racing when I see that Jack has sent me a message. I open it with a trembling finger.

Unknown Number: Hi, Annie. It's Jack Smith. I really need to talk to you. It involves the team.

There's a break where I see the moving dots that mean he's typing. I hold my breath.

He sends, isolated:

Unknown Number: Please.

"Holy shit," I mutter, thumbs hovering over the keys. Is this really about the team? Or is this a ploy to see me?

I hate the small part of me that really wants to go.

Daniel approaches me. "What's wrong?"

My mouth twists, remembering the strange joy of dancing with Daniel. Now, reality comes rushing back in. "It's Jack. He says he needs to see me urgently."

Daniel raises a brow. "Jack Smith? As in the Jack Smith you are supposed to be avoiding? As in Jack Smith, your father and the owner of your team?"

"That about sums it up." I rub my forehead tiredly. Is Jack on my side? What about his son, my brother Trenton, who is head of the board? Should we all be fighting this thing together? Or maybe I should be separating myself from them instead? I scan the room for Jadea, and Jeff, but don't see her. I just want to go home.

"Text Jadea." Daniel gently grabs my elbow, steering us towards the exit. "I'll take you home."

"Thanks." I sigh, leaning into his touch slightly. The cool air feels incredible on my skin and some clarity sneaks in. Whatever is going on with me is secondary. I have to protect Jadea and my girls, the Arrows. If Jack is doing something to jeopardize that, I need to know.

Sitting in Daniel's cool rental car, I finally type out my response and send it to Jack.

Annie: Okay. Tell me where and when.

Chapter 8

It does not escape my notice that Jack wants to meet with me at the Archers' offices. I shift nervously from foot to foot as I ride the elevator up to his office the next morning. All NBA teams, and those with WNBA counterparts, keep their team offices within their practice facilities. Ours are upstairs, with beautiful glass windows overlooking the courts below. I peek over my shoulder, through the elevator glass, and see my teammates getting started with their individual workouts. Per usual, Olabisi and Jadea are going first. As the team alphas, they want to talk to our coaches first thing in the morning and usually argue over plays that we haven't even workshopped yet. Today is a travel day, with a day game in Indiana tomorrow, so the workout will be light. We'll then watch film together to analyze Indiana's playing style.

The elevator dings, signaling my arrival on the top floor. I step out, nervously cracking my knuckles. I can hardly hear my footsteps as I approach the front desk; everything is drowned out by the pulse thudding in my ears. A young woman, a few years older than me, sits typing diligently on a computer. Her name plate reads *Jenna Green*.

"Excuse me?" My voice is trembling, quiet. I clear my throat again. "Excuse me?" The woman's head snaps up, eyes widening comically when she sees me. I thought long and hard about what I would wear to this meeting but decided on my usual practice clothes. Standard issue scarlet shorts and a reversible practice jersey over a white long sleeve. Boring, but extremely representative of how I want to appear to Jack. Not as his daughter, but a member of the Arrows. A player.

A hooper who bleeds for this team.

"You're here to see Trenton?" she asks, double-checking her notes on the screen.

My brow crinkles. "Trenton?" I echo. "No, I'm here to see Jack Smith. We have an appointment." I check my phone's clock, making sure it's the agreed upon 9 AM. It's in fact a few minutes beforehand, as my anxiety propelled me to try to beat Jack to the meeting he called.

She shakes her head. "No, *Trenton* Smith is expecting you in his office. He'll take the meeting instead. I'll walk you over."

I try to protest, but she efficiently ushers me down the sleek hallway, lined with unusually artistic pictures of railroads and steam engines, the industry that the Smith family made their billions in. I open my mouth a few times, but Jenna keeps a steady hand on my back, pushing me past the office that says *Jack Smith: Owner*. I crane my neck to peek through the door window, but I don't see anyone inside. What is going on? Did Jack ask Trenton to take this meeting for him? Or did Trenton pull this behind his back?

Jenna finally drops me off at Trenton's office, which says *Trenton Smith: Owner and President*. Jack transferred the day-to-day operations to his son a few years ago, prompting the media to praise his practicality and acceptance that young energy was needed to revitalize the franchise. The Archers did win an NBA championship two years ago, so Jack can hardly argue with the results. He's still involved with all the big decisions, but maybe Trenton took this meeting because he handles the daily operations. The small stuff. Me. Accepting my fate, I knock tentatively on the door.

Trenton's voice booms out. "Come in!"

I take a calming breath, smooth my customary braids, and push open the door. My frantic heartbeat matches my swirling thoughts.

What if Trenton hates me for possibly breaking up his family? Even though he's well into his forties, age won't soften that type of blow. Is my mom the first affair Jack has had? Is this a surprise to Trenton and his mom, Tiffany? What does he think about having a new half-sister?

Trenton's office is the stereotypical corner office: huge, littered with screens and framed newspaper articles about the Archers. I don't see any about the Arrows.

"Annie." Trenton looks up from the paperwork littering his desk. He notices me lingering in the doorway and gestures to the leather armchair across from him. "Please take a seat." I do as he asks, hoping the leather won't show my nervous sweat. Trenton gives me a practiced, almost plastic smile as he leans back in his chair. "Thank you for meeting with me."

I watch him warily. He looks like I remember from our passing interactions. Blond hair, just beginning to thin, striking blue eyes, enormous and expensive watch on his wrist. His tie is the perfect shade of Archers and Arrows' red. He looks too fancy for this type of meeting, and I try not to petulantly cross my arms over my jersey. "What's going on?" I finally ask, working to keep my expression neutral. "I thought I was supposed to meet with Jack."

Trenton picks up a pen, passing it back and forth between his fingers. "Right." He studies my face. "Dad told me yesterday that he intended to meet with you. He wanted to clear the air." He waves a dismissive hand. "Make amends or something." Before I can respond, he raises a cool eyebrow. "I think we can both agree *that* would be a waste of time."

Even though I've been thinking the same thing all morning, it stings a little coming from my half-brother. Maybe he's bitter that Jack didn't apologize to *him*. I keep my thoughts to myself and my eyes on Trenton. "That doesn't explain why *we're* meeting."

Trenton is testing me. He leans forward, blue eyes glinting viscously. "Did you think this was the first time Jack Smith betrayed his family and his legacy for a pretty face?" I freeze, hearing a thread of anger in the pointed question. "It's not. It's not even the tenth time. It's just the first one we haven't been able to clean up after."

"Because of me," I say quietly. I can't speak any louder, or Trenton will hear the wobble in my voice. I pray he doesn't notice how shiny my eyes have gotten. I try to blink it away.

It's not even the tenth time.

Trenton leans back, pleased with my answer. "Exactly. My father may be a brilliant businessman, but he's not quite sure what to do about you. So, I offered to help."

"Help with what?" I'm struggling to follow the conversation. "With the media?"

Trenton shakes his head. "No. The media attention will die down on its own. We just need to lay low." I nod along, relieved he doesn't want me to do family interviews or a press conference. "I'm more worried about the future and how you'll fit into it. Specifically, the Smith family's legacy: the St. Louis Archers."

I wait for him to mention the Arrows, even in passing, but he doesn't. He doesn't mention them even as I wear their jersey right in front of him. Trenton continues his monologue without waiting for my reaction. "So, I've asked my father to step away from the team, maybe take a little vacation." He drums his fingers on the edge of the desk. "We have a house in Bora Bora he particularly enjoys." There's a flash of Jack on the beach, sunglasses on, ignoring me and this mess forever. Hurt prickles in my chest. Trenton continues coolly, "The board agreed that is the wisest course of action. With the accusations of manipulation and bribery, it seemed best that he was no longer involved with the team at all. Maybe never again."

My mouth is officially open. Trenton finally notices my shock and hurriedly reassures me. "Of course, his legacy in this city is forever. But his direct oversight is no longer needed."

I've never truly known my biological father, but a small twinge of sympathy twists in my ribcage. Is it possible my mom was right? Was he just expressing his love for me through typical billionaire behavior? Jack probably should step down, especially if it's proven he did something underhanded. However, I wonder if Trenton is truly the best replacement. His smooth talking is almost too smooth. Like every word he says has been rehearsed in the mirror.

I eye him carefully. He almost seems energized underneath the cool I, as if his eagerness to take over is ripping him apart at the seams. "What do you need from me? I have nothing to do with the management of the team. That's between you and your father."

Trenton nods at me condescendingly. "I want you to keep doing what you're doing."

I narrow my eyes. "Which is what, exactly?"

Trenton opens his top desk drawer, pulling out a thin manila folder. "I want you to stay out of it. Forever. At this point, I believe I can sweep this scandal under the rug. Even if my father gets in trouble, I can keep you and the team out of it."

This all sounds too good to be true. "Why would you do that? Don't you want me off the team?"

Trenton shrugs. "I don't watch much of the Arrows' games, but my female assistant assures me you're quite good. You were an All-Star this year. It makes no sense to throw away a good investment."

In some ways, he's saying exactly what I want to hear. I can keep avoiding Jack. I can play with Jadea and the team I love. However, my brain catches every dismissive word he says about the Arrows, and his "female assistant", and I worry that there's something he's not saying.

He flips open the folder and shoves it towards me. "This is a standard-issue NDA. You're welcome to have your lawyer look it over. It says you will never speak out about any business pertaining to the Smith family." He flips the page. "*This* is a legally binding will. I had my father edit it to include you. If you sign the NDA, the terms of the will go into effect. You'll inherit five percent of Father's fortune when he passes, and in the meantime, you will receive an immediate trust of ten million dollars."

"Ten million dollars?" I almost choke on the words. "Right away?"

Trenton taps the papers patiently. "*Only* if you sign the NDA. The will and trust will only go into effect then." It's a mind-boggling amount of money. My rookie contract, which ends this year, has only a $78,000 annual salary. While that is certainly a survivable and welcome amount, it's piddling money compared to the millions that the men make when they're drafted at age nineteen. Shai Gilgeous-Alexander just received a supermax deal for four years of $285 million dollars. $285 *million* dollars. He makes more money in one game than Jadea or I ever will in a whole season.

On the other hand, it feels slimy to take the money. I don't need it. I play overseas too, in Hungary during the off-season, and while it's another exhausting reality women's basketball players face, it's also where I make better money. Financially, I do not need $10 million dollars.

"I don't want the money." I try to sound steady, even as every part of me wants to leave this room and escape Trenton's too-smooth expression. "It feels like a bribe." I leave the last word dangling, waiting to see if Trenton will take the bait and admit he's trying to trap me. Maybe he only wants me to sign the NDA because he thinks I know something about Jack? That my mom will tell me some of his dirty secrets and ruin the family business?

Trenton is nothing if not prepared. He smoothly pulls out another piece of paper. "I anticipated your resistance to accepting money for yourself. But, what about a nonprofit?" I tug on my braid nervously, then cross and uncross my arms. I wish I knew how to act in these situations. Should I play hardball? Should I let Trenton clean this mess up for me? Should I remind him that I'm his sister, or distance myself? I suddenly wish I had brought Jermaine with me. "Something we're considering is creating a nonprofit that funds scholarships for women or non-binary student athletes. This would also include other programs to improve women's sports, including camps,

Title IX celebrations, and other events. Instead of the money being transferred to you, it can be put into the funding of the nonprofit, and you will be given a board seat." This offer had to be for good press and to get me off his back, I *know*, and yet it is so tempting. To have millions going to women's sports and the growth of the industry I love so much.

"And I don't have to work with the family?" I sound pathetically hopeful to my own ears. Is this the way to pay the debt I owe for even being a part of this poisonous family? "I won't have to see...Jack?"

Trenton shakes his head almost vehemently. "No, in fact, we'd love to keep you separate from the family. I know that's what your mother wanted, and we agree." I wonder what "we" he's even referring to—him and his mom? He seems to have pushed Jack completely out of the picture.

Even though I secretly agree with him, a small part of me feels that sad, unwanted teen version of myself waking up. That girl who knew she had a father out there who didn't want her. Now, my half-brother sits in front of me, literally rejecting any offer to spend time with me. We're strangers, and we've just agreed to stay that way forever.

I swallow down those feelings and reach for one of his fancy fountain pens. I need to keep moving forward, and this will help me do that. "Where do I sign?"

As I do, trying to keep my hand steady, I feel like I might be making a mistake. The NDA looks pretty standard, and since I know very little about my biological family worth publicly sharing, it hardly seems a threat to me. Trenton might be handing me a hush nonprofit to stay out of this mess, but he doesn't know me. I've always been the ostrich with my head in the sand. Not the eagle on attack.

Once I've signed and initialed in the appropriate places, Trenton smiles too brightly. I'm suddenly itching to get out of his office. "Are we done here?"

He nods, calling his assistant in so she can take the damning manila folder. "I'll reach out when the scholarship fund is ready to go. For now, keep doing what you're doing." As I stand up, he seems to finally notice my apparel. "Do you have practice today?"

I bite my tongue, so I don't tell him to turn his head and look out his gigantic window. "Yes," I say through gritted teeth. "We leave for Indiana in a few hours."

I'm hovering in the door, unsure if I'm dismissed, when he asks distractedly, looking through his desk for something, "How's the team doing this season?"

My whole body flares cold and then hot at his question. I can't keep the anger out of my tone when I shoot back, "Aren't you an owner of the team? How do you not know?"

The situation only becomes worse when Trenton looks back up at me. He's puzzled, as though my anger is misplaced. He finally smiles. "I've always been more focused on the men's side of things. Sorry." Hollow words. My heart feels like it's being squeezed with a vise.

"Yeah, so is everybody else." I have to turn and slam the door behind me before I start screaming at him.

My whole body is fizzing with anger and unsaid words. There should be better comebacks, logical ones that make him seem small and ridiculous and misogynistic, but instead, I just leave. I've always been that way. I know how I feel, it's almost overflowing from me, but how to articulate myself? Women who are stoic and cold are heartless bitches. Women who are overly emotional are crazy. We never win, and so I shut my mouth and play. I'm always too afraid to say what I feel.

It's the shame that gets you.

When I escape the elevator and rush out onto the courts, Jadea is just finishing her individual workout. "Jadea!" I wave her over. She stops talking with Coach Zak, looking up from the tablet they're studying, and jogs my way. Daniel and his camera crew are in between our two practice courts, and he's wearing a suit, speaking to the camera. I can just hear some of his words about where we are in the season. "Today's August third and the Arrows have only five more games to solidify themselves as the number one seed in the East..."

Jadea approaches before I can hear more. "Where have you been?" she demands. "I saw you with Daniel last night and then you disappeared! I'd make some dumb sex joke, but the expression on your face tells me that wouldn't go well."

I shake my head sharply, and the meeting with Trenton comes spilling out. "What have I done, Jadea?" I'm shaking when I sink into one of the folding chairs on the sideline. "He looked so smug and sure, and I thought maybe this could all end quietly with some money put into women's sports, but now that I've signed it, I feel sick. He's terrible. I honestly don't think he cares about this team at all. Or me. His sister."

I look at Jadea for reassurance, but I'm surprised to see she looks faintly sick, too. "I don't like Trenton Smith," she admits, her voice sounding smaller than usual. "He's the reason I do the dunk show before every game."

She could have slapped me, and I would have felt less surprised. "But you *love* the dunk show. You love dunking." I know our coach and Jermaine think it's beneath her, as a professional athlete, but I always thought it was just Jadea's showmanship shining through.

She sits next to me, knocking her knee into mine. "I *do* love dunking. I loved our videos growing up, and I love the TikToks and social media stuff we do. I love experimenting with different dunks. It reminds me of when we were kids, imagining a league where we could be Michael Jordan or LeBron James. Where we were given every opportunity they had." I nod encouragingly. "But it was Trenton who approached me with the idea of doing the dunk show before home games. He saw the videos online, the high view count. He thought it would be great for selling tickets."

Logically, I know it *is* great for selling tickets. The WNBA uses Jadea on every branding item they can because she's the biggest star this league has. And a lot of that star power does come from her dunks. Jadea takes a deep breath. "I told him no. I would happily do videos for our social media and any other promotional marketing, but it seemed desperate and exhausting to do it all the time. They would never ask Steph Curry to put on a three-point shooting clinic before every game to sell tickets. Just seeing him play would be enough."

My heart is sinking, heavy as a stone. "But he made you do it?" I can't imagine someone making Jadea do anything.

She shrugs. "He told me that the team needed me and that more tickets meant good things for the WNBA. Technically, he's not wrong, but where do we draw the line? Why can't we just be respected for being the great athletes we are?" She clenches her fists. "I want this league to be the best it can be, so I do it. I convince myself it's fun and really *it is.* But it also makes me feel sort of ashamed. Like I'm a clown just begging for a scrap of the audience's attention." She shakes her head. "We shouldn't have to do that."

We sit in silence for a moment. I let her words course through me and picturing Trenton's smug face and my silence in his office only makes me angrier. I stand up and begin to pace, trying to release some of the tension flowing through me. "That is bullshit, Jadea!" My words are coming out fast and hot. "All of this is bullshit! NDAs and Twitter trolls and Trenton Smith with his plastic fucking smile! He doesn't even care about women's sports. He's just trying to squeeze the most money out of the team with the least amount of effort."

Jadea stands up, putting her hands up in a placating gesture. "None of this is new, Annie. Trenton just put a face to it."

She's right, but I don't slow down. "Let's be honest, Jadea, this is our dream, the fantasy we've had since we were kids, and it's magical. Every day feels like walking on fucking clouds!" I bark a bitter laugh. "But it's also complicated. You become resigned to the lack of equality. We're both lucky *and* unlucky. Lucky I can play and do what I love, unlucky that many men in the world refuse to even acknowledge us. There's no winning this!"

Daniel has stopped his spiel, probably because my insane ranting is bleeding into whatever he's saying. I'm practically panting with anger, and I'm sure my skin is a splotchy, raving red. Before I know what I'm doing, I march over to Daniel and his camera crew. "Are you looking for interviews?" I demand, focusing on Daniel.

He doesn't hesitate, his dark gaze unwavering. "Always." He motions at me to indicate that I have the floor.

A production assistant hurriedly hands me a mic. "Hello, America, this is Annie Larger." For a moment, all my angry adrenaline feels on the verge of crashing. This isn't live, but I'm still on camera, holding a mic like an avenging sword. I barrel ahead, for once letting those emotions spill out. "I would like to conduct a little experiment if our host is up for it?"

Daniel responds as any consummate professional host would respond to a crazy woman. A crazy woman who was once his girlfriend. "Of course."

I smile at him and then the camera, but it feels more like baring my teeth. "Would you mind getting out your phone and opening Instagram? You can all do it too!" I gesture to the crew behind the camera, including a displeased looking Iris Langley.

They all willingly pull out their smartphones and open the app. "Now, I assume you all follow ESPN?" Daniel nods, and so do some of his crew members. "If you could go onto their Instagram and find a video clip or post about the WNBA? Maybe the last one they posted?"

Daniel is the first to find one. I wonder if he knows where I'm going with this. Is he remembering those days we lay in bed, and I flipped through the channels trying to find a WNBA game and couldn't? Is he remembering squeezing my hand and buying some weird streaming service so we could watch the games together? I shake the memory off. "Here's one." He shows me the video on his phone. "It's a New York Liberty clip. A defensive trap that stops the other team from tying the score. The Liberty win at the very last second." He watches the clip for a second time, analyzing the motions. "It's an amazing read of their opponents' plan with a Breanna Stewart block to end." There is a warm dose of admiration in his tone.

I hear Iris muttering something about putting the clip in during post so people can see it on TV. "Awesome." I'm feeling eerily calm now. "Can you click on the comments for the video and read the first few? And please ignore the bots." A wry smile twists on my face.

I point the mic towards Daniel, like every reporter has always done to me. I can tell Daniel is uncomfortable with the comments he reads when he hesitates and clears his throat. "The first one reads: 'Is this supposed to make me want to watch the WNBA?'" Angry tears begin to glimmer in my eyes, but I refuse to let them fall. Crying and yelling never make for a logical experiment. Daniel continues, keeping his voice even. "The next one says: 'I've seen middle schoolers play better." My fingers tighten on the mic, but I don't waver. Daniel's eyes are glued to his phone. "This one says: 'Go back to the kitchen.'" When he looks at me then, I swear I see my own anger reflected in his own eyes. "That's horrifying," he finally says, his cheerful disposition effectively smothered.

I take back the mic. "The WNBA has lots of amazing fans. If you check the WNBA Instagram or even ESPNW, you will see evidence of those wonderful people. However, when mainstream media posts anything about women's sports, especially team sports, the post receives dozens of hateful comments. When people ask me how I feel about playing in the WNBA, I want to say it's a dream come true. Because it is." I look squarely at the camera, my voice quivering. "I swear, it *is*. But really, it's way more complicated than that. Sometimes it feels like playing in a vacuum, like screaming into the void. They're analyzing the NBA draft weeks before it happens on SportsCenter and not even mentioning what's happening in the WNBA during our *actual season*." I swear Iris Langley looks irritated in a different way now. Like she's remembering some suit at HBO, wondering how a woman could lead a show about sports. Like maybe, she understands every flame licking my ribcage right now. I take a deep breath and soften my tone. "There have been some amazing strides in women's college sports recently, but professionally, things are stIll moving so slowly. Caitlin Clark's rookie salary is $76,000. Fellow number one pick and generational player, Victor Wembanyama's is $12.2 *million*. She's making less than one percent of his salary." I let that sink in before I continue. "And while some of you may be hearing about my biological father and his alleged misconduct and wanting to turn away from us, please don't. Whatever happens to me, I love this league. Stop comparing the NBA and WNBA like only one can exist. These women are worth it, I promise. Give them respect. Get them paid." There's an awkward pause. I try a tremulous smile. "Thank you."

Satisfied, I hand the mic back to Daniel. He says a few things after I walk away, but my ears are ringing too much to hear him. I feel like I just played in a championship game, and my adrenaline finally crashed. How could I do that? It's still a few weeks until Daniel's piece airs, but this goes against Jermaine's plan. No one will want to hear what a billionaire's bastard child has to say about the gender pay gap. I also didn't even call Jermaine about Trenton's ridiculous NDA. My life is spinning out of control, and I'm only egging it on. I sidle up to Jadea, who has been watching the whole thing. "How did I do?" I ask nervously. "Did I say the right things?"

Jadea wraps an arm around my shoulders, pulling me off the court and towards our film room. Coach Rembert is probably wondering where the hell we are. "Annie, there's not just one way to say something important. You were great."

While her words reassure me, I do hear the tension underneath. It hasn't solved any of our real problems. I still hastily signed Trenton Smith's NDA without knowing his plans for me. Jadea is still being forced to put on a show by the very same half-brother. I'm still being questioned in the media. The league is still investigating Jack for misconduct, and I still haven't spoken to him.

I'm still pretending not to care that Daniel ghosted me after I sat by his hospital bed for days and signed his cast with a heart.

When we sit down in the dark room, the projector screen already lit up with Indiana's plays, I feel utterly defeated. There must be a right play, the perfect one that I'm just not seeing, but it continues to elude me.

I put my head down and listen to Coach Rembert and my teammates discuss tomorrow's game. For once, I don't find their analysis comforting.

How close am I to losing all of this?

Chapter 9

We're supposed to be boarding the bus to Indianapolis in twenty minutes, but I'm still on the court shooting. I've decided to practice my free throw, because out of all my shots, they feel the most rhythmic. My three-pointers are streaky, and my jumpers are rare. But at the line, I almost never miss.

Everyone else already boarded the bus, and most of the lights were turned off by the facility manager. It's dim in here, with pockets of low lights reflecting off the court.

That's where Daniel finds me.

I hear him walking across the courts, quiet and steady. I don't turn to look at him; instead, I inhale and exhale when I see the ball swish through the hoop. My brain needed a vacation from Trenton, Jack, and all the men out there who are just like them.

He doesn't say anything, hovering at the baseline. His face is half in the shadows, but I can see that he isn't smiling. He rebounds a few balls for me, cleanly passing them back so I can shoot again.

Finally, when I've made eight shots in a row, I stop. Some of that adrenaline-fueled rage has settled, and basketball serotonin is surging through me instead. "I'm sorry," I say, turning the ball over in my hands. "For blowing up in that interview."

"Don't apologize." Daniel's voice is firm. He takes a couple of steps towards me, into a pocket of fluorescent light. "Everything you said was true. We took screenshots of the comments to show our viewers. You shared what you were feeling in the moment. Nothing wrong with that." He smiles then, though it looks a little softer than I've seen these past few days. A little more personal, a little less man-on-the-silver-screen.

I huff and throw another shot up. It clangs off the rim loudly. Daniel wordlessly passes it back to me. "I can't just say how I feel. Sometimes I don't even *know* how I feel. I know that the WNBA is frequently ignored. I know that some of the most amazing fans in sports struggle to find our games on TV. I know that when one of us gets hurt, the injury might not even make mainstream news. I know that every time we dunk and prove ourselves, men get more disgusted that they might have to tune in." I dribble emphatically with each point. "But the WNBA also isn't perfect. I know that straight, white girls like me have more media and sponsorship opportunities. I know that there are sometimes toxic coaches or teams. It happens. This scandal with Jack, Trenton, and my...family, where does that fit in? If the league's investigation confirms all the mismanagement Jack has been accused of, what will this team do? They would not be remiss in getting rid of me. I understand that. I benefited from underhanded activity, even if I knew nothing about it. But..." I trail off, feeling like I'm talking in circles. If I were trying to be a moral person, a good person, what would that hypothetical person do? Should I bow out of the season? Should the league suspend me for a few games as punishment? Am I being selfish if I want to play?

If that's what I want to do forever?

Daniel steps even closer to me, effectively blocking my next compulsive, agitated shot. He opens his hands, and I pass the ball to him. He turns it over, admiring it, and then looks at me. "But..." he continues softly, "you were an All-Star this year. You're second in the league in assists and fifth in steals. You and Jadea have created an exciting identity for a new team, with the help of Lynn, Olabisi, Allyson, and all your teammates. It's okay to admit you love what you have, and you feel like you deserve it, Annie. It's okay to fight for it."

My eyes are watering as usual, though it's difficult to tell what kind of tears they are. Desperate, angry, sad? Hopeful, when I really look at the belief shining in Daniel's face?

I'm about to respond when Daniel asks, "Do you want to play some one-on-one?" There's a teasing quality in his tone, even if I can't fully see the sparkle in his eye.

"Right now?" I say, barking out a laugh. "Sure, why not?"

"You first." He bounces the ball to me, and we start at the top of the key, both trying to score on the same basket. Half-court play.

I don't want to brag—but I am a WNBA player and All-Star, as Daniel just pointed out. So, I start small. I dribble the ball a few times between my legs, switch hands, stalk back and forth across the top of the key. Daniel keeps his eyes on me, the distance between us less than a foot. I carefully avoid his bad leg, the left one, but then dart past him and score the easy lay-up.

Daniel groans good-naturedly, and I pump my fist. "Your turn." When Daniel has the ball at the top, I give him a bit more room to breathe.

It only seems fair.

What doesn't seem fair is Daniel taking advantage of that space and shooting an easy three-point shot. The ball swishes through the basket behind me, and I spin around to face him, mouth open. "You didn't use to be able to do that!"

In fact, Daniel used to have abysmal aim. As a track star, he could absolutely keep up on defense, but his shot was terrible. The Daniel of today shrugs, a cocky smile tilting up the dimple. "I play pick-up every weekend with some people in New York."

I huff impatiently at his response, and we go again, playing the first to ten points. In the end, I win. It's close enough to make Daniel happy, and with a decent enough gap to make *me* happy. When I win it 10–6, I jump a little in excitement. "Yes!" I point at him. "Victory for Annie Larger! Just like the old days!"

It's a familiar routine from our time together at Stanford, one that usually involved the loser pouting for a few hours, but Daniel isn't pouting. Instead, there's a softness in his face, his eyes. He looks like he's proud of me. For winning *pick-up basketball.*

"You're different now," I blurt out, discombobulated by his graceful and kind losing face. "Than when we were dating."

Daniel freezes for a moment, clutching the ball hard. I can see the whites of his knuckles. After a strange moment of tension, he releases a sigh. Straightens. Smiles, just a little. "I *am* different. The accident changed me. I had to start over."

I want to protest, but instead I wipe some sweat off my brow, stalling my quick tongue. I couldn't have been a part of that future? Or he couldn't have at least let me know he needed to move on? I don't want to ruin the moment by arguing over the past, so I say, "You were so intense, mostly about track. Not to say you couldn't be social when you needed to be, but you smiled less. You were moodier, more focused on your goals than partying or meeting with friends." I tilt my head, studying him and wishing he weren't so beautiful. He looks like an angel standing in the strange, low fluorescents, eyes shadowed and skin gleaming. "We just stayed in every day and watched sports. Hit the gym together. I went to your track meets, and we analyzed your times. You went to my games, and we analyzed my shots. Now, you've lost that obsessive edge. That frenetic energy." It's difficult to describe how I feel about the softer, kinder Daniel. He's wonderful, but I thought he was wonderful before. I thought we were wonderful together.

Daniel's smile wavers a bit. "I had to lose it, remember? I couldn't run hurdles with a steel rod in my leg and a partially collapsed lung." I remember arguing with a nurse about Daniel's accident when I was first called to the hospital. I said numbly that it couldn't be possible that he had been hit; he always wore reflective strips when he ran. He was always cautious, focused, *safe*. The nurse told me Daniel had a broken femur, three broken ribs, and a collapsed lung. He was lucky to be alive, and he would never run hurdles again.

"Is that why we broke up?" I try to say it tactfully, but the words still have that bitter edge. "Because we couldn't do the same things anymore? Would it be too painful to watch me play?" A small part of me can understand that.

What would our relationship have been like? Would he have resented me? Would I have made myself smaller to fit into his new environment?

"Annie." Daniel's eyes are burning as he looks at me. His voice is strangled. "I'm so terribly sorry for how I left things. My life was falling apart, and I took it out on you."

"And now my life is falling apart, and you showed up to help," I volley back at him. "But would you have shown up if Jadea hadn't called?" It's a cutting response, but one he doesn't duck away from. The Daniel I used to know was a bit of a sore loser, someone who avoided giving in and saying sorry. Now he appears calm and contrite. He feels like a stranger, albeit a likable one.

"Do you remember your first game in the league?" Daniel smoothly changes the subject. I blink and then nod. I was so nervous before we went out that I started bawling incoherently in the locker room. When I blubbered apologies to my teammates, Jadea put her arm around me. Olabisi rolled her eyes and put a Sarah McLachlan song on the speaker, causing me to snort with laughter. Coach Rembert looked at her watch and told me, "Thirty seconds of fear. And then forty minutes of fearlessness." I looked at them all, and it hit me. This could be my second family, if I let it. We'd fight and get tired of each other and sometimes let the politics of the game get to us, but we'd love each other. I scored four points in the 12 minutes I played. Even better, I passed Jadea the winning assist.

It was a different kind of lightning in a bottle. More like the brewing of a spectacular storm.

Daniel interrupts my musing with his own recollection. "Of course, I had to pay for some ridiculous TV streaming service to get the game because it wasn't on any of the main channels." My mouth falls open. My first game was only a month after his accident. That story about me playing at Gonzaga, that makes sense. But watching me in the WNBA, after he disappeared on me? I struggle to believe him. "I even shared my account information with the Stanford Athletic Department, and they had a viewing party for you and Jadea at the student union. I desperately wanted to see you achieve your dream, and the utter disbelief on your face when you made your first basket and Jadea pointed at you...it was that same magic as when I first saw you play against Gonzaga."

There's a pause. "There was pain that time, when I watched." He doesn't elaborate on what kind of pain he means. "But I couldn't miss it. I never had that moment of achieving my dream. I never ran at the Olympics or at the Diamond League, but you're in the WNBA. Now that your dream is in jeopardy...I would have found a way to be here now, with or without Jadea."

"But-but..." I'm stammering, completely thrown off by his admission, "...you're a Liberty fan."

There's a beat where he's giving me a confused look, and then he lets out a huge laugh. "Annie." He's fully grinning now. "That's all you can think to say?"

I cross my arms petulantly, trying to hide the blush suffusing my face. "You are a confusing man." I want to sound grumpy, but there is an undeniable note of affection in my voice. Maybe Daniel just needed to get his head on straight after the accident. While I don't agree with the methodology he chose for that fresh start, maybe I understand it. Plus, he still cared enough to watch me play, even when we weren't together. I try to let my guard down a bit. "Thank you for being here. It helps."

The smile he gives me in response is out of a movie. A victorious, glorious smile. I blush even deeper. Trying to distract myself and make the moment last, I pass him the ball. "Switch with me. I need to study your new and improved shot."

We shoot in contemplative silence for a few beats, me with the mid-range jumper and him at the free throw line.

He frowns in concentration, staring down the hoop. "I think I need the adrenaline to shoot well. Just standing here and shooting feels off." Spoken like a true runner. I stifle a smile.

When his third shot in a row pings off the rim, I walk over. "Here, let me." I hand him the ball. "Put your arms in a shooting motion."

He raises the ball, not looking at me. I step into his space. He emanates a pleasant heat. I gently push his elbow out and straighten his wrist. I nudge his back foot and push it forward so they're equally toeing the line. I lightly push his waist so he's facing the basket more head-on.

Every place we touch seems electric. My fingertips burn. "Try it now," I say, breathless.

The ball falls through with such a perfect swish that it hardly touches the net.

I know I should step back from Daniel, but the moment feels heavy. Heavy with our past and our present. Heavy with that lightning in a bottle feeling. Would it be so bad to try again? Could I ever trust him? Has he really changed, like it seems he has?

The ball bounces right back to Daniel, and he hardly moves as he holds it, maybe waiting for me to step back. We're only inches apart. I could wrap my arms around him, feel his warmth course through me. I step carefully around him, reaching for the ball.

Our hands touch, surprising me. I meet his gaze, and I see that sparkle in his eye and the endearing mole on his jaw and his beautiful dark curls and that tiny white scar over his brow, and I've never wanted to kiss someone more in my life.

There is something about Daniel and me that just works. I can feel it.

I'm leaning in, the ball pressed between us, and I can feel a whisper of his minty breath. "Annie," he whispers. There's something in his voice, wonder or awe or that same desperation I feel.

"Daniel," I murmur back, voice trembling. My whole body is trembling.

There's a beat where it seems like we'll drop the ball and kiss and press together so tightly, and then we'll back into the basketball hoop and kiss harder, but then I hear a voice.

Jadea's voice.

"Annie!" Fortunately, she sounds far away, like she's in the tunnel, which means she hasn't seen us yet. "The bus is going to leave without you!"

My brain fires all at once, and I back away from Daniel abruptly. The game. Indiana. Trenton. Jack. He drops the ball, letting it bounce between us, running a frustrated hand through his hair. "Coming!" I shout to Jadea. I start walking backwards towards the locker room, where I'd stored my luggage. "I'm sorry," I tell him. "We have a game tomorrow." It's a ridiculous thing to say, because he's going too. His crew will be filming there, but they're flying out tomorrow morning with their equipment.

I look at him apologetically, trying to communicate that even though this conversation was difficult, it was necessary. The first step. "Any time, Annie." He steps towards me, grabbing my hand. "You have my number."

I'm lost in Daniel's dark eyes, an emotional black hole that's threatening to swallow me up. I don't know how long

I stand there until I'm interrupted by, "Annie? We need to leave." It's Jadea's voice, curious and wary at the way Daniel and I are standing.

I leap back from him, dropping his hand. Again. I try not to look guilty like I wasn't about to throw away past trust issues and make out with Daniel right there on the court.

I tug on my braid. "Sorry. Daniel was just rebounding for me. Helping me get out my feelings."

It's the wrong thing to say. Jadea's expression grows mischievous, eyes lighting up. "I've just had the most incredible idea." She points between us. "We'll talk, the three of us, after we get back from Indiana."

"What idea?" I try to sound casual, but Jadea doesn't fall for it.

She shakes her head. "It's just that maybe your animosity towards Daniel has led to some more useful feelings." Useful might not sound like a scary word to most people, but from Jadea any number of things could be useful. A dunking contest to end practice? Thirty pairs of Jordan sneakers? Matchmaking her best friend and her ex, when she doesn't know it's her ex?

"Don't go anywhere." Jadea beams at Daniel, and he smiles sheepishly in response. "We'll talk soon."

She puts an arm over my shoulders and pulls me away. "Sorry," I mouth to Daniel over my shoulder. I have to admit that even though his past mistakes make me uncomfortable, the secrecy surrounding our past relationship is probably making him uncomfortable, too.

As we board the bus and take our seats, Jadea gives me that same teeth-baring smile I gave to Daniel's camera crew a few hours ago. "We don't need Trenton Smith's bribes, Annie. We can make waves of our own."

The feminist sentiment makes my heart thud with a fierce pride. The scheming expression that accompanies it makes my stomach drop.

Suddenly, I wish we were playing in Indiana for weeks. I don't want to know whatever Jadea is planning when we come home.

Chapter 10

The trip to Indiana is a story of highs and lows.

High: Jadea has four dunks during the game, including a fast break assist from me. We beat the Fever 109–101. Coach Rembert tells us we have four games remaining until the playoffs, and we only need to win two of them to secure our number one seed in the East and earn a first-round bye. Olabisi and Jadea get into a water fight, and the locker room erupts into chaos. I apologize to the janitor, asking for more towels, but I'm hiding a smile.

Low: We walk towards the tunnel during halftime, talking animatedly to each other and waving to the few Arrows fans in the crowd. I've barely stepped into the tunnel when I see a man moving closer to the railing, as though he's desperate for an autograph. It does happen sometimes, especially to Jadea, who is just a few steps in front of me. I'm about to point him out to her when he shouts, "Nepo bitch! Tell your father to go to Hell!" It only takes a beat to realize he's talking to me, and then I'm knocked out of step by a plastic cup that he's thrown at my head. I feel the ding of pain on my temple and then the sweet stickiness of what smells like Dr. Pepper trickling down my neck onto my red uniform. Taherah is walking next to me, and grabs hold of my arm. "Annie! Are you alright?"

I blink at her once in confusion and look at the man who threw the cup, who is now arguing with some fans by the bleacher railing. "I-I think I'm fine." My voice is trembling. I'm genuinely shocked, unsure how to react. Occasionally, heckling leads to something this extreme, but I've never been the target of it before. It's also more common at high-tension games with lots of people, like at NBA games.

Jadea whirls around, and the rest of the team notices it too. "What happened?" she demands, her eyes tracing over my wet, red face and the cup on the ground. "Who did this?" She sounds furious, and I react the exact opposite, eyes welling with tears.

Typical.

Taherah looks up at the stands again, but the cup-thrower has disappeared. Probably knew that he was about to get into trouble. "It's fine," I choke out, taking a step forward. "Let's just go." A confrontation is beneath us, especially when I'm not hurt. It's not unusual for people to hate billionaires and their offspring.

Taherah doesn't let it go, glancing between Lynn and Jadea. "He called her a nepo bitch. It sounds like he hates Jack."

Lynn looks at me sharply, and I can't help the embarrassment that almost chokes me. This scandal has gotten so out of control that now fans are throwing drinks at me as if I'm the bad act at an open mic night.

Jadea is incensed. "We have to find this guy and tell security. Coach Rembert!" Jadea is looking around, but our coaching staff has already walked ahead into the locker room. "This isn't okay. You haven't done anything wrong."

The best response is to keep moving, not make a fuss. I swallow and hook arms with Jadea. "Come on." I pull her, still protesting, to the locker room, ignoring the curious gazes of fans nearby.

We're about to step out of sight of the court when Taherah says, "Wait, look." Her voice is low with awe. Jadea and I turn around, my other teammates clustered at our backs like soldiers. It's Daniel, standing on the sideline with a camera in his hand. He's with two security guards, gesturing between what's on the screen and the crowd. We're too far away to hear what's being said, but Daniel eventually points out someone in the crowd, and it's definitely the man who threw the cup at me. Security nods resolutely and calmly collects the angry man, who shouts at Daniel and the security staff as they escort him out.

Daniel glances at the tunnel as he crosses the court to be with his crew, and I swear we hold glances for a moment. I feel avenged. He didn't make a scene. He didn't punch the guy out or have a macho shouting match over my honor. He just did what needed to be done.

Sexiest thing ever.

"That was amazing." Taherah sounds breathless, the romantic she is.

Now Jadea pulls *me* back towards the tunnel, even as my gaze feels attached to Daniel. I watch his walk through the crowd, his gesturing to his crew, his laugh and smile as they exchange jokes.

Jadea's voice snaps me back. "He's *perfect*." She doesn't say it as a compliment, but as though he's the perfect pawn for her scheme. Like she has a plan and wants him to be the star of it.

High: Jadea doesn't mention her scheming after that, and I hope that in the flurry of basketball and her caring for me (i.e., helping me wipe off a lukewarm, syrupy Dr. Pepper stain), she's forgotten about it. She does sneak a few extra looks my way, but I'm hoping it's only out of emotional concern.

Low: The moment where I get hit in the head by the drink and the man's aggressive, "Nepo bitch!" goes viral on Twitter. I just can't escape social media. Jadea shows me several clips of them debating the attack on ESPN and various other sports shows. While those clips are more professional and agree that the man should be banned from the stadium for his obscene behavior, social media is not so kind.

One tweet reads: *I think the drink is kind of extreme, but people shouldn't ignore what he said. Why is she still playing?*

High: Daniel texts me a video link to the first-ever U.S. women's basketball game at the Olympics, which we won triumphantly. I watch the game three times on the bus and try not to give in and call Daniel. Shouldn't these feelings be gone after all this time?

The final low of the 48-hour road-trip: My mom calls twice, and I don't call her back. I remember reserving her tickets for this Indiana game, since it's not too far from St. Louis, but I didn't see her in her usual spot next to Jadea's mom. We never fight, and so it turns out that when it finally happens, neither of us is a good fighter. I'm still that ostrich, with its big, dumb head in the sand.

*

Jadea and I have a tradition on off days during the season. They are few and far between. The WNBA has a 44-game schedule, and we usually play two or three times a week. And if we aren't playing games, we're practicing or having team meetings. To have a full day to ourselves feels like a breath of fresh air. No Twitter. No hecklers in the stands. No Trenton or Jack. No Daniel. Just Jadea and I relaxing.

We usually go to brunch at an old-fashioned diner, Suzy's, just down the street from our apartments. Then I drag Jadea thrifting, which she has just enough interest in because of the possibility of finding a vintage sneaker or a t-shirt with Michael Jordan on it. Mostly, we laugh and try on the most absurd things we can find. Fuzzy bucket hats. Mom jeans with small mirrors up the leg. Elton John-style sunglasses. Platform sneakers with rainbow rhinestones on the toe.

I may or may not have bought all of those things at one time.

I'm sitting in our usual booth, the one with a small tear in the baby blue leather seat and a coffee stain on the table. I'm not surprised to arrive first, and neither is our usual waitress, Bethany, who waves at me before going back to her other tables. She knows Jadea will probably show up in a flurry of activity in the next few minutes.

My best friend does not disappoint.

She looks like she possibly sprinted down the block, her braids whipping behind her and her chest heaving. She nearly topples into our booth, and I smile apologetically at the other people eating nearby who look our way. "Sorry!" Jadea huffs. "I meant to actually be on time today so you wouldn't feel ambushed, but unfortunately, I saw him walking and I was only a few steps ahead, so, sorry—"

"Jadea!" I wave a hand in her face. "Slow down! I have no idea what you're talking about."

She readjusts so she's sitting up straight and breathes in deeply. I gesture with my hand for her to continue. "Daniel," she says simply. "He's on his way." I gape at her, not understanding a word coming out of her mouth, but then I see him.

His tall and lean body, stepping foot in *our* little diner. He's still wearing his customary black, though this time it's black track pants, black Nike sneakers, and a black Stanford T-Shirt with red lettering. He's also wearing a baseball cap and those glasses I like so much. Even with the incognito look, heads still turn when he walks in. It's the presence that emanates from him that makes him so compelling to watch on TV, that makes me want to lean towards him and smell his signature sage and mint cologne.

What makes it worse is that when Daniel spots me in the booth, he gives me that movie star smile. The one that shows off the mole on his jaw and that half-dimple in his right cheek. I try not to melt into the seat. I should smile back, but instead I just manage a half-hearted wave and a glare at a cat-who-ate-the-canary looking Jadea.

"What were you thinking?" I whisper at her. "This is our day off. *Ours.*" Not only did Jadea inadvertently invite my ex to brunch, she also ruined one of our only girls' days this season.

Daniel is walking our way, but Jadea manages to make me nervous before he even sits down. "This is *for* us," she insists in a calm, normal voice. "I have a great idea, and Daniel can help us with it."

Jadea's last great idea was to invite Daniel into town and that has only caused me romantic confusion and increased levels of anxiety.

Daniel slides into the booth next to me, and our thighs touch. I jump in my seat like I've been electrocuted, and he gives me a strange look. "Hi Daniel," I murmur. We haven't spoken since Jadea interrupted our almost-kiss two days ago. Despite the tension, I know it would be a mistake to kiss Daniel. It would just remind me of all the best parts of our relationship, rather than the pain and dip in self-esteem I experienced when he left me. For other reasons, I'm sure he feels the same way. We dodged a bullet.

Then why can't I stop thinking about it?

"Annie." There's a smile on his lips, like he's thinking about the same thing I am, but maybe in a more positive light. I glance away, furiously blushing.

Jadea claps from the other side of the booth. "This!" She gestures enthusiastically. "This is what I'm talking about."

I blink at her slowly. "What is what you're talking about?" Even Daniel looks confused.

She points between the two of us again. "You two. Every time you and Daniel are together, it's like fireworks. Electricity..." She trails off absently, trying to think of something else to say.

"Lightning in a bottle?" Daniel offers up innocently, avoiding my gaze and focusing on Jadea. I want to crawl under the table.

"Exactly!" Jadea snaps her fingers at him. The older woman at the next table jumps in her seat at the sound. "We need to capitalize on this."

I'm practically sweating now. "Daniel and I don't even like each other!" It's a poor defense considering some of the positions Jadea has seen us in, but I can't have her going any further with the hare-brained scheme in her head.

"Well," Daniel interrupts casually, leaning back a bit to look at both of us, "I quite enjoy Annie. She's the one who doesn't like me." When he catches the fury in my gaze, he clears his throat and adds quietly, "For good reason, too."

Jadea nods firmly. "Annie told me all about your little drama, Daniel. But that was years ago. I wouldn't worry about it."

Daniel's eyebrows are almost to his hairline. "She did?"

I wish I could give him a subtle signal, but instead I awkwardly intervene by blurting out, "About the project. Our class project. How you left me to do all the work."

Daniel winces at the analogy, but I'm not sure Jadea notices. She barrels on. "The past is the past. What *I am* interested in is the future. Annie and I want the WNBA and the Arrows to be successful. Win championships. Bring attention to women's sports. Play the game we've always dreamed of." Jadea lays her hands on the table, making sure she has our attention. "However, it's difficult to do any of that with meddling billionaires and sports pundits dismissing our hard work at every turn."

Daniel and I are following so far. "Right," he agrees cautiously. "That's why you asked me to come do the profile on you."

Jadea smiles sweetly. *Too* sweetly. "And it's been wonderful. I think it could really help the team." She scants a look in my direction. "However, it doesn't do much to help Annie's current PR nightmare. Everyone just keeps complaining about a family that she isn't even a part of instead of noticing the awesome things about her. Her playmaking ability. Her clothes. Our friendship. I want to change that."

I get that cold, anxious feeling in the pit of my stomach. "Jadea, wait—"

She finishes her scheme, laying it all out there. "I think you and Annie should date."

Daniel and I are shocked into silence. A small part of me wants to clear this whole thing up by saying, "We already did."

Instead, I look at Daniel. His expression tells me that this is my fault, that I've gotten us into this mess by lying to Jadea about our relationship.

My expression tells him that this is *his* fault for ghosting me after I visited him in the hospital for over a week.

I win our silent standoff, and he's the one who turns to Jadea. He's trying to keep his expression neutral. "How would your matchmaking help Annie's PR nightmare?"

I'm glad I let Daniel speak. My response would be way less coherent and much more embarrassing.

Jadea looks at us like we're slow. "I don't care if you actually date for real. You should *fake date*. For the good press."

Now, I really feel like I'm in a nightmare. "We're not celebrities, Jadea! No one follows us around with cameras. TMZ does not care what we're doing."

Jadea rolls her eyes. "Think bigger, Annie. We're talking about social media dating here. Daniel has a huge following. In the span of four years, he's exploded onto the scene as not only a sports commentator, but also a TV host and journalist. He had seven million YouTube subscribers before HBO snatched him up, and he won an Emmy last year! He has nearly twelve million followers across all of his platforms. We need to put your relationship out there, and it will be believable because you already have chemistry. Instead of everyone talking about Jack and Trenton, they'll be posting #Dannie."

I groan and slump into my seat. This is a disaster. When Daniel was actually my boyfriend, he didn't want to be with me, and now Jadea is asking him to *pretend* to want to be with me? I cover my eyes to hide from the humiliation.

"I don't know if it would work," Daniel says cautiously. "I may have a following, but they're mostly sports fans looking for commentary. I'm a D-List celebrity, if that."

"That's perfect." Even without seeing her, I can imagine the animation in Jadea's face. "Your fans are just the community we want to reach. By bringing their attention to Annie in a positive way, they're more likely to see her as a basketball player and badass woman, not some villain of the league. People are fascinated by romantic relationships, especially with eligible bachelors such as yourself."

I groan again. "Jadea. Stop. Please."

"What?" Her voice is innocent. "Is there some problem I don't know about?" An idea occurs to her, and she asks, almost accusingly, "You are single, aren't you?"

"Yes," Daniel answers, and I feel a strange flutter in my chest that takes some effort to tamp down.

"Excellent." Jadea sounds smug. "Now you just both have to agree."

I uncover my eyes and take a deep breath, ready to tell Jadea that this is the worst idea in the history of the world when Daniel silences me by saying, "I'm in."

I whirl on him, panicked. "You're in? What do you mean you're *in*?"

He shrugs casually. "She's right. If we want people to see you differently, we need to change the narrative. I don't know if I really have the sway she believes I do, but maybe our collective social media power could help. Your Instagram isn't bad, but you hardly use it. We could both try to boost our online presences." He softens when he sees the anxiety on my face. "I'll do anything to help you, Annie. I owe you, remember?"

Jadea claps her hands in delight. "Amazing!" She turns to me, pleading. "Come on, Annie, we can do this. I promise."

I look between the two of them, torn. The reflex reaction is to give a firm refusal and walk out. That's what the ostrich would do. Burrow deeper. Ignore the problems in front of her. But a small part of me, growing louder each moment, thinks this actually could be a good idea. If no one will tune in to see me play, they might tune in to my romantic life. Sadly, that type of gossip gets the most attention.

And...I'd get to see Daniel more. Despite my reservations about our past, I still crave his presence. I still want to talk to him. To laugh with him. To stare into those deep, dark eyes of his and run my hands through his curls. I could do that in a safe way. I could test the waters. Maybe we could be friends. Maybe I could learn why he left.

I find myself nodding. "Okay," I say cautiously. "We can try."

Jadea is beyond herself with excitement, but I find myself peeking at Daniel. He looks almost relieved. As if he thought I would say no. His arm lies across the back of our booth, and his fingers just brush the top of my shoulder. I suppress a shiver.

Fortunately, Jadea doesn't notice and comment once again on our "chemistry". She's already moving on to stage two of her elaborate scheme. "In this day and age, a relationship is only 'real' to the world if it's put on Instagram." Jadea says this with all the wisdom her two million followers afford her. "So, we need to make a cute post for you two that subtly acknowledges your relationship. It shouldn't feel forced. We have to post just the right amount, so no one gets suspicious. We want everyone to feel the chemistry and genuine tension between you two."

I shift uncomfortably at her words. Is it really that obvious to everyone? I'm hoping Jadea's just more observant because she wants this scheme to be successful.

Before Daniel and I can chime in with any ideas, her eyes light up. "I've got it! Follow me." She slaps down some money on our table, even though we've only been served coffee at this point.

*

Considering that Jadea is staging a romantic picture, I'm immediately brainstorming possible places we could be going. She called a cab, but I didn't hear the address she gave, too distracted by Daniel's warm body beside mine, and the insane scheme I just agreed to. The St. Louis Arch, maybe? It is the most notable landmark in our hometown. One of the numerous parks or gardens in the city? The basilica? I'm pretty sure Jadea has filmed some sort of TikTok at all those locations.

When we finally pull up in front of our destination, I don't know why I'm surprised. It's Arch Arena, our home stadium, where we'll play again in two days. Our sleek, silver stadium looks fresh and shiny. Jack's company logo of railroad tracks broken up into an S-shape graces the side, which makes me wince a bit. Could the world stop sending me signs about my biological father abandoning me?

"Isn't this a little on the nose?" I ask dryly as we hop out of the cab. I have to admit that the brand-new stadium was a lovely addition to the city and is nicer than many of the other WNBA stadiums I've visited. It even has some garden features encircling the stadium and an outdoor bar that's open during the summer.

Jadea shoots me a *look*, not appreciating my cynicism. "This is the perfect place. One, it reminds people who you are and that we're in season. Two, it tells people that Daniel came to visit you, and he cares about your success. Three, it's not too obviously romantic or staged. We'll take a picture under the sign announcing our game Sunday." There's a tall electric sign looming above us, flashing our scarlet colors and advertising our next game. It is pretty amazing to see our team's name in lights, I have to admit.

Daniel's nodding like this is all perfectly normal. "What will the caption say? How long have we been dating? We can't have just started dating now, people would be suspicious."

Jadea falls silent at his good point.

"We could have met at Stanford," I offer tentatively. "It would make sense that you would know Jadea and me." I shift a bit from foot to foot. "People at school saw us together."

Daniel is giving me a searing, pained look as if he knew this was the future I imagined for us. I look away. Jadea crinkles up her face. "No, a mysterious relationship of five years is too difficult to explain." It does sound pretty unrealistic; I have to admit. Maybe that's why it never happened.

Daniel rubs his chin. "Maybe we met at Stanford, but reconnected recently? Maybe six months ago? We could be celebrating our anniversary, and that's why we're posting now. It's a reasonable time frame to keep it to ourselves."

"Good." Jadea nods her approval. "We could say we all met again at the ESPYs. That was a little over six months ago. You were presenting, and Annie was my date. You could have reconnected then." I want to laugh and admit that when Daniel walked past our group at the ESPYs, I casually sprinted to the bathroom to avoid him. Instead, I just nod.

"Okay." I take a deep breath. "How should we do this?"

Jadea immediately whips out her phone and works on the scale, making sure Daniel and I are visible with the glittering sign in the background. She insists he take his hat off, and I resist the urge to help him fix his curls. I adjust the sundress I'm wearing, decorated with a print of tiny multicolored daisies. My red hair tumbles in fresh curls down my back. The day is clear and bright above us, the sky a beautiful blue. It would be such a strange reality if this were true. If Daniel and I had reconnected and were celebrating our love. Instead, I feel unsure and awkward at his side.

Jadea is a few paces from us, phone in hand. She flaps her free hand at us. "Well, don't just stand there! Pose!"

I try to put an arm around Daniel, but it feels stiff. He gives me an incredulous look. "We can do better than that! I'll pick you up."

"Pick me up?" I nearly laugh. "We're both too big for that. I am *six feet tall*. And so are you."

"Are you questioning my masculine strength? I'm wounded." He lays a hand on his chest, eyes sparkling.

I scoff. "If anyone is picking anyone up, it will be me. I'm the professional athlete."

He laughs then, bright and shining. I can't look away. "That would be amazing."

I'm stunned into silence. "Really?" I can't imagine most men would enjoy their girlfriend, fake, ex, or otherwise, picking them up. However, Daniel seems genuinely delighted.

"Now, don't back down so quickly, Annie. Do you doubt your *feminine ferocity*?" I start giggling then, too, at the alliteration, and he spreads his arms as though ready to be cradled.

I crack my knuckles, warming up to this picture more and more. "Let's do it."

I may have spoken a little too quickly, because while I am a badass professional athlete who lifts weights and works out several hours a day, I don't usually lift a six-foot-tall man. I almost lift him too quickly, arms under his knees and back. I stumble back a step at the momentum. He quickly wraps his arms around my neck, his warmth suffusing through my chest. I adjust and then we're standing still, my arms straining, but holding him securely enough.

Daniel's delight continues. "I want you to carry me around everywhere. You'll never get away from me now that you offer this kind of service."

I'm giggling still, looking down at Daniel's grinning face. All that love and joy he brought to my life senior year; it's still protected in a glass bubble in my chest. I know it's there in my memories, but I never let those feelings out. Every moment we're together, the glass bubble cracks. Those feelings flood my veins.

"Guys!" Jadea is calling to us. "I think we got it."

The moment shatters, and I hurriedly put Daniel down. This is just business. He's helping me out because he feels guilty. That's all. We don't love each other anymore.

Daniel, Jadea, and I find a table at the stadium's outdoor bar. Over drinks and some greasy bar food, we decide on the picture. The sign looks great, bright and enthusiastic, but Daniel and I look even better. I can't stop staring at it. My arms under his knees and wrapped around his shoulders. My face angled down a little bit and laughing at

Daniel. He's staring, expression content and soft. We look like a couple.

We create a shared post on Instagram with the simple caption, "Six months," and a heart emoji. As soon as the post goes live, I begin to sweat. This is no longer a theoretical scheme cooked up by Jadea, but an act I will have to keep up for at least the next two weeks. After that, Daniel and I will have to decide when to reveal our subsequent "break-up".

Daniel gets a call when we're planning and steps away. It's Friday, and we have a day game on Sunday. Daniel will film the game and then fly to New York to film his late-night show that evening. I know most of the package is pre-made and researched weeks in advance, but he still has to prep for his monologue and other live elements of the show. I wonder more and more how he transitioned from track star to YouTuber to host of an Emmy-award winning show. And in between all that, he abandoned his girlfriend. Was that a necessary part of the process?

Daniel returns to the table. "I'm sorry, but I need to go meet with my writers on Zoom. The meeting starts at one, which I now realize is in twenty minutes."

He's about to exchange goodbyes when Jadea interrupts. "Wait! What are you doing tomorrow night?"

"Are you asking me out, too?" he says dryly. I smother a snicker, and Jadea shoots us a reprimanding glare.

"You just posted a six-month anniversary post, but it was really only *one* cute picture. It would make sense that you'd go on a date, too. A grand one to celebrate your anniversary. You can post about it on social media."

"A date?" I squeak out nervously. When we were in college, our dates usually involved pizza and watching bad movies. Or sports, obviously. An actual, real-world date sounds seriously intimidating.

"I have some really great ideas." Daniel smiles. "I'll plan it and pick you up tomorrow?"

He says it too casually, like he already has a dream scenario in his head. I narrow my eyes at him. "No, *I'll* plan it." I don't want him to have all the control. Fake dating an ex is already anxiety-inducing enough without adding the surprise element.

Jadea rubs her hands together in anticipation. "Why don't you both plan half of the date and surprise each other? Make it big so it looks good on your socials."

I nod slowly. "Sure."

Daniel reaches out his hand, shaking mine. I'm shocked at the frisson of electricity that goes through my body. Our eyes lock. "Game on, Annie." Before I can say a word, he leans in and presses a quick kiss to my cheek. Face on fire, Jadea and I wave as he quickly heads to his taxi.

Jadea gives me side eye. "Are you sure you don't want to date him for real?"

I groan into my hands in response.

What a beautiful mess I've created.

*

I'm lying in bed later that night, racking my brain for great date ideas. A small part of me wants to torture Daniel and take him paintballing or laser-tagging with pre-teens, but I figure Jadea wants something more romantic for our so-called anniversary.

Tired and restless, I open the anniversary post on my phone. It already has over three thousand likes on my page, more than any of my other posts. When I flip to Daniel's page, I see that he has over 150,000 likes, which makes sense considering our follower ratio. I'm tempted to click on the comment section, but I want to bask in the purity of the picture and not have it potentially ruined.

I scroll through my Instagram and click on Jadea's most recent story. I'm surprised to see it's a video of Daniel and me. We're standing in front of the sign, bickering about the pose. You can hear Daniel's delight at me picking him up and my overt giggling at his reaction. You watch us stumble and then steady ourselves, laughing even more. Jadea put a caption on it: *Thanks @ESPYs for reuniting these Stanford lovebirds. Happy 6 months!*

It's almost too convincing. My heart feels like it might beat out of my rib cage. Why am I holding on to this fantasy? Daniel left and didn't look back. I should do the same.

For the second time this week, I throw my phone onto my nightstand and try to quiet my mind.

*

The next morning, my phone buzzes endlessly. I finally have to turn off the vibrate feature and go fully mute. There are comments on our Instagram post that make my heart sing when I eventually give in and look at the notifications.

@CandaceParker: You two are a thing? Shut up [fire emoji] [heart emoji].

Candace Parker, three-time MVP of the WNBA, and all around incredible human being, is *shipping* us. I played against her just twice before she retired, but I've always been too shy to say anything more than a lame "Good game". Belatedly, I remember that Daniel did a deep dive into her career and personal life last year on his show. His social media shows they've kept in touch.

@MinaKimes: Finally, Dan! Get it you two!

Now, this is a more interesting response. Mina and Daniel are friends who have collaborated a few times. Has he talked about me? It's too insane to consider, so I move on.

@PatrickMahomes: Amazing pose dude [cry laughing emoji].

I've had very few crushes in my life, but Patrick Mahomes makes that list. And he's friendly with *Daniel*. Maybe I should reconsider this platonic thing and just date him to meet all my heroes?

No, Annie, focus!

Daniel's Instagram reads like a who's who of A-list sports stars, commentators, and other people in the business. Steph Curry, Venus Williams, Sydney McLaughlin-Levrone, Oksana Masters, Michael Wilbon, and John Oliver, who executive produces Daniel's show, all wrote something supportive or hilarious on the post. I guess the attention makes sense, as both Daniel and I rarely post such personal things on our social media. His page is almost entirely focused on work, with some sprinkling in of his family wolfhound terrier Dustin. It's charming, but mostly professional. My page reads more like a ghost town with a few basketball pictures every three months to show proof of life.

The comments and likes are much more subdued on my page, but still higher than any other post I've made. Fans are commenting on how cute the photo is and how cute Daniel is and how cute my dress is and just generally emphasizing the cuteness overload. I don't want to give Jadea too much credit, because she'll just cheerfully throw it in my face, but her scheme seems to be working. If there is negative feedback about Jack and the team and me, it seems small in comparison to the fun and bubbling happiness surrounding our relationship.

Our fake relationship.

My group chat is also blowing up with my teammates'
responses:

Taherah: Is this real life? Annie, respond to us!!!!

Olabisi: Bitch, how dare you?

*Lynn: It was obvious, y'all, did you not see them at
practice??*

Allyson: The pic [heart-eye emoji]

Jadea: I took it! Isn't it incredible?!

*Olabisi: Where the hell is Annie? Are they still in bed? Get
it girl [fire emoji]*

*Allyson: So, it's true? They've been dating all this time??
Come on, Annie, details!*

I feel the guilt that's been eating merrily in the back of
my mind surge to the forefront. I'm already partially lying
to Jadea about Daniel. Should I lie to my team about this
relationship? Clearly, Jadea expects me to. I understand her
point of view, as not all of them could keep this a secret,
especially when he's around us all the time filming.

I finally decide on a neutral, but playful response, one
that doesn't make me feel like throwing up from guilt.

Annie: Eat your heart out, ladies!!

They immediately start sending R-rated memes and
internet pictures of Daniel running track with hideous
innuendos as the captions. It should make me happy that
the deception is working so well. It means this might
actually help my reputation and steer focus away from the
scandal. Instead, I feel hurt blooming in between my ribs.
This could be my life. Daniel, who I trusted and grew with
and supported when he was hurt, was the future I always
imagined. We had only dated for a few months, but we were
together almost every day. We enjoyed all the same things,
we met each other's families, we took a mini road trip to see

the giant Sequoias and sniffled a bit at their majesty. This *should* be us. But he left.

The hurt only grows worse when I see one text from my mom, who I still haven't spoken to.

Mom: Are you and Daniel back together?

It's a gut-punch. I accused her of keeping secrets, and now it looks like I've been keeping one. It was my mom who loved Daniel when she first met him and cursed him every day when he ignored me. And since I never had the courage to tell Jadea about our relationship, it was my mom who picked up the broken pieces and called me every day for weeks after Daniel disappeared. To her, this is not a fun relationship. It's complicated and full of mysteries neither of us can explain.

It's time to come clean. I need my mom. She kept secrets, but I've kept some, too. It isn't always easy to open your mouth and be vulnerable. Especially when it's clear that Jack Smith was never going to be my mom's happily-ever-after. I wonder if she knows that he's had many affairs, each with a young, vulnerable woman like my mom. I decide to respond before I can change my mind and avoid her again.

Annie: I'll explain everything. Come to the game tomorrow and we'll talk after.

She sends a thumbs-up emoji, and that's proof enough of our strained relationship. She tends to be an effusive, paragraph-style texter. Brevity is rarely considered, efficiency never on her mind. I have to make this right.

A weight is lifted off my shoulders when I imagine us talking tomorrow. That's one problem solved.

The next on the agenda: the date. Daniel and I are going out at 6 PM, and I have exactly four hours to get myself together. This morning, inspiration struck, and I planned the second half of the date. Daniel assured me in a text this morning that he had planned something he knew I would love. I just responded with a "Game on". Easy enough to think of our fake relationship as a competition. Daniel and I always did have a competitive streak.

I tended to win then, and I intend to win now.

Chapter 11

It's ten minutes to 6 PM, and I'm wondering if I should put on a third coat of deodorant. Am I wearing too much perfume? Not enough shimmery lip gloss? Should I take my hair down? Did I pack the clothes we need for my half of the date?

An hour ago, I texted Daniel.

Annie: What's the attire for this date?

Daniel: Fancy. Give me your very best, Annie.

His response skyrocketed my pulse, both due to anxiety and because he knows I find dressing up to be *very* sexy.

I take one last look in the mirror, checking for any missing details. I chose a baby pink satin dress with spaghetti straps, a sweetheart neck, and three petal-like tiers in the skirt. I'm wearing white leather platforms with red hearts stamped on the monster heels. Chopsticks made of faux pearls loosely hold up my hair. I have a red velvet clutch hung on a chain that matches my lipstick.

It's a bold look and one my other boyfriend Evan never liked. He once said, "I don't mind it. But it's kind of a lot." I grimaced and redirected the conversation, but his words stuck with me. On the flip side, Daniel always seemed to enjoy my concoctions in college. When I'd work on something for my independent study he'd listen closely as

I described it or would send me articles about sustainable fashion that came up on his feed.

Hopefully, he still feels the same way.

My phone buzzes with a message that Daniel is downstairs. I take three deep cleansing breaths, throw a couple Twizzlers nibs in my mouth, and head downstairs. I send a quick picture of the look to Jadea, and she sends back exclamation points in response.

I expect to see Daniel sitting inside his sleek rental car, but instead he's parked it on the street in front of my building. He's leaning against it casually, holding a bouquet of flowers.

"Daniel." The word falls out of my mouth like a sigh. "Are those for me?" Shy, shy, shy. Why can't I sound casual?

Fortunately, he's fidgeting, too. He smiles bashfully and hands me the bouquet. "I hope you like them." I look at the beautiful arrangement, a dizzying array of different flowers and colors. Purples, pinks, and reds.

"They're perfect." I still sound breathless, but I can't help it. Seeing him like this is like being hit by a car.

"I know you don't like boring." His smile eases a bit. His eyes roam over me and then settle on my face, warm and dark and full of that shine. "You look just as I imagined."

"Too much?" I force a laugh, plucking at my skirt.

Daniel's brow crinkles. "No, perfect. Colorful. Freckled. Taller than me." That one makes me grin. "Amazing, Annie. You look amazing."

My face may be freckled, but the flush creeping up my neck is probably overshadowing them. "You look amazing too, Daniel." And he does. I see Daniel in suits all the time for his show, but this is different. The suit is slim, dark, and hugs him just right. He's wearing a charcoal silk tie, and his curls ruffle a little in the wind.

I focus on breathing evenly as we get into the car. I carefully lay the bouquet on my lap. "So, where are we going?" I try to sound as normal and cheerful as possible.

Daniel takes my bubbly attitude in stride. "It's a secret. Here, put this on." He hands me a sleep mask, the cheap ones from an airline.

I narrow my eyes at him playfully. "Have you turned into a serial killer in the time we were apart?"

He rolls his eyes. "I want it to be a surprise. You've been very secretive about your half of the date as well. All you told me to bring was sneakers and running shorts."

I begrudgingly agree to the blindfold, only because he's right about my half of the date. I want this date to be the best one he's ever had, even if it's fake, which is why a surprise seems the best route. People love surprises. "Alright." I put the sleep mask over my eyes. "But be warned, St. Louis is in my blood. I'll probably know where we are just based on my other senses."

Daniel snorts. "I'd like to see you try."

I pretend to listen to the city. "Are we heading to the hot yoga studio on Olive Street run by Ms. Nancy?"

That startles a laugh out of Daniel. "Is that a real place?"

We turn again. "Are we heading to the St. Louis Zoo to look at the penguins and ponder their mating rituals?"

Daniel hums. "Closer. Try again."

"Are we attending the underground poetry reading in the basement of the Urban Outfitters on Park Avenue?"

I can imagine Daniel rolling his eyes again. "Now you're just making things up."

I shake my head profusely. "Don't doubt St. Louis, Daniel! You're just not listening to her hard enough."

"I don't remember you being this chatty last time we were together," Daniel muses. "Time really changes a person."

I'm about to retort when I feel the car stop. It was a short ride. "Are we here?" I'm surprised at my feelings of anticipation. Even though this is all for show, I'm still excited.

"Yes." His cool fingers brush my temple and an errant curl as he delicately pulls off the sleep mask. I appreciate the concern for my hair and make-up.

I blink a few times, surprised at our dim atmosphere. "Oh, so you are a murderer?" I look over at him.

He huffs a laugh. "This is the parking garage. Come on, or we're going to be late."

We get out of the car and take the elevator down, spilling out onto the street. I'm just about to look around and get my bearings, but Daniel puts his hands over my eyes. "No cheating!" he insists. We shuffle down the street, Daniel nudging the back of my legs towards our destination.

I'm laughing at his antics. "This is ridiculous!" His body feels warm and solid against mine, and I almost trip several times at the distraction.

"We're here," he finally announces, lifting his hands from my eyes. At first, all I see is the street to my left and some people milling on the sidewalk in front of me. But then, I look up. There's a sign lit up with Broadway bulbs. The marquee for tonight reads "St. Louis Ballet Company performs *Swan Lake*". A beautiful dancer in a white tutu stretches her leg up in the air on the poster, serene and graceful.

I feel strange, like I'm no longer in my own body. I can feel Daniel hovering behind me, unsure of my reaction. I can't formulate words, and instead, tears start welling and then slowly falling down my cheeks.

Daniel rummages through his pockets. "I hope those are tears of joy and not disappointment." He finally finds what he's looking for and pulls out a travel-size tissue pack. He offers them to me; his face creased with worry.

There's a pause when I reach for them, and the tears slow. He brought tissues on purpose. For me. If I have a movie star smile, I try to show it to Daniel then. "You like it?" he questions, and then rephrases it into a statement. "You like it."

I can't contain myself then and throw myself into his arms, tissues still clenched in my fist. "I love it, Daniel. Really." I pull back, using a tissue to wipe my face. "How did you know?"

He shrugged. "You mentioned once that you and your mom go and see *The Nutcracker* every year. A Christmas tradition. I figure you're usually too busy to keep up the tradition now, since you have your European season then. It seemed like a good idea."

I'm grinning foolishly. He's describing a story that I told *once* in the five months we dated. And he *remembered* it. "It was a *great* idea," I say enthusiastically, grabbing his hand and tugging him towards the theater.

"Wait," he says, laughing, "We need to take a picture, remember? That's the whole point of this."

Though he says the words with warmth, they make me go cold. I try not to let the change show, smiling brightly and pulling out my phone. "Right, of course!" I snap a selfie of us with the ballet marquee in the background. I post it to my Instagram story with the caption: *Anniversary surprise!* Daniel posts it to his with: *Happy Anniversary, Annie [heart emoji].*

After the picture, I feel a little deflated. For a few heart-stopping moments, this all felt real. I was sucked right back into Daniel and me, together and romantic and fun. Daniel either doesn't notice or pretends not to. "Ready?" he asks easily, grabbing my hand again. "This performance is getting rave reviews."

We go inside and take our seats, which have a wonderful, close view of the stage. "How did you even get these tickets so last minute?" I ask as we settle in. We still have about fifteen more minutes until the ballet begins.

"A D-List celebrity still has some power, Annie!" he chastises me, winking. Then he leans in conspiratorially and adds, "I also asked local superstar Jadea Jones to help me."

This makes me smile, too, and I flip through the ballet program, excitedly reading the dancers' bios and the numbers they'll be performing. It's all so amazing. I know ballet has its highs and lows, just like the WNBA, but the athleticism, the artistry, the power—it's mesmerizing. My mom always loved it and used to dance when she was growing up. Despite my lack of coordination, I fell in love with it, too. The body control, the power, the precision. Whoever says dancers aren't athletes clearly hasn't seen them perform.

Daniel has been watching me. "You really do love it, huh? Why?" He doesn't say it skeptically, like he thinks it's boring or something, but with genuine curiosity like he wants to climb inside my mind.

"I always wanted to be a ballerina growing up," I admit, surprising myself. I rarely dive into these childhood memories. "I saw the Nutcracker for the first time in fifth grade, and I became obsessed. I made my mom sign me up for classes at the rec center, and I watched the *Barbie in the*

Nutcracker movie about a hundred times." Daniel cracks a smile, eyes focused on me. "Unfortunately, I told some 'fellow' dancers in my class that I wanted to be a ballerina, and they made it clear that I didn't quite fit the mold." I shrug. "I was crazy tall at that point and not model thin. None of my clothes fit right, and Jadea hadn't moved to town yet. I wasn't confident enough to push back and say that I could do whatever I wanted." The memories feel hazy, as if I'm recalling them through a fogged mirror. I do remember the strange, sharp turn in my self-esteem and how I refused to go to the dance class that my mom had so lovingly signed me up for. I remember crying in front of the girls who insulted me because I had even less control over the tears then than I do now. "Fortunately, Jadea moved in next door a few months later, and I found basketball. The love of my life. It all worked out."

"People made fun of you for how you looked?" His expression is bewildered.

I try to remain casual, like it doesn't still haunt me sometimes. "Yeah, a little. I mean, by the time I was in seventh grade, I was 5'10", ginger, and straight up and down. Not exactly the body type most normal teenage girls are looking for. And my last name did not help. The boys used to say, 'Could she get Annie Larger?' Get it?"

Daniel winces but doesn't say some platitude about how it made me stronger or how I'm in the WNBA, so who's laughing now? Instead, he shakes his head. "Larger has so many great possibilities and that's what they go with. They lacked imagination."

I let out a shocked laugh. "And you don't, sir?"

"Absolutely." He nods seriously. "I'll workshop a few and let you know."

He's making it light, which I appreciate, but he squeezes my hand, too. I look away, blinking back a few more tears. This all doesn't quite feel real.

I snap a picture of the ballet's program and add it to my story, so Jadea sees I'm taking this fake relationship seriously. After that, I'm done with the socials. I just want to watch the people on stage and try not to drool too much.

The lights dim, and the first scene unfurls. All the dancers are beams of light, power, and grace, everything I admire. I know they sacrifice for this life, and I feel that ache in my heart when I see how perfect they are at what they love.

Daniel doesn't let go of my hand the whole first half, his thumb lightly tracing the back of my hand. I tell myself it's because he's so engrossed in the performance he forgot to let go. This is fake. Fake.

Fake.

But, as we sit there and take in the performance, it doesn't feel that way. It feels like that memory Daniel had of us winning at Stanford. Lightning in a bottle.

Except, instead of feeling struck on the head, it's a slower sensation. Creeping. Seeping in my bones. My heart. Slowly cracking that glass bubble in my chest.

I cannot let it shatter like before.

*

I force Daniel to change his outfit for the second half of our date in the theater bathroom. I've already changed, decked out in black leggings, my favorite running shoes, and a neon pink racer-back tank top. Daniel brought his own running shorts and shoes, but I've procured him the perfect shirt for tonight's activities.

When he walks out of the bathroom, I snort with delight. The lemon-lime neon running top I found for him is perfect. The people who are milling after the ballet give us strange looks, but my heart is beating fast with excitement. Daniel told me I would love what he'd planned, and boy, did I. Now it's time for me to level the playing field.

"Where are we going, Annie?" He surveys himself with genuine concern. "An athleisure rave?"

I suppress a smile, gesturing for us to walk out. "That's actually not a bad idea."

We walk to the garage to stash our fancy clothes. After putting our outfits in the back, Daniel heads to the driver's seat. I tug his arm, pulling him away. "We'll come back for the car. Our starting place is only a few blocks away."

It's well after 9 PM now, the ballet having been around two hours long, and the sun is just starting to dip behind the horizon. It's perfect outside, crisp and draped in shadows. Our activity starts as soon as the sun fully sets, so we should be okay on time.

Daniel continues to guess our activity, mirroring my own act in the car. "Are we going cosmic bowling and you're trying to convince people that bowlers are athletes with these outfits?"

That one startles a laugh out of me. I glance his way, smiling. "We used to go bowling all the time in college, remember? In the union?"

Daniel nods sagely. "For two broke college kids with a competitive streak, it was the perfect date."

"You never let me win!" My mind flashes back to those early weeks when I was nervous to be alone with Daniel, and then he'd set me at ease by suggesting bowling. We'd compete and tease and laugh and it felt amazing.

"Let you win?" Daniel shakes his head. "You always won everything; I had to take the edge where I could!"

"Everything?" I snort. "Like what?"

"Mario Kart, kickboxing, who bought the better birthday present, Settlers of Catan—"

"Settlers of Catan?" I point his way accusingly. "I didn't win that! We were invited to *one* board game party by your track team, and you were the one who ruthlessly read the entire rule book ahead of time and sucked the joy out of the game. You decimated everyone!"

Daniel grins at me. "Okay, so maybe we were more like 50/50."

"Equals." I nod in confirmation. "Agreed."

Daniel's about to respond when I notice we're approaching the St. Louis Arch, the river, and the surrounding park. I can already see other people dressed like us clustered around a check-in table. "We're here!" I clap my hands in anticipation. "Let's go!"

I can tell Daniel is trying to figure out what we're doing. There's a sign that reads "Check-In" above the table, and the pamphlets on the table are for the nonprofit Love for St. Louis' Children. "Is this a charity event?" he asks quizzically, glancing around at everyone in their neon running gear. One of the perky organizers comes over and hands us a stack of glow sticks. Now, if there's something I know how to do, it's accessorize. I begin making glow stick bracelets and necklaces for Daniel and me. I even make myself a halo that I perch around my messy bun, a replacement look for my previous pearl chopsticks.

"It's a Charity Run," I finally give in and tell him, bubbling over with excitement. "Love for St. Louis' Children is a non-profit that helps foster care or emancipated kids transition from a life in the system into being an adult. Finding jobs, schools, housing. The Arrows do work with them, and I got an invitation to this event a few weeks ago. I didn't have anyone who could go with me, but once Jadea said we needed a unique date activity, this seemed perfect. For every mile we run, the team matches it with $500. We get to run through the city, and people will know what we stand for." I'm babbling now, trying to read his neutral expression. I start to trail off, "And, as you can see, the theme is 'You Light Up My Life'! As in, the kids do..."

The longer I look at Daniel, the more concerned I become. He's not just expressionless; he looks a little sick. His face has lost all its color. "Hey," I say gently, tugging him towards a nearby bench, "is everything okay? I know your bad leg probably isn't up to hurdles, but sometimes you still post your running times on social media, so I figured this would be okay."

A little bit of Daniel's expression clears when he hears my voice. "I do still run, but only on the treadmill." He says it like it's a shameful confession, looking at the sidewalk and fiddling with his neon green glow stick bracelet.

It takes a few moments for me to connect the dots and when the epiphany finally strikes, I sit down heavily next to him. "Daniel." I don't even know what to say. "I'm so sorry. I didn't even think about running outside. We can leave. I understand."

When someone is hurting and you're the one trying to support them, it almost feels like you're trying to will your empathy onto them. Not pity but understanding. Daniel was in the hospital for weeks after being hit on a run outside, and while I didn't see the full aftermath, he likely had months of physical therapy before he could even walk normally, let alone run again. That would obviously be a time you don't really want to remember. The guilt makes my skin crawl. I was thinking of the old Daniel, not the new one.

Daniel takes deep breaths, slowing himself and his thoughts. I recognize the technique from my therapist. I keep my voice even and quiet. "I'll do whatever you want, Daniel. If you want to run and face it, I'll run with you. If you want to leave and watch Olympic reruns, I'll do that, too. I know this run might be triggering."

He nods at my words but continues to focus on his breathing. I sit with him for a few minutes, waiting.

"This is different. It was dark, raining, when that car hit me," Daniel finally says. His words are steady, almost like he's trying to reassure himself. "I was on the side of the road, not on the sidewalk. I was wearing a gray reflective jacket that was dampened by the rain. Visibility was poor, and it was after 11 PM. There were lots of young drivers in that area, and the one that hit me was driving twenty over the speed limit. It's unlikely all of those circumstances will happen again." It's almost a mantra, the way the sentences fall from his lips. I wonder if he's had to tell himself these things before. He smiles wryly. "And it certainly did not have the fun energy of tonight's 'You Light Up My Life' theme."

"Even if that's all true, it doesn't mean we have to run," I say, words fierce. "Sometimes feelings overrule logic." I try to pose my next question gently, without judgement. "Do you *ever* run outside?"

Daniel surveys the excited buzz of people around us, the glow sticks and neon apparel, the light twilight of summer. His expression is far away. "Sometimes. If I'm running on a trail where there aren't any cars nearby, and it's light out. That feels very different from the accident." His eyes catch on some of the cars racing by. "I was always a stress runner, and it was finals week. It was too dark and too rainy to be running without proper reflective equipment. I should have gone home or to the track or something. I had the walk sign crossing the street, but the car didn't see me and was in a hurry. I just remember blinding pain and then waking on the wet asphalt. I was in and out of consciousness, lying in the street for what felt like hours as paramedics prepared me to leave. I still have dreams of going on that run. Or not. That decision feels paralyzing now."

I wish I had planned better. This isn't a marathon or anything, so we just run on city sidewalks. They planned a safe running route, but there will be cars driving nearby. I never even considered that Daniel would be bothered. I feel so disappointed in myself.

I reach out and take his hand. It's cold, but I hold steady. He meets my gaze, surprised. "I believe in you, Daniel. Whoever you are in this moment, I believe in. We can leave and set boundaries and be strong. Or we can run together and fight back and be strong. Both are honorable. Understandable. I'm with you."

I squeeze his hand, and he looks down at our intertwined fingers. The green and pink glow stick bracelets I made to match our outfits.

Finally, he looks at me. His eyes are lit up, his expression glowing. "I want to do this, Annie. This is my chance to take back something I lost. I had to say goodbye to a dream I'd had since I was a kid. I've come to terms with that. But *this*, I can have. Running outside with you, laughing and feeling better. Feeling better than I have in years." Daniel's eyes brighten with each word he says, and a relieved smile grows on my face at the sight.

There's something inexplicable snapping between us. Like we're balancing on the precipice of sharing exactly what went wrong between us. Delving back into the accident and the hospital and the silence afterwards. I almost open my mouth to let loose the barrage of questions, but instead all that comes out is, "I'm proud of you."

He gives me that movie-star smile. "I couldn't do it without you, Annie. You help. This helps." He gestures to our clasped hands. "Everything we do together feels like the greatest thing I've ever done." I'm blushing at his honesty.

I struggle to say something, to not let these new feelings mix with my old ones. I open my mouth, but then the last of the sun dips and a sharp whistle rips through the calm evening.

We both get to our feet, a bit unsteady, but brave and sure. The woman in front shouts for our attention. "Everyone ready to run for something they believe in?"

The crowd around us roars, and so do we. There's something healing in sports and collaboration and caring for others. The route has already been set for us, largely along the river and downtown, with patches of neon sidewalk paint marking our way.

The pack starts running together, dozens of people looking ridiculous and loving it. I gently bump Daniel's hip with mine, checking in, and the look he gives me is loaded. Mostly, it seems warm with determination, grit, and gratitude. I put myself between the street and Daniel, giving him the grassy side. We run at an even pace, one I know is much slower than Daniel's usual, but he seems to be enjoying it.

One of the front runners is holding a Bluetooth speaker in the air, and it's pulsing with different rainbow lights.

Whitney Houston is the first song to play, and the whole group sings together, Daniel and I included.

Everyone cheers when we reach the first mile marker. We're heading closer to the city now, and I see Daniel's first flash of apprehension when we run across the intersection. He seems to run a little faster, so I use it to distract him. "Let's try to go to the front." I nudge him, and he jolts a little as though lost in thought. "Show them what we can do."

My distraction seems to help, and we flow back onto the sidewalk. Some pedestrians seem irritated by our sidewalk takeover, but lots of cars and passersby cheer or smile when we pass by. "I'll race you," I offer and then take off before he can respond.

I hear Daniel's surprised laugh and then we're racing through the small crowd, apologetically pushing through to the front. We pull even with the guy with the speaker at the same time, but I try to argue I had the edge. "I was first!"

Daniel scoffs, and we merge to the front. "You just *want* to be first. Very different."

The run is a 5k, and we run all five with delight. I'm sweating pretty heavily by the final mile and so is Daniel. We're definitely pushing the pace a little at the front, but the tunes and enthusiasm from the group never waver. It feels like we're flying down the sidewalks.

As we near the end, I take a celebratory video of the group running, making sure to get Daniel's gleaming and grinning face in the clip. In retaliation, he takes one too, focusing on me next to him. I try to block the camera, but he just laughs and zooms in more.

A surge of disappointment goes through me when I see the finish line. That half hour of running was without thought. It was joyous, ebullient, freeing. I thank the organizers of the event profusely and they thank the

Arrows for their $1500 donation. Daniel, to show me up and because he's a good person, writes them a check for another $5000.

We walk back to the parking garage in contented silence. I'm humming Whitney quietly as we reach the last block before the car. Daniel is the one who speaks first. "Annie." I'm so surprised by his tone that my head snaps in his direction. He sounds soft, nervous. "Thank you. I really couldn't have done that without you."

I shake my head immediately. "You did it, Daniel. The only thing I did was believe that you could."

He takes a deep breath. "I should tell you the truth, the reason why I never reached out after the accident, the reason I just left the hospital without a wor—"

I put a finger to his lips. We're entering the elevators now, climbing up to our very last few moments of the night. "Daniel, I want to hear all that. I do. But tonight...it was one of the best nights of my life. And I kind of want to keep it that way, you know?"

It's an awkward explanation, but I want him to understand that sparkling feeling in my chest. I want him to see I need this uncomplicated joy, and I think he does, too.

The elevator dings to tell us we're on our floor. "Yes," he finally says, softly, "I think I know exactly what you mean."

The short ride back to my apartment is filled with more of that warm silence. I lean my head against the window, trying not to think about tomorrow. About seeing my mom, about winning our last few games, about Jack and Trenton.

He pulls up in front of my building, and I startle. "Oh, we should probably post those videos we took at the run," I tell him, forlornly taking off my glow stick halo. "Jadea thought it would look so great on camera."

"I will," he promises, and there's an awkward moment where we're automatically leaning towards each other, as though to kiss or embrace or melt into each other.

This time, it's me who remembers the scheme. The farce of our relationship. "Thanks, Daniel," I say evenly, getting out of the car. "I had a wonderful time."

"Me too." Another whisper of a smile and then he's off into the night. I climb the stairs up to my apartment and flick on the lights inside. I rummage through the cabinets until I find my only vase. The flowers in the bouquet Daniel gave me puff up proudly in their new home, and I wish I didn't miss Daniel as much as I do. I wish I could have asked him up. I wish we could go back and redo all the mistakes we made.

Instead, I hurry to bed. It's only a little after 10:30 PM, but I have a noon game tomorrow, so I'll need to be up pretty early. I set my alarms and lay out the equipment I'll need for tomorrow.

I'm about to put my phone away and turn off the light when I see I've been tagged in Daniel's Instagram post. It's the video of me running beside him and then a quick cut to the rest of the group who cheer when they see the camera. A very cute and happy video. Jadea will be pleased.

I almost miss the caption, but when I finally read it, my heart skips a beat.

@DanielChan: Thanks @AnnieLarger for lighting up my life. Best date I've ever had.

Daniel Chan. Why does he make this so hard? Why do I? We're caught in a romantic web of our own making, but as we get more tangled, we'll only start hurting each other to get free.

But I don't regret the date. How could I?

Chapter 12

There is nothing like being on the court with my team. The lights, the fans, that moment where the referee throws the ball up for jump ball, and everyone flows into their game. I love that feeling: the sweat that drips down your temple, the thudding of your heartbeat in your ears, the gasp of your breath.

I'm not a daredevil. An adrenaline junkie. But sometimes, out there, I feel like I'm chasing a competitive high that is unreachable. Like my fingers are stretching both towards the ball and towards that feeling of flying.

Tonight, I don't feel any of that.

The first thing I notice when I head to the court for warm-ups is two neon green posters held by Indiana Fever fans. The first reads: *Jack Smith = Another corrupt billionaire.*

The second reads: *Annie Smith = Washed-up nepo baby.*

I wait to feel something. Jack probably deserves to be taken down a peg, but couldn't they leave me out of it? The moral dilemma is endlessly messy, and I understand that some fans are frustrated that I was drafted by my father. Even if I didn't know what was happening behind the scenes, I still potentially stole another player's spot in the league. It's an agonizing prospect to imagine someone losing their dream because my billionaire sperm donor had a crisis of conscience in his old age.

Fortunately, Jadea has enough anger for both of us. The two signs are only a few rows into the stands, and she looks ready to climb up there. "Washed up?" she growls, aggressively dribbling the ball during warm-ups. "You were an All-Star this year! You're only behind Caitlin Clark in assists, and she's a future Hall of Famer."

"Nothing to say about the nepo baby part?" I try to joke, but it comes out bitter.

Jadea shoots me a look but quickly refocuses on the two sign-bearing fans. Her glare would be enough to scare me, though I can't tell from here if they're shaken at all. It's Lynn who talks Jadea down. "There will always be some idiot with something to say," she counsels us. "We're here to play. Don't forget it."

There's nothing more powerful than some of Lynn's wise words, and I wait for them to wash over me, fill me with fire and courage. Instead, I continue to feel cold. The only spark I feel the whole warm-up is when I see Daniel, and he waves at me tentatively. I can see him working with his crew, as they'll use some footage of the game in their piece, getting extra cameras set up around the game broadcast's. They're mostly focusing on bench conversation, locker room huddles, and other in-between moments. They don't want to step on the toes of the ESPN2 broadcast. Daniel is wearing something strange for the occasion: black joggers, black sneakers, and a white T-shirt with something printed on it. A quote maybe? I can't catch a good enough look of him during warm-ups, but it certainly deviates from his usual dark wardrobe.

The game starts horribly. We just beat Indiana at their home stadium, and they feel energized, ready for revenge.

My fingers are cold, my chest numb, everything feels far away as we take the court. Allyson sends the ball my way during the tip-off, and I would usually tear down to our basket, Jadea even with me. I would pass it to her, and it would look like she's going to slam the usual dunk down. Instead, Jadea would pass it back to me for the easy lay-up. It's a triple deception, and it always swings the momentum our way from the get-go.

Instead, the ball slips through my fingers and all-around superstar Catilin Clark snatches it up. She has Jadea-level speed herself, if not the size, and runs away for her own lay-up. Our defensive response is sluggish, and Jadea fouls Clark early. "Shit." Jadea looks my way, and I'm surprised to see the unease in her expression. We're down 2–0, not exactly a blowout. But we both feel something, a series of mistakes waiting in the wings.

We're not wrong.

At the top of the key, I throw two turnovers in a row. One, a bounce pass to Olabisi, where I didn't see Kelsey Mitchell streaking up the lane. 4–0. Another effort, this time I wait at the top of the key a little longer, trying to slow the pace. Typically, our pace is blisteringly fast, but I'm trying to get us back in rhythm. Settle. We pass it around endlessly, reaching no conclusions, until I'm back at the top and trying desperately to throw a high-arching pass to Allyson in the lane. It goes over her head and into the hands of Indiana's center behind her. 6–0.

I can hear Coach Rembert shouting from the sideline, but it's not reaching me. I feel a strange urge to walk to the bench and sit down. I shouldn't be here anyway, right? Am I the reason we're out of sorts? Is my team questioning whether I should even be on the floor?

The Indiana Fever is a younger team, just like us, so they're hungry and growing fast. They've settled into the middle of the standings and would love to take down the current number one seed. Lynn goes for a three-pointer that dings horribly on the rim and falls right into Lexie Hull's hands. She runs away with it, and I give chase. I search for that fire within myself, but I can't catch her. She scores again, and we're officially down 8–0. It's only been two minutes of play.

The rest of the first half continues in the same style. We have 14 turnovers, and I've contributed six of them. We're shooting only 28 percent and miss five free throws, two of them being mine. I have zero points and two assists. Jadea has eight points and three rebounds. When we have a time out with two minutes left in the half, Jadea throws her water bottle, and it explodes all over the ground. I cringe.

"What is going on?" She glares at the court. "We're supposed to be the best team in the league, and instead we're embarrassing ourselves."

Coach Rembert is barely controlling her own frustration. "We just need to adapt and try to get through to halftime. Do not let them get to you." She and Coach Zak give us a suggested out-of-bounds play that should lead to an easy Jadea dunk.

I'm trying to pay attention, but my eyes keep darting to those electric green signs waving in the air. Was I deluding myself all this time about my skills? Was I puffed up by making it into the league, and all my stats are simply the product of the placebo effect? It feels like any ounce of pressure might break me. The sweat dripping down my neck feels cold and I clench my fists, feeling the nails dig into my palms.

Coach Rembert wraps up our time out, erasing the Xs and Os on her whiteboard. Jadea and the girls start heading back to the court, but my gaze is locked on the scoreboard. 46–24. A 22-point deficit. We haven't been down this much all season. We also haven't lost in eight games. To get back into this game would take a miracle.

Coach seems to sense the swirling cloud of my thoughts. "Annie?" Her tone is sharp. "Do you need me to sit you?"

I snap my gaze back to hers. She looks fierce, but not exactly angry. More like she's testing me. To sit now, at such an important moment in the game where we need to shift the momentum before halftime, would be shameful.

I need to fake it. I straighten my spine and jut out my chin. I imagine it's how Jadea would stand, or Lynn, or Serena freaking Williams. "No, Coach." I hold her gaze for a beat, even as the referees are whistling emphatically for us to get moving. "We'll score here. Turn it around. I promise."

She nods and shoves me towards the referee holding the ball. I'll pass it in. We have two minutes until half, and we need some easy buckets. A quick turnaround so that the second half doesn't feel like such an uphill battle.

Once I have the ball in my hands, I have five seconds to pass it in. If I don't do it in that time, we forfeit the possession. I take a few breaths, standing next to the referee and surveying the court. Jadea and Aliyah Boston are pushing each other ferociously. Taherah, who we decided to put in for her three-point shooting ability, is balanced on her toes, ready to run. Olabisi has her arms spread wide, her knees bent so she's crouched low. Lynn stands all the way in the back, the furthest target, and the last resort if our play doesn't go well.

I'm just about ready to fake it and hope I don't turn it over again, like the bad luck charm I am, when my gaze snags on a white shirt across the court from me. Daniel stands next to one of his cameramen, but he doesn't seem focused on work. Rather, he seems focused on the game itself.

We lock eyes in that split second, and Daniel looks as fierce as Jadea a few minutes ago. Beneath his kindness and friendly demeanor, Daniel is as competitive as they come. This game must be killing him. My lethargic play must be killing him. I feel myself shrinking away from him, wanting to hide. But before I can look away, he taps his chest with one finger. I look down again at that strange white T-shirt and, for the first time, I can see what's written on it.

Larger Than Life.

My heart turns over. He promised that there were better things for Annie Larger, and he delivered. He clearly made the shirt himself or went to a T-shirt shop to have it custom-made. The font is aggressively dark and bold. There is no hiding his thoughts on me and my play.

She is larger than fucking life.

He's telling me without saying a word how he feels. It doesn't feel romantic exactly. It feels like life. Daniel said I saved him yesterday at the charity run, and now it feels mutual. I don't need to listen to fans, to pundits, to Trenton Smith in his glass office. I need to punch back and show people who I am. I need to stop shrinking and start growing.

The referee puts the ball in my hands, and there is a small spark of magic. It's difficult to shake off two bad quarters of play, but I feel determined. This is my team. My life. My game. I have to own it, even when it doesn't feel like my own. Indiana expects us to pass to Jadea since she's our star, which is not a bad gamble, but Coach Rembert had something more brilliantly subtle in mind. Instead of Jadea getting a screen so she gets open, she gives the screen to Taherah. Taherah, our shortest player, spins around the screen and comes close to me at the sideline. I quickly pass it to her, then screen the defender, Lexie Hull, who is chasing. Taherah is left with a moment of solitude just outside the three-point line.

Just as I push back on Lexie Hull and everyone is turning towards Taherah, she lets loose the three-point shot. It isn't perfect, it doesn't swish, instead it rattles inside the rim, taking its time to go through the hoop. It feels almost poetic, seeing it fight its way through—just like we'll have to for the rest of this game. Despite the fact that we're losing by so much, the crowd roars at the spectacular basket. Everyone wants a close game—hopefully, we can give them that.

I look at my girls, surrounding Taherah for a fist bump, and that fighting spirit rises up. Yes, we will. I'll make sure of it.

The last two minutes of the first half are chaos. I can't say we're playing cleanly yet, but we are pushing back. We play tougher defense, and I get a steal that has me streaking down the court with Jadea in tow. Just as my defender is about to catch me, I bounce pass it to Jadea, and she goes up for a showstopper dunk.

SLAM!

The crowd is frenzied now, and Indiana shows their first sign of nerves. Aliyah Boston goes up for an easy bucket under the basket and misses. Lexie Hull shoots two threes and misses both. Caitlin Clark steals the ball from me, but I stomp after her and snatch it right back. The look she gives me is almost scandalized.

We go into halftime 48–33. Fifteen down. It's still a pretty decent lead on their part, but I feel a shifting of the momentum, both in myself and the game. We can do this. Daniel's extremely cute, extremely bold T-shirt is branded into my brain. I have to think of myself differently. I have to block out the noise.

Larger than Life.

When we get into the locker room for our fifteen-minute halftime, Coach Rembert is angrier than I've seen her in months. "Where did the St. Louis Arrows go? Because I don't see them out there."

She turns her heated gaze on each of us in turn. Most of my teammates look away or just keep wiping their sweaty faces with towels, but I stare right back. I want her to see that I'm sorry for the way I played and that I intend to bounce back.

Whatever she sees seems to inspire her. "Annie, get up here." A shiver of nerves trickles down my spine at her words. I step up next to Coach, and she gestures to me, her tone calmer. "Annie played an abysmal first half, I think we can all agree. Until those last few minutes, she was oh for four in her shooting, missed two free throws, had six turnovers. We all agree on that, right?"

My teammates rightfully look nervous for me. No one wants to be made an example of. But I try not to fidget. I'm the first one to say, "Right." My voice hardly wavers.

There are a couple of muttered agreements, but nothing rousing. Our spirit is currently doused. "But then, she changed," Coach Rembert continues, tucking her clipboard under her arm. "The last two minutes, she made two easy baskets, had three steals, and was tougher on defense. Our gap closed a little. We have a chance here, a real one." Some eyes are looking up at her now, her words resonating. I nod too, listening hopefully.

So, I'm especially surprised when she turns the floor over to me. "Annie, tell them why that happened. Why you started to play better."

"Oh." I fidget back and forth, swiping some sweat off my upper lip. I take a deep breath and shoot for honesty. "Someone reminded me that even when you're being labeled, that doesn't mean you have to listen. Besides my own current family issues, this team has to contend with labels, too. We're the best team in the league, and when we don't play like it, our feelings get hurt. We're embarrassed. Angry." I pause, thinking of the right words. Jadea is looking at me like she's never seen me before, and I hope that's a good thing. "I think that label, of being the best team in the league, is almost hurting us. We shouldn't be playing for that label; we should play for ourselves, for our fans, for each other."

I rarely make speeches and certainly not in such tense situations. I notice that Lynn is smiling softly, and Allyson gives me a tentative clap. I duck my head and look at Coach for her approval. She seems pleased, as though I said exactly what she wanted and more.

Jadea's expression has been more shuttered than usual today. But my words seem to prompt her into action. I'm never going to be a hype girl who shouts the team into excitement. So, when Jadea does it, I follow along happily. "Annie is right!" Jadea works herself up, leaping from her seat on the bench. "We can't play like a sword is hanging over our heads. We'll fight no matter where we are in the standings. We'll play our game no matter what our record is. It's us. It's our game."

She puts her fist out into the air. I'm the first person to touch mine with hers, and then my teammates' sweaty, warm bodies are closing around us. I love seeing all our fists together, together and bleeding for the game. "Arrows on three!" Jadea is shouting now. "One, two, three!"

"ARROWS!" I let loose that scream inside, and we all dissolve into whoops and cheers.

Allyson grabs my hand on one side and Jadea on the other. We run back onto the court and shoot a few warm-up buckets. Some don't go in, but the attitude has already turned. Failure is part of the game. And while Jack and Trenton are making my failure feel particularly uncontrollable, I will yank back whatever control I can.

When I see Daniel on the sideline, I do what any heart-full girl would do. I blow him a kiss.

Movie-star smile in return. I can't even bring myself to care about the fake nature of our relationship. About the ghosting in the hospital. Actions speak louder than words, and his in the present speak volumes.

When the whistle blows for the second half, I get redemption for our first jump ball missed opportunity. Our triple deception with the tip-off looks better than ever, and my lay-up kisses off the glass cleanly. 48–35. Indiana starts to glare a little more our way, and we glare right back. I respect every single woman in our sport, but right now, it's only fire in my veins and the need to win beating a drum in my brain.

The rest of the half feels like a comeback tour. Jadea dunks three times in the third quarter and at the break in between the third and fourth we're all grinning. It's 63–57 them. We're only down by six points, which is an extremely surmountable number when we still have ten minutes of game left.

Coach Rembert calls us to order. "We have one more quarter to prove our worth." Her words are clear, clean. I can feel Daniel's crew hovering a respectful distance away, recording our huddle. "Annie, I want you cutting more to the basket. They've been losing you underneath, and it's a great opportunity. Jadea, keep it up in the paint. Watch for your fifth foul, because you could foul out if you're not careful. Taherah, catch and shoot from beyond the arc as much as possible." Her words are quick, and she's honestly said some variation of them dozens of times. There's something comforting in the familiarity. She surveys all of us and then gives a grim little smile. "Let's win this one. Please."

We head back onto the court for the fourth quarter, and Indiana's game plan quickly becomes clear. They begin pushing Jadea as much as possible, trapping her in the corner, double-teaming her on every opportunity, hacking at her arms to strip the ball away. We're a few minutes into the quarter, and she gets her fifth foul.

"That's BS, Ref!" she shouts at the official nearest her. "They've been doing the same thing to me all game!"

"Crap," I mutter. I reach for her and yank, Olabisi doing the same on her other side. She's straining, trying to talk more to the referees. "Stop it, Jadea! You'll get a technical. You only have one more foul to give."

"They're all over me." She seethes in frustration. "I can't get a clear shot anywhere."

Indiana shoots their two free throws, and the score is 71–63. I try to recalibrate us and get Jadea back into the game. I pass her a quick one under the hoop, but to my surprise she passes it back out to a lonely Taherah who has been abandoned by her defender. An easy swish, and it's a three-pointer. Taherah grins, and Jadea points at her. 71–66.

When Caitlin Clark takes it over the half-court line, I press close, lingering on one side. She pulls the ball to her back hip, trying to look for an open lane to pass to. My teammates must have clamped down enough that there's no easy pass to make. I take advantage and press her back two more steps. When she tries to spin away, she turns into my outstretched hands, and I take the ball away. For once, I don't look for anyone while I sprint down the court. This basket is mine and that resolve burns brightly when I easily make the lay-up. 71–68.

Indiana calls a time out, and I check the clock, chugging my water. 3:48 left. Some of my teammates are in foul trouble, with both Jadea and Lynn having five. Allyson has four. If anyone gets six, they'll be out for the rest of the game. The Fever knows this and will likely try to goad someone into fouling. Coach warns Jadea of the possibility. "Watch your back, Jones. They'll want you gone."

Jadea nods seriously. This team is impressive, fantastic really, but Jadea is practically born for these moments. She can make something out of nothing. We can't lose her.

The next three minutes pass in a blur. Indiana scores first with a set play that has so many passes and cuts we lose track of the ball. Taherah shoots another three, and electricity crackles on my skin when it falls through the hoop. 73–71 them. I can see Daniel pacing anxiously on the sidelines and my mom in the stands, recklessly throwing her pom-poms in the air.

There are a few more plays, a few more steals, and time feels like it's slipping through our fingers. It's tied with 34 seconds left. 77–77. Indiana calls a timeout, and then we do. Both trying to throw the other team off. Freeze their momentum and slow them down.

We have the ball. I'm coming down the court, watching my defender, Kelsey Mitchell, carefully. She's one of the toughest players in the league, and she won't back down in these last few plays. I dribble across half-court and look for the first pass. I see Olabisi lingering on the wing, and my first thought is of her quickness and how easy it would be for her to pass it to Jadea for the easy bucket. The ball shoots out of my hands, but I make the same mistake as the first half. I forget that Olabisi's defender is just as quick. Caitlin Clark jumps the lane and snatches my pass out of the air.

She barrels down the court, feeling that hunger for an advantage in the final minute. I race after her, but I'm not quite fast enough. Jadea was standing in the corner, but she's so fast, she races past me. Just as Clark is about to score, Jadea throws a hand in the air. I wince, hoping it will be a clean block, but Jadea clips Clark's hand, and the whistle blows.

Clark missed the shot, but she has two free throws. Jadea is escorted to the bench since she's fouled out. I grab her hand before she leaves. "I'm sorry." I shake my head. "That was my fault."

We won't have our star player these last few moments, and it's because of me. Jadea looks more serious than I've ever seen her. "We'll win." She leans in, eyes locked on mine. "Not you. Not me. *We* will win. I promise."

I'm startled by her declaration but manage to turn my attention to Clark's free throws.

She makes the first one. 78–77, them.

She misses the second one. Unusual. Still 78–77.

There's 23 seconds left in the game, meaning we have just one go at this. One full shot clock run at this. We don't have any timeouts. We need to move.

I think about Coach Rembert. About her familiar directions. About Jadea's fevered promise. About Daniel and his T-shirt. My mom and her pom-poms.

This is for them.

I shock Indiana by practically sprinting down the court. I should be wasting time by their account and waiting for one perfect shot to end the game. Instead, I force my team to pass.

To pass and pass.

To their credit, they don't seem surprised. Despite my eight turnovers tonight, passing is what I do best. I can see every teammate and anticipate their opportunities for success. The paths to the basket.

The clock is counting down, and I'm still standing at the top of the key, directing our passing. The girls are running around, pushing themselves to the limit in these last few seconds. Their defenders are giving chase.

Finally, when the clock reaches ten seconds, I leave the top of the key. I bounce pass to Taherah, who is my backup point guard anyway, and I run as fast as I can. I rush behind Allyson and Flo, keeping their position under the basket. I push past Indiana defenders and come out on the other side of the basket. Taherah has directed the pass to my side, Olabisi's wing, and she has the ball.

I'm open, my defender two steps behind me, just a few feet away from the basket. Too far for the easy lay-up, but close enough for a fairly basic jump shot. When I catch the ball there's three seconds left. My pulse is so loud in my ears.

I spring up on my toes and shoot.

It doesn't swish. It doesn't go down easily. It bounces and bumbles and bumps the backboard. Then it rattles home. Basket made. 79–78, us.

The buzzer goes off, and the crowd goes wild. Jadea jumps off the bench, running to hug the breath out of me. I'm laughing and laughing, my chest light. Taherah and Olabisi are suddenly there, and we're all screaming, crying, laughing. We won. It wasn't a playoff game, but it felt like one.

I pull myself free from the pile, smiling brightly. My eyes seek out Daniel, and when I find him, across the court, near the media table, I find myself running. It's a strange instinct, but I don't tamp it down. I fling myself into his open arms, and then we're laughing together. My sweaty cheek sticks to his newly minted t-shirt.

When I pull back, I admire his shirt. "When did you have time to make this?"

Daniel frowns in thought. "Hard to say. It might have been a rush job that my assistant and I struggled with. The letters might even be iron-on."

The giddy laughter finally flickers out, and the moment grows more serious as I look at him. "It's perfect. Thank you." He smiles a little, studying my face as though to see if my words are genuine. I hope he sees every little bit of hope he's given me reflected in my face. I lean in close to him, savoring his minty scent and the reappearance of his half-dimple. "Best date I ever had," I say softly.

Daniel's expression melts, and he looks at me with galaxies in his eyes. He reaches a hand to my cheek, and I inhale sharply as he tucks a wayward baby hair back into place. Before he can say anything, there's a tapping on my shoulder. Someone with an ESPN media badge on. "An interview, Ms. Larger?" They gesture to a smiling Holly

Rowe. You know the game is being nationally televised when you have the brilliant Holly Rowe interviewing you.

Daniel nudges me encouragingly, but some of my confidence has deflated. Just because I'm getting better at talking to my teammates and to Daniel doesn't mean these interviews feel any easier. Especially since the last one I had basically upended my life. I nod hesitantly and accept the microphone so I can talk to Holly.

I nervously flip a braid over my shoulder as Holly and the camera turn their attention towards me. "Annie, I think we'll start with this game. I have to say it felt like one of the most exciting of this season. Do you agree?"

Familiar territory, and I want to pull Holly aside to thank her. "I'm sure it was very exciting for the fans, Holly, though I'll say it was a little more nerve-racking for the team."

This gets a small chuckle from Holly. She continues, "You started off the game struggling with your passes and shots. You finished with 14 points and nine assists. What changed?"

I try very hard not to look at Daniel, standing a few feet away, talking to his cameramen and pointing to my team, who is finally heading off the court. "Someone reminded me that I can change my mindset. It's been a hard week, and my game felt off as a result."

Holly's eyes are sparkling. "Is that someone Daniel Chan?"

"No comment," I respond, but my voice is teasing.

She switches gears, growing a little more serious as she looks down the camera lens. "The hard week Annie is referring to is the recent investigation into her biological father's misconduct when it comes to the ownership of the Arrows." It's a kind and efficient summary. She turns her attention back to me. "But, as far as I understand it, you don't even know Jack Smith?"

I think about Trenton's warning to stay out of his family's business, but I still feel compelled to say something. Holly is looking at me seriously, like she knows this isn't just jokes about being a "nepo baby".

"That's correct," I finally say, trying to keep my voice even and to show no sign of tearing up. "I didn't know he was my biological father until a few days ago."

Holly presses me, but in a surprising way. "And do you feel like your father's scandal, which may or may not have anything to do with you, is taking away from your team's recent success?"

It's a thoughtful question and exactly what you'd expect from consummate professional Holly Rowe. Jadea will be pleased. Her fake dating scheme and our win today seem to have boosted my reputation already. "Yes, I think it has," I say softly. "Jack isn't my father. He didn't raise me. He didn't coach me. I've never said more than a few words to him. Maybe he thought he was helping me, but instead, he's distracted everyone from the incredible games being played in the WNBA right now. I think it's shameful that the WNBA is getting more press than ever right now, and it's all because of a scandal that most players have nothing to do with."

With that, I pass back the microphone. I don't know if I said enough or explained it in the right way, but I tried to be honest. As I walk away from Holly, I see my mom is still in her seat, waiting to talk to me.

I know we need to hash things out. I need to explain Daniel and our entanglement, and she needs to talk about Jack. I want to be friends with her again, to tell each other everything again. I've hovered over the call button so many times these past few days. But my mom and I hardly ever fight, which means we're not used to making up.

Daniel sidles over to me. "Is that your mom?"

I nod nervously. He reads my expression. "You're still not speaking?" His words are laced with sympathy, maybe because he's also close with his family. His parents and younger brother William.

I take a deep breath. "It's time. We need to talk it out, but I don't know what to say. It's hard to be disappointed in someone you love, you know?"

As soon as the words are out of my mouth, I regret them. It sounds like I'm talking about Daniel, about how disappointed I was when he left. Before I can open my mouth and say something, anything, he says, so softly and achingly, "I guess you just have to hope they'll acknowledge how they hurt you. And promise yourself that you'll try to understand their reasons." There's a moment of fraught silence, fragile as spun glass. He clears his throat, looking away from me and towards the stands. "Your mom wasn't honest with you, and that hurts. But she didn't do it intentionally. If anything, she was probably scared that you'd be disappointed in her when you heard about Jack. And so, she became trapped in a paradox of her own making."

Every word that comes out of his mouth is empathetic and kind.

Like always.

Is there a reason out there that would make up for all the pain I suffered when he left? If there isn't, is time enough to heal our wounds?

We can't have this conversation now, with my mom watching us from above. There's a few more breaths of tension before I try to smile for him. He returns it tentatively. "I'm sure you're right. She's my mom. How scary can she be?"

I take a deep breath and start my ascent.

Chapter 13

I climb up the bleachers to talk to my mom, going up to her now empty section. She seems so alone there, her pom-poms deflated, her mouth drawn down. She looks like she's aged years in one week. I feel a twinge of guilt and hurry to her side.

I open my mouth to say, "I'm sorry."

But she beats me to it.

I sit down in the stadium seat next to her, and she immediately turns to face me fully. "I'm sorry, Annie." Her voice is wobbly, her eyes glassy. "I didn't handle any of this right, and now you're facing the consequences. I—" she muffles a sob, pressing her hands to her eyes, "I saw those signs at the beginning of the game. Those green posters, and I thought about people saying those things to you, day after day, and I—"

"Mom," I cut her off gently. "I stopped looking at those posters. I was looking at that instead." I point down at Daniel, who's pretending like he's not watching us by checking his phone absently. When he catches us both looking, he waves, showing off his Larger Than Life t-shirt.

My mom sniffles and then squints. "Did he make that himself?"

"He had some help from his assistant Derek," I explain wryly.

She smiles a little. "It's wonderful, honey." There's a lull where we're both sitting there, not sure what to say. It's difficult to fight with your mother when you've hardly ever done it before. Our usual tiffs revolve around vintage fashion finds, period-related hormones, or whoever ate the last of the Twizzlers.

I think about Daniel and his advice. She never meant to hurt me. She never could have anticipated the mess this secret being unearthed would create. She has just as much of a right to be angry with Jack as I do. We should be on the same team; we always have been before. "Mom," I finally gather my courage, "why didn't you tell me about Jack? I don't mean anything big, like making new custody arrangements or even giving me his phone number; I just mean, why didn't you mention that he was a businessman? The owner of a sports team I cherished? A billionaire? A married man? Any details of his life. It might have prepared me for this nightmare. Even just a little."

I keep my eyes on her, steady. It's hard, watching her fidget and seeing the glitter tears track down her cheek from her red sparkly eyeliner. For a moment, it doesn't seem like she'll answer. But then, she meets my gaze. "I was terrified," she says, and it falls like an anvil in between us. "Terrified that if you knew anything about him, you'd want him in our lives. That you'd want to meet him and understand him and that you'd..." She swallows. "That you'd forgive him."

"Forgive him?" I parrot back, open-mouthed.

She laughs bitterly. "Because the truth is, Annie, that I've never forgiven the man. He promised me every love in the world, every life and dream I wanted, he said we could have it all. We seemed like the love stories you see in the movies. Dramatic, maybe. Full of obstacles, definitely. But I thought we were made for each other. When he said he didn't want to be with me, I was the one who shut him out. I won't say he was exactly excited to be in your life, but I was the one who told him no. No money. No birthday cards. No contact." She wipes her eyes with the back of her hand. There's glitter everywhere. "He might have done the bare minimum if I'd let him."

It's not the first time this week that my life feels upside down. Daniel was right. I feel like I'm seeing my mom for the first time. "You never said one bad thing about him." I marvel at her. "You always said we didn't need him. That we were perfect on our own."

"We were," she insists, smiling shyly at me.

"We *are*," I correct her. I lean my head on her shoulder, a struggle with her 5'9" frame, but I make it work. I grab her hand and squeeze. "I don't want Jack, Mom. I don't *need* him. I have you and Jadea and my team." I don't include Daniel, but I know my mom is thinking it.

I pull back after a few heartbeats of closeness, of motherly comfort. It's my turn to be honest. "I don't need Jack. Or Trenton or a whole new family. But this is *extremely* complicated. Jack seems like he wants to make amends, but I've yet to meet the man. Trenton wants me to stay away, and I have no idea how Tiffany feels. This story has hurt lots of people and disappointed even more." I try to hold her gaze. "I have the family I need. But I might have to see Jack one day. He'll never be my dad. But he might be *something*. I just don't know."

It feels good to say it. I'm not lying when I say there is no dad-shaped hole in my life. I don't need Jack to come into my life and start coaching my little league team and ordering me to clean my room. He missed that time in my life. But there is a small part of me that's curious. He did something terrible, manipulating the draft and the team, but why did he do it? Guilt? Misplaced devotion?

My mom's expression clears. She nods resolutely. "I understand. You do what you have to do."

I gnaw on my lower lip. "The league is still investigating, but Trenton told me that Jack is no longer involved in day-to-day operations. Do you think he did everything the source says he did? Insisted on my draft? Blackmailed journalists? Screamed at the board, so I got a starting position?" It sounds horrible, all laid out like that.

Her gaze goes unfocused, looking out at the stadium, which is currently being cleaned and deconstructed. "I want to say that I know one way or the other. The man I loved did not seem demanding, high-handed, or manipulative. But that man was just an illusion, hiding the real him." She purses her lips grimly. "I have no idea what he's capable of."

"Comforting," I murmur, my gaze zig-zagging across the staff cleaning the floors and Daniel, who has finally dismissed his camera crew. It's sweet he's waiting for me when I know he has a plane to catch. He's flying back to New York to tape his show.

"Annie." My attention snaps back to Mom, who looks serious all of a sudden. She hardly blinks, gripping my hands tightly. "You and I, we're the same, but different. You've always been quieter and more independent, but we deal with our problems the same way." There's a pause, and I know she's making sure I'm listening. She gives me a ghostly smile. "*We don't.*"

There's a lump in my throat. "I'll figure it out," I promise. "I won't just sit on the sidelines."

She seems to believe me and changes the subject, her features relaxing now that we're back to normal. "You played beautifully tonight, Annie. And I'm certainly not the only one who noticed." Her eyes focus on Daniel, lingering down below.

"I wanted to tell you," I reassure her, "because it's not what it seems." I quickly fill her in on the highlights of Jadea's scheme. I don't say much else about Daniel and our date, but something must bleed into my tone.

"He left you, honey. He left and didn't say anything, even when you called and texted for weeks." It's a gentle reminder, a loving one.

I keep my eyes on Daniel. He's taken a ball from one of the racks and goes to the free throw line. I remember the ways our bodies glanced off each other as I showed him how to shoot.

He swishes the first shot.

I look back at my mom, who's been watching me curiously. "I know what he did. And he's offered to talk about it." I remember being in the parking garage and insisting we didn't talk about the heavy stuff.

How do Largers deal with their problems?

We don't.

"You didn't let him?" she asks, brow furrowing in confusion. "He wanted to explain what happened?"

I sigh. "It's all fake, I know, but it's been so nice. If he tells me what really happened, it will pop our bubble of happiness. All those ugly, messy feelings will spill out."

Mom stares at him, shooting aimlessly on the court. "I didn't like what he did to you, Annie. It was horrible." I think she's going to leave it at that, and my chest aches. If my mom can't see redemption for Daniel and me, maybe there is none.

When she continues, that ache turns to a fluttery hope. "But he had just gone through something equally horrible. You and I both know from this week that sometimes we don't act like ourselves in the face of something terrifying."

Daniel and I creep closer and closer to the precipice of this whole facade. Maybe Mom is right, and we should just leap together.

"Besides," Mom's voice has grown light, "I always liked Daniel."

*

I'm exhausted when I get back to the apartment that night. A little shot of pleasure goes through me when I see the bouquet from Daniel still preening in its vase.

I shower and change into my softest pajamas. I even pull out my unicorn sleep mask, saved for those nights where I want to crawl under the covers and sleep forever. We have a light practice tomorrow and then another game on the road Tuesday. I need my beauty sleep.

I'm checking the alarms on my phone when I notice my Twitter is blowing up. There are mentions everywhere. I open the app and see a trending video of the game. It's from after the game actually, a few moments post-buzzer beater.

I'm hugging my friends and grinning like a fool. It's a good quality clip because it was taken from the ESPN2 broadcast. They zoom in on my freckles and flushed face and my long red braids in a disarray. I look disarmingly happy.

You can see me search the sideline for a moment after extracting myself from the excited huddle. There's a spark in my eyes, and then I'm running to get to Daniel. ESPN managed to capture our long hug and the soft conversation that ensued. The clip is barely 45 seconds long, but it makes an impact. For those who don't follow my Instagram or haven't been keeping up, now they're in the know.

Jadea texts me: *#Dannie?*

And I check and see that it's the ninth trending topic in my location for the evening.

A fan with the username *@JJonesObsessed* retweets the clip with the comment: *@AnnieLarger @DanielChan what is happening here???*

I should feel ashamed that my fake relationship with Daniel is fooling the world. Instead, there's a strange mix of pride and confusion. It doesn't really feel like a fake relationship. He didn't have to make that gesture. Jadea did not insist on it. He ironed on those letters because he thought I needed it, because he cared about me.

And so, when I respond, I don't hold back, but I don't give any information either.

@AnnieLarger: Eat your heart out, St. Louis.

Chapter 14

The next morning, I wake up anxious. It happens sometimes when I dread my tasks for the day. Getting my oil changed. Filming a team promotional video. Going on a date. Getting a cavity filled. Arguing with someone I love.

Today's anxiety has to do with my biological father. The conversation with my mom rattled me. We both agree that we avoid our problems, so shouldn't we try to change? Try to be brave and actually confront our problems head-on?

I don't ever have to like Jack Smith. But I'd like some information from him. I don't want to be ambushed again once the WNBA is finished with their investigation. I want Jack to tell me the truth. I want him to explain how he treated my mother and his own family. I want him to explain the risks he took that have ultimately jeopardized both our careers.

I deserve all of those answers and more.

I stare at my phone for a long time, the numerous missed calls from him. Strangely, I haven't heard anything from him since I talked to Trenton. Did he and his son come to an agreement that we shouldn't be in contact? Is that another reason why Trenton swooped in and met with me instead of Jack? Maybe he doesn't want us talking at all. But it's not against my NDA to talk *with* Jack. Just *about* him.

Or maybe Jack just got the message that I didn't want to talk to him unless it was about basketball. I can change that message if I'm the one to reach out.

I take three deep breaths, burrow my feet deeper into my pink fuzzy slippers, and press the call button. I'm buzzing with anxiety as I listen to it ring.

And ring.

And ring.

There's no answer, and the answering machine lists the number itself, not some damning personal message such as, "This is Jack Smith, meddler in the life of the daughter I never wanted." When the beep sounds, I hesitate for a moment. Is this his way of telling me he doesn't want to talk? That Trenton handled everything in his office a few days ago? Does that matter?

Finally, I say as evenly as possible, "Hi Jack, this is Annie *Larger*." Do I put some emphasis on my mother's surname? I sure mean to. "I'd like to talk if you can find the time. Thank you."

I sound like someone's secretary, but I guess it's better than sounding like his hot mess of a daughter.

I get ready with one ear tilted towards my phone, primed for it to vibrate and Jack's number to flash across the screen. It never happens. I braid my hair, no call. I put on my combo moisturizer/sunscreen, no call. I put on my favorite slides with the glittery Arrows logo, no call. I swing my backpack over my shoulder, phone clutched in my hand, no call.

I drive to practice, trying to push the whole thing out of my mind. I was brave and tried to reach out; it's not my fault if he doesn't respond. Just as I'm about to get out of the car, I see I have a text message. I expect it to be from Jack, but instead it's from Trenton.

Trenton: Hi, Annie. It's Trenton. I thought we agreed that you needed to stay out of my family's life. Please don't call again, especially if you want that scholarship fund we agreed on.

My heart starts pounding at the vaguely threatening tone of the message. How did Trenton know I called his dad? Are they together and having a big laugh about it? Did Trenton convince his dad to avoid contact with me...forever?

As I exit the car, I slam the door extra hard behind me. All that matters is basketball. Winning the championship. At this point, everything else is a distraction.

*

Practice seems normal when I arrive, at least at first. Maybe a little extra exhausting. Despite our miracle victory against Indiana, Coach Rembert is still putting on a clinic. Even cardio goddesses like Olabisi and Jadea are sweating buckets.

And, of course, for karmic reasons, Daniel is really delving into one-on-one interviews today. Our schedule from Iris reads that he'll be doing a half hour interview with Olabisi, Lynn, and Allyson today. He rotates through them as we do our early morning individual workouts. I can see him intently questioning each of them up in the bleachers—the venue he chose for the interviews. Tomorrow night, we have an away game. The following day, Taherah, Jasmine, and Flo are on the schedule. Jadea and I will be interviewed last, at the end of the week.

I'm chugging my second Gatorade of practice, this one a battery acid yellow, when Jadea practically runs me over in her haste to talk to me. "Jadea!" I yelp as a splash of Gatorade hits the floor. "Where's the fire?"

"We have a problem," she says without preamble. "With our..." She leans in to whisper, "*Special project.*"

I look around the court for Daniel, expecting him to *literally* be on fire or talking fervently on the phone to an aggressive reporter. Practice is just winding down, and his crew is packing up. He *is* on his phone, but in the casual way most 21st-century Americans are. If there's anything strange going on, it has to do with my teammates huddled up together across the court from us. No doubt Olabisi is sharing a sordid dating story, or Taherah is showing them a new TikTok dance. "What's the problem?" I carefully screw the cap on my Gatorade. "We were on People.com this morning. It's even more mainstream than we could have hoped."

I don't know why I'm repeating myself. Jadea was the one who sent me the link today. It wasn't like we were *People's* number one trending story or anything, but in their "What's New" section, there was a small blurb with the headline "HBO's Daniel Chan and WNBA player Annie Larger confirm relationship."

Jadea shakes her head dismissively. "It's the team. They've gotten sort of carried away, and I couldn't nip it in the bud. And then they talked to marketing and the Arrows social team, and it just got...out of hand."

"Marketing?" I croak. I'm getting goosebumps as I associate all these words with public speaking and another hellish interview. "What do you mean?"

The words flood out of Jadea. "They're about to ambush you and Daniel into playing a game of Who Knows Who Better. They want to film it and put it on the team's social media."

I almost sag with relief. That doesn't sound so bad, does it? "What's wrong with that?" I ask curiously. You'd think Jadea would be jumping for joy—she lives for social media.

She gives me a bewildered look. "I know you two kind of knew each other at Stanford, but I don't think you'll be able to fool anyone into thinking you've been together for *six months*."

"Oh." The lies that have swirled around Daniel and me are finally coming back to bite me. I try to reassure Jadea. "We've talked a lot this week. I think we can wing it convincingly." I've seen these challenges before on social media and half the fun is when a couple gets an answer wrong and bickers charmingly. We could always lean into that, right?

Jadea's face grows a bit suspicious. "You're being very calm about this, Annie."

I try to sound flippant. "Maybe I'm just getting better at this whole public speaking thing?" She narrows her eyes, but she can hardly disagree without insulting me. I keep my tone cheerful. "I'll go warn Daniel about the ambush."

I sidle over to him, and he smiles beautifully when he notices me. I struggle to keep my steps even. "Daniel!" I'm whispering like we're undercover spies. "We're about to be attacked."

He leans towards me conspiratorially, eyes wide. "Where are the troops coming from, General?"

I stifle a snort. "The girls have convinced the Arrows social media team that we need to play a segment of Who Knows Each Other Better."

Daniel nods gamely, as one who has seen these challenges in every form on social media and YouTube. "Like the newlywed game?"

I keep my expression dead serious. "I believe so."

When all my teammates come over and explain their grand idea to us, Daniel and I try to act shy and surprised. Truthfully, I'm trying hard not to laugh. They force us into two chairs placed next to each other. Taherah has a stack of notecards so she can read off the questions. Olabisi is holding her phone up, entirely focused on getting our "best light".

Once again, this fake relationship feels like the best relationship I've ever been in. I always imagined Daniel knowing and laughing with my friends, Jadea especially, but I could never explain either group to the other as well as I wanted. Despite my nerves about getting these questions right and acting like a true couple would, I'm also genuinely excited we're all together. There's a sort of warmth in my chest that I would not normally associate with being on camera.

Taherah orders everyone around behind the camera. I'm not surprised this is her brainchild. She's always been the true romantic of the group, and she's obsessed with game shows. "Social told me they'd put up a title at the beginning to introduce the game," she tells us earnestly, a smile on her beautiful face. "So, we can just jump right into the questions! You get a point for each question you get right."

Once she introduces the competitive element, it's like Daniel and I both immediately sit up straighter. Daniel rubs his hands together gleefully. "You're dead, Larger. I know you better than anyone."

I squint at him. "I think you're overconfident, Chan. We only got back together a few months ago. How well do you know the in between?" It's a little snarky, but I can't help it. He's so confident.

The girls are giggling a bit behind the camera, signaling to me that our sassy interaction is being recorded. I roll my eyes at Daniel's cutthroat expression and turn to give my attention to Taherah and the camera.

She clears her throat. "First question is easy. Daniel, you'll answer first. What is your partner's favorite color?"

His answer is quick and sure. "Hot pink." My cheeks flush that same lovely color when he looks me in the eye. "Or rainbow, if that's an option." He smiles charmingly at the camera.

"Too easy!" I scoff. "My wardrobe is a dead giveaway."

Taherah's calm voice cuts through our squabbling. "Annie?"

I state my answer in the same confident manner he did. "Black if we're talking clothes, green if we're talking in general."

Daniel nods slowly, as though pondering the merit of my answer. "Fair enough."

Taherah reads the next one. "What is your partner's go-to take-out order? You first, Annie."

This is an interesting question. I really haven't seen Daniel order take-out in years. And he lives in New York. His tastes could have changed. I decide to go with my gut, a taste of home. "Saara's tandoori chicken with basmati rice. Dr. Pepper, extra ice." I wink at the camera, surprising myself. This is even more fun than I thought it would be. "He loves to chew on it." I grin victoriously as Daniel nods along.

"A bad habit, I'll admit," he says grimly. He then ponders my take-out order, his expression sweeping me up and down. I have something in mind, but he'll never get it.

My jaw drops when I hear what he says. "Suzy's Belgian waffles with sliced bananas and Nutella. Cold brew coffee."

It's my usual cheat day meal from Suzy's. He joined us there a few days ago, but we didn't even get around to ordering.

"How did you know that?" I demand and then freeze. If we'd truly been dating six months, he'd likely have fed me those very waffles in bed. "I love all takeout," I finish lamely, hoping to cover up my misstep.

Daniel's eyes are twinkling at me, his half-dimple popping and taunting me. "You like taking pics of it, Anna-banana." And there it is, a small and unimportant memory of Jadea bringing me the meal when I was in bed, sick, a few months ago, and posting it to her Instagram stories. She even called me Anna-Banana in the video. Damn Daniel's ridiculously hot brain for remembering.

Taherah doesn't even bother hiding the laugh in her voice when she continues. "Daniel, what records does Annie hold at Stanford?"

This question is in his wheelhouse, and yet I'm still slightly turned on when he rattles them off easily. "First freshman to have 150 assists in a season, career assist record for the women's basketball program, All-Academic team Junior and Senior year."

Some of the competitive juice has depleted, leaving behind softness. Daniel and I were going to pretend we knew each other, wing it the best we could. Instead, we're doing well. We're crushing it. I'm so busy looking at him with heart-eyes that I don't hear Taherah's question. "Sorry," I apologize, giving her my full attention. "What did you ask?"

She raises a brow knowingly. When my gaze darts to Jadea, I'm surprised to see she doesn't look happy. Maybe our acting is too convincing.

It's certainly starting to fool me.

Taherah repeats her question. "Annie, what made Daniel want to run track?"

The question catches me off guard in its simplicity. I know the answer; Daniel has told me the story a dozen times. However, post-accident, I imagine it's now a very painful story. I dart a glance his way, and he gives me a small nod, as if to say, "go on."

"It was the 2008 Olympics." My voice is a little softer, and I try not to look away from the camera. "Track and Field excitement was at an all-time high. Usain Bolt had just set world records in the 100- and 200-meter sprints. The U.S. 4 by 400 team had set an Olympic record that had the announcers shouting with excitement. I know because he made me watch a clip of it early on in our relationship." A true story from our days at Stanford. I look at him teasingly and find he's already looking at me. His expression is so affectionate that I almost falter. His eyes are like pools of ink. "He asked his mom what Track and Field was. His mom said—"

"Track and field is the purest form of sport in the world." Our voices mingle together over the words.

I stutter a bit as I finish the story. Daniel's eyes never leave me, and it's making me nervous. In a good and bad way. "And so, he joined his middle school's track and field team. He tried every event he could, but the 400m sprint and hurdles suited him best. He ended up competing in hurdles at Stanford. And then..." I gloss over the accident, "When his time competing was over, he set his sights on broadcasting about what he loved. He's always wanted to go to the Olympics. I know he will one day, even if it's a little different than he imagined."

The words surge out of me, fierce and protective. I should take them back or apologize, but I think Daniel needs to hear them. He always wanted to compete in the Olympics, and unfortunately, the accident got in the way. But he can still get there. He can cover it. He can go behind the scenes. He can still see the magic he saw before.

"Is that true, Daniel?" Taherah asks him tentatively.

Her question draws his attention back to the game and the camera. "Yeah," he says, sounding a little dazed. "It is. I hope it is."

We manage to get through a few more of the lighter questions and end the video with the expected tie. The girls didn't seem to notice the strange shift in the mood, except Jadea, whose expression is puzzled. They put the camera away, finally separating to leave practice.

Taherah is practically bouncing with excitement. "That was great, you guys! I'll send this to social today."

Daniel, who has been lost in thought, focuses on her. He smiles. "Thanks, Taherah. That was fun."

"Absolutely!" I chirp, though really, I'm focused on Daniel's strange mood. Should I not have mentioned the Olympics at all? I crossed our unspoken line by bringing up the past. We've been swerving those topics as much as possible in our fake dating bubble.

"If you'll excuse me," Daniel says, that polite smile still on his face. He gets up from his chair before I can say anything, heading back into the hallway that houses the locker and laundry rooms.

I'm about to follow him when Jadea corners me. "What was that?" she demands.

"What was what?" I say innocently, hiding a wince. This lie gets worse and worse every day. But surely this isn't the time or place to come clean.

"You guys scored 100 percent. Neither of you even wavered." Her tone is accusing. I curse Daniel and I for not coming up with a better strategy. We should have answered at least one or two wrong, squabbled about our answers a bit.

"We did know each other a little bit at Stanford, remember?" I try to rationalize it. "And you made us go on those dates."

It's a weak argument, but not impossible. Her aggressive posture softens a little. "I guess." It's hard to read her expression, something I don't usually struggle with when it comes to Jadea. Does she believe my lie? Does she believe that Daniel and I are falling in love during our fake dating scheme?

None of it makes sense anymore.

Unfortunately, I can't get into any more with her. "Talk later." I give her a reassuring smile. "I've got to find Daniel."

She gives me one more suspicious look but then waves me away good-naturedly.

Chapter 15

I speed off the court and into the attached hallway. I can hear my teammates getting ready in the women's locker room, so I know he's not in there. The men's locker room would be a great guess, but some of the coaches and practice players are in there. Daniel was probably looking for a place to be alone. Either he left the facility, or he went into one of our two laundry rooms. I look in the first one, but it's empty.

I'm surprised at what I see when I open the second. Daniel is leaning against one of the washing machines, taking deep, measured breaths. He looks upset, hands pressed over his eyes. I hurry inside, closing the door behind me.

"Daniel." I cross the room to be at his side. My body feels like it's vibrating, trying to say what I really mean. "I'm so sorry about that. I shouldn't have talked about the Olympics. Your track career." I reach a hand to comfort him but drop it when he abruptly lowers his hands and looks at me fully. He hasn't been crying, but his eyes look a little glassy. His face is pale in the fluorescent light. His curls are in disarray from running his hands through them.

"How can you say those things?" His voice is a little hoarse, his expression intense.

I stutter again, apologetic and rushed. "I know. I know it probably hurts—"

He laughs in disbelief. I freeze, watching him. "No." He looks at me with affection. "It doesn't hurt when you believe in me, Annie. It doesn't hurt when you still remember all my dreams and say that I can achieve them. It doesn't hurt when you smile, and it's not on some screen. You're right next to me." His smile fades a little. "But it should *hurt* you. That's all I've ever done. Hurt you, abandoned you, hid the truth from you." Shame bleeds into the words, mingled with his disbelief. "Why should you care whether I ever go to the Olympics? Why should you care whether I'm lying somewhere in a ditch?" He looks at me beseechingly, as though he really needs an answer.

My mouth trembles a little, but I try to smile kindly. "Daniel, if I've learned anything during our little scheme, it's that you've changed. That man who left me, who hurt me, who blew up my life," he winces at the assessment, "isn't the man you are now. You may have been broken by the accident, but you still have a real chance to achieve your dreams." The words spill out of me, bold and unyielding. "I know you'll go to the Olympics one day. I know you'll keep fighting your PTSD and win most of the time. Maybe you'll even share your story with the world. I hope you will. I hope you'll keep dreaming and not regret what could have been."

The fluorescent light flickers above us, as if sensing the tension. Daniel steps a half step closer to me. We're only a breath apart. The laundry room, which is normally warm, suddenly feels hot. "Annie," he whispers. I tilt my chin up defiantly, looking into those starry eyes.

"Yes?" I whisper back, trying to hide the tremble in my voice.

His words are a tender murmur. "I do have some regrets."

And then we're crashing into each other. His lips are on mine, hard and soft at the same time. My hands crush into his shoulders, reaching up his neck and sighing when I find his decadent curls. His hands roam up and down my sides, and I find I don't even care that I'm still wearing my sweaty practice clothes. Daniel is backing me up, both of us trying to find some solace as we press closer and closer.

The back of my legs hit the dryer behind me, and in one quick, exhilarating movement, Daniel hoists me so I'm sitting on top of it. I hum a sound of pleasure as I wrap my legs around his waist, pulling him even closer to me, lifting his chin. I can feel his heart pounding against my chest.

"Annie," Daniel says again, but this time it almost sounds like a groan.

My skin feels like it's on fire with him, and I break off our frantic kiss to rip off my practice jersey. I'm wearing an entirely too no-nonsense sports bra underneath, but it's heaven to feel my skin against him. He begins kissing down my neck, tickling a sensitive spot below my ear, and I can feel his smile against my likely splotchy and flushed skin. His hands, which have been firmly on my hips, begin to inch up my body.

They feel wonderful, scalding to the touch and almost electric on my skin, but then his thumb just grazes my breast. The pleasure that shoots through me is more than I'm prepared for. Everything is tingling, from between my legs to the ends of my eyelashes.

"Daniel," I gasp out, pulling back to look at him. "Wait—we need to—" He looks at me for a moment, eyes huge and lips swollen. It's almost enough to stall my racing brain and instead go back to our frenetic kissing. But I know we really need to talk. We've danced around it. We've alluded to it. But if we're going to be together, really *together*, I have to trust him. That mental block won't go away with just hormones, at least for me.

I take too long gathering my thoughts. Daniel's face falls a fraction, and he takes a few steps away from me and the dryer. The air between us feels suddenly cold. "Annie," he's stumbling over his words, avoiding my gaze altogether, "I'm sorry. I got carried away. It won't happen again, I promise."

"Daniel, no—" But my words betray me again. They always do. I can't make myself ask him to stay and talk about why he left and how it made me feel, and yet I also can't stop remembering his scalding hands on my hips, his tongue in my mouth.

He backs out of the room. "I'm happy with your friendship, Annie. Your belief in me." He smiles, even as he's looking past me, not *at* me. "I won't ask for more."

And then he practically runs out of the room.

Somehow, I'm the one being left again.

*

The next day's away game is a disaster. Despite our miraculous comeback in the last game, we're still working through some kinks. Teams have been reading our plays more and more. Jadea is being double-teamed any time she has the ball, which leads to her racking up unnecessary fouls trying to get free. Lynn makes a run towards the basket but is slammed by a Dallas Wings' defender. She practically topples into the base of the basket, leaving her with an aching head and a probable concussion. I can see her wife and new baby in the crowd, watching nervously as she's led off the court. I play okay, with nine points and six assists. Not an atrocious game, but a quiet one. We ended up losing by eleven points. It felt like sand running through our fingers. We almost had it but couldn't grasp the elusive victory.

Daniel and his crew were absent as well. They're pretty much finished with any game or practice footage. Besides their interviews, Daniel is just working on his own narration. I find myself imagining him on the sideline, wearing the Larger Than Life t-shirt. I fantasize about his hands raking down my sides, his body between my legs. In general, I don't think I've ever thought about a man so much.

And despite the obsessive nature of my thoughts, I don't hear from Daniel until we're on the plane ride home later that night.

Daniel: Sorry about the loss, Annie.

I look at it, strangely disappointed that's all it says.

Then, another ding.

Daniel: And sorry again about the laundry room.

Daniel: Friends?

Jadea leans to look at my phone from her seat next to me, but I quickly tuck it back into my sweatshirt pocket without responding. "Is that Daniel?" she asks, once again suspicious.

I fidget a little. "Yes."

It's dark in the plane, the lights dimmed for sleep-mode. We speak in hushed whispers. I try to read Jadea's expression in the shadows. Her brow is furrowed. "You really like him, don't you?" I don't answer, and she pushes. "Like in real life? Outside of our little PR stunt?"

I lean back in my airplane seat, closing my eyes briefly. I can feel a headache forming. "I guess I got over my Stanford grudge a little quicker than I expected."

Truer words have never been spoken.

To my surprise, deviating from her usual strong opinions, Jadea reaches out and gently holds my hand. I turn to look at her. "What do you want to do?" she asks softly.

There are a lot of unspoken words between Jadea and me. She understands my frequently lukewarm feelings about romance and sex. When I imagine my future, I imagine a partner, a best friend, someone I cuddle up with as we watch Netflix. I imagine lots of Twizzlers, maybe a couple kids, a cozy apartment or house. But I don't get excited about some guy on the street. A man who's only on my screen, with five pictures and three funny quips about his personality, all wrapped in a swipe-right formula. I really can only imagine that life, that future, with somebody once I get to know them.

That applies to sex, too. I've never had a one-night stand; it's just not in me. I almost never self-pleasure or use sex toys. I had sex with my last boyfriend, Evan, because I trusted him and liked him, and I knew him a few weeks before we even started dating. The slow approach worked best for me. When I was with Daniel at Stanford, I began to feel attracted to him in that way. I would have slept with him if given the chance.

Some people think I'm afraid, and I probably am, to some degree. Sex is a scary, intimate thing. But it's more because I want people to understand me and not think I'm something unusual or unnatural just because I'm not very sexually motivated. Jadea has never treated me that way. She never told me to just "get it out of my system" or "jump into bed" with some guy, which some of my high school and college friends tried out when I complained about the lack of physical sparks.

But... Daniel.

I trust him. I loved him. Now, I care about him again. And...I can't stop thinking about how sex with him would probably be wonderful. Mind-blowing. Romantic and hot and fun.

And for someone like me, those thoughts alone are shocking.

I don't have the guts to tell Jadea about our past, but I do find my voice to speak about the present. "I want to be with him," I tell her quietly. "I can't stop thinking about him."

Jadea's eyes definitely widen this time. "You want to sleep with him?"

I smile a little at her expression. "Before we left, we made out in the team laundry room." Jadea lets out a low whistle that has Olabisi glaring at us from two seats ahead. I shush Jadea, but for her this *is* quiet. "And now I can't stop thinking about it. I was the one who pulled away because I wanted to clear the air, but nothing came out. He thought I stopped him because I didn't want it. Him. Now he says we can just be friends."

Jadea manages to whisper, but every word is fierce. "Annie, this is your chance to have everything you want. You shouldn't ignore these feelings, especially when they don't always happen for you." It's a pep talk at first, but then she softens a bit. "You deserve it, Annie. Daniel is special. I know it."

Weirdly, I'm tearing up. Or not weirdly, considering my propensity for crying during life's pivotal moments. "My chance," I echo. "Maybe I should talk to him?"

It's a weak response, but the best I can muster. I just need to explain to Daniel what I want. Possibly with my tongue.

No, no, focus. Words first.

Jadea cheers me on, silently raising a fist. "Text him now!"

Trying not to hyperventilate, I pull out my phone. I immediately notice another message from Daniel. I must have missed the buzz.

Daniel: I'm working on the narration for your piece...do you want to read it?

The offer seems to be two things: a peace offering, in case I was truly upset about our laundry room tryst, and a genuine offer for collaboration. Back when we were at Stanford, we'd read each other's papers and mark the parts we liked with pink hearts (me) or red stars (him). It was a wonderful routine that he probably thinks we can recreate platonically.

This seems as good an opportunity as any.

Annie: I'd love to! We don't have practice until noon tomorrow. Want to come to my apartment tonight to go over it? I should be home by 11 PM?

I think to anyone else it would sound like a booty call hiding within very professional words, but Daniel knows me and is probably taking me at my word. He agrees, and I tell him where the spare key is in case I'm running late, and he needs to let himself in.

Once our exchange is over, I put my phone away with a relieved sigh.

"Nervous?" Jadea asks, voice low and excited.

I press my heels to my eyes. "I think I'm going to be sick."

Jadea cannot contain her giggles now. "My girl is going to get laid tonight!"

Her announcement is met with many shushes and serious side eye from Allyson in the row over.

"Like it will be so easy," I mutter. I slump in my seat and wait anxiously for the last hour of our flight to pass by.

196

Chapter 16

I seriously regret inviting Daniel over to my apartment. First, getting our baggage takes a little longer than expected, and by the time I'm back in my apartment building, it's almost 11:30 PM. Secondly, I can't remember if the apartment is clean. I should have made him wait in the hall. Thirdly, the idea of confronting Daniel is making me feel physically ill. I had to take off my hoodie because I was cold sweating so much.

Maybe Daniel flaked, and I won't have to deal with him? Honestly, it's not impossible, considering our past.

Instead, when I open the door, toting my carry-on suitcase behind me, I see beautiful Daniel waiting. He's sitting at my tiny kitchen table, scribbling on some printed pages of what is likely a rough draft for our piece. He's wearing a soft gray Stanford Track and Field sweatshirt that I used to borrow all the time when we went out. Black framed glasses. Sneakers neatly lined up by the door. Socked feet crossed at the ankles as he works out a new idea.

And that's not all.

There are dozens of my favorite snacks on the table next to him. Three different variations of Twizzlers, including some blue-colored ones that have to be a special edition. My favorite kettle-cooked potato chips. A fruit tray, packed with strawberries, blueberries, and pineapple. A six-pack of Watermelon-flavored Propel.

My gaze travels just past him and the kitchen, into the living room. The lighting is soft, and it's because he strung up some tiny paper lantern string lights in my favorite shade of pink. There are a couple of my blankets on the floor and a crazy number of pillows. Some mine, some he must have brought up in what—a garbage bag?

I must make some sort of noise, some precursor to surprised crying probably, and he turns to look at me. It's a strange moment. Like we're suspended in time, crystalline versions of each other. I wish this was our true reality. Working together. Setting up surprises for each other when we come home from a hard day at work.

But instead, I just feel confused.

Daniel stands up from his chair but doesn't approach me. I softly close the door behind me, my mouth still gaping. "Did—did you do all this? Why?"

He looks shy and a little guilty. He rubs the back of his neck. "I know these last two games haven't been going your way, and all of this is so overwhelming, and I just thought..." he trails off, as though gathering his thoughts or his courage, "I just thought maybe you needed some comfort. Comfort food." He gestures to the table. "And a comfortable place to sleep. Maybe not for the whole night, considering we're no longer spry twenty-one-year-olds, but I remember the time we built a pillow fort senior year, and you said it was the best night's sleep you'd ever had."

My mouth clicks shut. He's right, of course. One night, driven to insanity by midterms and extra-long conditioning, we built a pillow fort in Daniel's apartment and watched old movies. We fooled around, but only a little, and then we slept nestled in the fuzzy blankets, pillows, and each other. It certainly felt like the best night of sleep I'd had when I woke up the next morning.

I breathe through my nose, so I don't cry. "It's amazing, Daniel." The emotion is still thick in my voice. "I love it."

This is the Daniel who just wanted to help his friend. Or is hiding his feelings because he thinks that's what I want. Either way, it's incredible. He had no expectations for tonight except for some collaborative editing. He did this for me. Because he thought I needed it.

He cleanly sidesteps my emotions. He smiles and lifts up his pile of papers. "I have a few pages of my narration for the piece here. I thought maybe I could read it to you, see if it needs anything?"

There's a little shimmer of nerves in his voice, and I realize he really wants me to like it. I swallow the lump in my throat and try to smile genuinely. "Sure. Go ahead and get started while I put my suitcase away."

We never get closer than a few feet. I try not to look longingly at him as I pass by the table and head into my bedroom, suitcase dragging behind. Daniel sits down and clears his throat. "Good evening, world, this is Daniel Chan and tonight's episode of *Our World Through Sports*."

His voice has smoothed, the vowels rounded, each word unfettered and practiced. It sounds like my TV is on. I hide a smile as I quickly unpack my clothes. "Sounds great so far!" I tease, shouting at him.

"Focus," he admonishes, trying to regain his composure. "Tonight's episode focuses on the WNBA and a recent team's struggle for composure as they pursue their championship dream." Struggle for composure is a very poetic way of describing our last couple of weeks, and my smile stays firmly in place. I unravel my phone charger and plug it in next to my bedside table. Daniel continues, voice raised a little so I can hear him. "The St. Louis Arrows seem like a team with an electric presence. Unstoppable momentum. Young, exciting players. Veteran leadership and coaching. In terms of sports, this is a team reaching for the top with every resource they need to get there." More pretty words, but they do make my heart thump a little. Sports need inspiration. Motivation. Drive. All of those things keep the machine moving and hearing Daniel ignites all the live wires in my body. I zip my suitcase closed, almost finished.

"At the heart of the team are two of the best players in the league: Jadea Jones and Annie Larger. Best friends since childhood, Jones and Larger challenge every misogynistic remark they can. Jones can dunk in spectacular fashion. She and Larger frequently streak down the floor entirely in sync. They want Arch Arena to be swelling with roars, for the team to be talked about on social media or ESPN. They want every opportunity women's sports are frequently denied."

I abandon the suitcase, mesmerized by Daniel's voice. I walk slowly out of my bedroom, hovering in the doorway to listen. Daniel hasn't noticed me yet.

"Many of you may know from social media that Annie Larger and I have a relationship off the court. I won't add anything personal to this piece, but I hope you'll indulge me with one little anecdote." I freeze in place, shocked that he's including anything specific about me in the piece. "My junior year at Stanford, Annie's junior year as well, I was tasked with writing an op-ed about the most exciting sport on campus. I wanted to write about track and field, for obvious reasons, but a few classmates told me it would be crazy not to write about the women's basketball team, which was about to head into March Madness. I went to see them play, hearing a lot about Jadea Jones before I even got there. To my surprise, Jadea was on the bench with an injury." I've already heard him tell this story, but I'm still leaning towards him, drawn into the magic of the memory. "It was Annie who was leading the team. Who scored bucket after bucket, like she had wings on her shoes. She scored the last basket of the game, and the stadium was on fire. Her teammates dog piled on top of her. Jadea was crying softly on the bench, watching it all unfold." He pauses, still looking doggedly at the paper in his hands. "It was the first time I realized that I loved not only track and field, but sports in general. It was a life-changing moment. Lightning in a bottle. When I talk about the St. Louis Arrows, I'm talking with that feeling still sizzling in my veins. That's the feeling I hope this piece gives to you."

He finishes there, finally looking up at me. I'm still mute, standing a few paces away. "What do you think?" he asks as if he doesn't already know.

"You're going to share that story?" I ask hoarsely. I tuck a few loose hairs behind my ear, trying not to fidget. "About us? Stanford, I mean? All of it?" I don't even know what I'm asking.

Daniel shifts in the chair. "I thought the piece could use a personal angle."

It's a laughable response, purely polite and political. I almost *do* laugh. Instead, we just stare at each other. I'm gathering the courage to say more when he stands up abruptly from his chair. It scrapes against the hardwood floor. "I'll leave you to rest up." He smiles that same polite smile, and I want to scream.

"You're leaving?" There's something rising in my voice—anger or disbelief or humor again, humor at this whole voiceless pattern of behavior.

"Well," Daniel keeps that smile on his face, "I probably should go, keep working on the piece, and you have practice tomorrow—"

I practically growl my response. "Daniel!" His eyes widen, and the smile drops. "You're driving me crazy!"

I start pacing, agitated and frustrated. "What?" He sounds bewildered.

I throw my arms out. "What do you mean, what? What the hell are we doing?"

Daniel is growing more uncertain by the second. "We're friends—right?"

The words stop me in my tracks. "Is that what you want?"

A fraught second, where I beg him with my eyes to be honest, for my sanity, please. His voice nearly cracks when he finally says, "No."

I should feel a romantic gooiness in my chest, a sense of relief. Instead, I'm still angry. "Then why are you leaving me, *again*?"

I wonder if he can hear all the hurt hurled at him in that question. He walks over to me, gentle, like I'm a wild animal. He grabs my wrists, slowly lowering them from their current frantic condition. He leans in very closely, our noses almost brushing. My heart trips over in its chest. "I didn't want to leave you, Annie. I've regretted it every single day."

I blink at him. "What do you mean?" How could he have regretted it every day? I hadn't seen or heard from him until Jadea called.

"Come sit." He releases me and gestures to the nest of pillows. "Please?"

I nod, warily following him and sitting with a few feet between us. I gesture for him to continue.

He startles me with a direct question. "How did I seem in the hospital? After my accident?"

I rack my brain, thinking over those memories of him smiling weakly from his hospital bed and me perkily bringing him the best cookies from the vending machines. "I don't know," I answer honestly. "As expected, I guess."

I'm trying to connect the dots, but Daniel switches track again. "Did you know that when I met you, I had been on anti-anxiety meds for nearly four years?"

It would have shocked me less if he had told me he was on steroids. "N-no," I stutter. I'm not upset by this reveal; people should get whatever help they need. I was in therapy during my early high school years to discuss my self-esteem, which really helped. I still have e-visits with my therapist every few months to check in. It's just... I didn't feel that type of camaraderie with Daniel. He never mentioned a past history of mental health or depression. He never seemed to have anxiety about anything. He reminded me more of Jadea than myself. Confident, sure of himself, competitive, kind.

Perfect.

It's strange to consider an extrovert as someone who has anxiety, but I know it's possible. Maybe even frequent.

Daniel takes a deep breath. "It started pretty early on. My parents noticed it as I got into middle school and high school. Every time I failed or did something imperfectly, I would get bouts of anxiety or even have a panic attack. If I failed a test, didn't say the right thing to a friend, disappointed my parents... I had this amazing family, a good life, but everything always felt out of control. I needed to get things in order. To do things right to deserve that life." When he notices my surprised expression, he adds, "Or at least that's how it felt."

"My parents started taking me to therapy and that helped. It was amazing to talk to someone who didn't have a stake in the game. Who I wasn't afraid of disappointing. I also went to a psychiatrist who recommended anti-anxiety meds. We put them off for a while, unsure if they were right for me. But as I got further into high school, the anxiety only got worse. Besides the meds and the therapy, the only thing that gave me relief was—"

"Running," I whisper.

Daniel's eyes are bright with emotion. "It was the only time my brain was quiet. I got on the meds, and I ran track, and I talked to my therapist. I spent more time with my family. Things got better. When I went to Stanford, I grew even more confident. Anxiety would always be in my life, but I had found ways to manage it. I had more joy in my life than I could have imagined. I met you and you were amazing, like a shooting star—" His words grow strangled. He grips his knees and takes a deep breath.

I reach out and take his hand, threading our fingers together. I finish the story, as best as I can imagine it. "And then, you got hit by a car. And your running career was over. That control you had perfected was gone. The patterns of your life had been ripped apart."

Daniel looks at me, expression open. "Annie, I knew I would need help after the accident. I realized I knew how to manage my anxiety when life went according to plan, but not when things got hard. Those days in the hospital with you, I knew you were being wonderful and kind, but I felt so far away. I couldn't be with you the way I wanted. You were about to be drafted. Your future, your *dream* was just weeks away. I couldn't bring you down, drag you to physical therapy, and have you visit me at my parents' house as I reimagined my future." His voice falls to a harsh whisper. "It was excruciating, imagining a life without my Olympic dream. No professional track. No racing. I went to a week of in-patient treatment. Then I had therapy and physical therapy several times a week for *months*. It wasn't meant for you. I couldn't do that to you."

We're both misty-eyed now. I squeeze his hand, almost too tightly. "You wouldn't have brought me down. You're a fighter, Daniel. You might have been down, but not for long." I smile at him, a little watery. "What's the rest of the story?"

His brow crinkles. "The rest of it? What do you mean?"

I keep my voice kind, even. "You did grow. You found a new dream, and you have your Emmy-award winning show. How did that happen?"

Daniel runs a hand through his hair ruefully. "It was luck, really. I was missing sports, and I found that old op-ed I wrote about you on my computer. After reading it, I remembered how exciting it was to be an observer of sports. I figured I could capture some of that magic again, just from a slightly different perspective. My YouTube channel's success steadily increased during those first two years, and then Iris found me. She's brilliant, and she basically co-created the show with me. I still go to therapy once a month and take my meds, but it doesn't feel so crushing. I've learned to adapt." His smile is wry. "Even if it's just a little bit." There's so much about Daniel that I understand now. Nuance to his every word, his every action. The reasons for his precision, his facade of perfection.

"I go to therapy, too," I tell him, surprising myself. A hint of surprise flashes across his face. "I went more often when I was a teenager, but we still check in occasionally. There's no shame in it, even if the world sometimes makes us feel like there is. Thank you for telling me." I bite my lip, wondering if I should be honest. He waits expectantly, as though he knows I have more to say. Finally, I add, "I just wish you'd told me before. I would have understood if you needed a break from us for your mental health. I would have been disappointed and missed you, but I would have understood. Instead, I was sure *I* had done something wrong."

It's an almost impossible situation. Daniel was hurting, and he did what he needed to do to help himself. He did all the right things, really. I just needed a text message. A quick call. A sticky note on his hospital bed pillow. Some clue that he was okay and that he actually cared for me.

Daniel's eyes close at my words, as though they pain him. "I'm so sorry, Annie. I should have done better. Even when you're hurting, it's not an excuse to hurt other people. I told myself I never texted or called for your sake. Because you needed a clean break, and if I texted or called, you would figure out what was going on, and you wouldn't have let me leave. You would have been there with me."

"Damn straight," I whisper, smile a little wobbly.

He smiles then, too, genuinely. "But I think I was just scared. To say those words, to explain that I was mostly happy, but also mostly anxious...it seemed impossible." He shakes his head ruefully. "Everyone has their own experience with mental health, and I figured mine was small in comparison to other people. I didn't need to bring it up—I had it handled. Unfortunately, it was probably more the stigma than anything keeping me quiet."

I nod thoughtfully. "People rarely bring it up, especially in sports. Only a few brave people, like Simone Biles or Michael Phelps, have really been willing to go there."

He runs his free hands through his curls. "I've had this piece on the back burner, ever since I started my show, about mental health in sports. I thought I might even mention my experience with the accident. But I always put it off, too afraid of what people will say. What if people thought I was just looking for attention? Or that I didn't fight hard enough? Sports are all about competition and grit. What if my anxiety took away my ability to be a competitor?" He shakes his head. "And being Asian...there's a lot of layers to it. I didn't want to be the representative for a whole community. What if I misrepresented someone else's experience? What if someone made me the stereotype? What if they blamed my parents?" He's rambling a bit now, and he seems to know it. He laughs. "And that's probably all my anxiety talking, anyway. My therapist would say I'm just feeding it over and over again by avoiding it."

It sounds like a beautiful piece, perfect for his show, though I certainly understand his reservations. Aren't I just feeding my anxiety by avoiding the scandal and avoiding Daniel? I look at him. "Maybe it's time we both stop feeding the beast."

The smile spreads across his face again, like a light flickering on in a dark room. "Maybe you're right."

We stare at each other, and I don't know what he's thinking, but all I can say is, "Daniel, will you kiss me?"

I've surprised him again, but he recovers quickly. He cups my right cheek, releasing our clasped hands. He tucks my hair behind my ear, trailing a finger down my ear and side of my jaw. I suppress a shiver. "Annie," he whispers, leaning closer to me so I can feel his words on my flushed skin, "kissing you is my favorite thing to do."

And then we're pressed together again, our lips hot and greedy. My hands immediately reach under his shirt, sliding over his smooth skin. Daniel's fingers are threaded through my hair, angling me towards him. The lights and the blankets and the pillows suddenly seem too perfect for the moment, and I remember we did not fool around much in our last love nest.

Time to remedy that.

I pull back an inch, both of us panting and looking at each other. Just when he's about to open his mouth and possibly ruin the moment, I curl one sweatpants-clad leg around him, pulling so he's flat on his back and I'm straddling him. "Whoa." Daniel looks up at me admiringly, "That was smooth."

"All credit to you." I wink and hover over him, my long red hair tickling his face. He's laughing when I kiss him again. Our kisses are almost frenzied, the hint of a five o'clock shadow on his chin rubbing my face raw. I work my way along his jaw, peppering him with small kisses and even biting his ear lightly. I remember him liking it last time, and his groan does not disappoint.

I pull my Florence + the Machine t-shirt over my head, tossing it aside. I'm unnaturally pleased at Daniel's reaction when he sees me. He looks up at me with awe, like I'm powerful and beautiful. "You're amazing," he says, eyes wide. "Did you wear that on the flight?"

It's a deep burgundy lace bra with pink flowers embroidered throughout. I laugh then, too. "I might have changed in the airport bathroom. You're just lucky I packed something nice at all."

"Lucky is right," he says with those starry eyes, and I can hardly contain myself. I feel like I'm jumping out of my skin.

Daniel must be feeling the same way because he grips me tightly and rolls us again, so we're on a different blanket, this one is soft and white. I'm now underneath, peering up at Daniel who is braced with only some of his weight on me. He begins kissing me again, with that same fervor and passion that makes my head spin. I arch my back, aching for him, and he reaches a hand underneath. He fumbles once, then unlatches my bra. I help him take it off. "I prefer you over the lingerie, Annie," he breathes, touching my breasts just the way I like. I grit my teeth when he takes my nipple in his mouth, swirling his tongue over it. My brain feels like it's on fire.

He takes the same care with the other one, while I grip his shoulders and swallow down some whimpers. When he finally stops, I find myself scrambling for his shirt, wanting more of his skin on me. He pulls off the black T-shirt and Stanford sweatshirt in one go, tossing both behind us. I kiss down his chest, admiring his lean physique. He might have lost track, but he could never quit running.

My eager hands find the waistband of his pants, and Daniel stills, reaching for my hand. "Annie," his voice is hoarse with wanting, "are you sure? I understand who you are. We don't need to do anything you don't want to do."

My heart swells up, almost stopping me from responding. It's sweet he remembers our conversation from so long ago.

A couple weeks into our relationship when we had hardly shared more than a few kisses, I talked to Daniel about being demisexual. I explained that I wasn't always sexually motivated, and certainly not by people I hardly knew. He nodded at all the right places, asked some thoughtful questions, and we decided to create the pace we wanted. Just about the time he had his accident, I was feeling ready to move our relationship to the next step. I slept with Evan about four months in, and it was good, just not great. We both knew it wasn't the right romance for us. We weren't bad together; we just weren't great.

Daniel makes me feel like greatness itself.

I look him in the eye, so he knows I'm telling the truth. "Daniel," I keep my tone even, "it's unusual that I'm sexually attracted to someone, that's true." He's already leaning back, trying to give me space, but I grab his jaw, pulling him back down so he can hear me. "But you're pretty unusual, Daniel Chan. And I've never wanted you more."

At my words, he gives me that movie star smile and I want to fan myself, a blush spreading down my chest. He leans down, gives me a peck, then we begin to move slower. Everything becomes less frantic and more sensual. I appreciate the savoring. Every moment feels weighted, tension-filled, and it makes my body writhe with wanting him. The eye contact as he slowly peels off my socks. When we both take off our pants and he eyes my matching burgundy underwear hungrily. When he delicately runs his hands along my lower stomach, teases the band of my underwear, traces a finger up my upper thigh. My breath comes shorter and shorter. When he disappears for a moment for protection, which, like any ridiculous boy, he had stashed in his wallet, we both shiver as I help him roll it on.

I lean back on my elbows, feeling the soft plush of the blankets underneath. I wonder how I appear to Daniel, nearly naked and hungry and flushed and freckled and almost out of my mind with needing him. I can understand the appeal of sex now. It's clouding any coherent thought. Daniel's fingers dig into my hips for a moment, skimming the faded stretch marks there. He kisses them softly, pulling down my underwear and putting them aside. "Ready, my beautiful Annie?" His voice is achingly soft, his body just as ready for me as mine is for him.

"Yes," I say tremulously. He kisses his way up my body, his erection just teasing at my entrance. I whimper at the lack of pressure. "Please," I say, my nose skimming his cheek, whispering in his ear.

When he finally enters me, it is slow. So slow, I see spots. I clutch his back, and he kisses me searingly, and then we find our rhythm, moving faster. He adds a few fingers just where I want him, making the pleasure almost unbearable. I wrap my legs around him, increasing our closeness and the angle.

I wish this moment would last forever, this feeling of closeness and understanding between us. The night feels perfect, untouchable and sacred. We started with emotional, intellectual closeness, followed by a more physical, subconscious closeness. I cherish every place we touch, the grip of his hand on my waist, his teeth just grazing my lower lip, his chest pressed against mine, my ankles interlocked in the small of his back. The rhythm of us, the bliss of us.

Then there is a blistering amount of pleasure, a starburst in my brain, and we're both sighing at the finish. His body is heavy on top of mine for a moment, but then he pushes up a fraction. I raise a trembling hand, smoothing his eyebrows, tracing the angles of his face. He looks beautifully undone, curls flopping in his eyes, eyelashes so close to me I can count them.

He gives me one more kiss, then leaves for just a moment to clean up, and the chill makes me shiver. I wrap myself in one of the blankets, blinking in surprise when I see that the living room clock reads 12:34 AM.

I'm already dozing when Daniel comes back and re-wraps the blanket around both of us. I nestle into his shoulder, feeling more content than I have in years.

*

I wake the next morning feeling hungry and cold. Daniel and I spent all night in the living room, waking up a few times to kiss and more. We even talked for a lovely hour at 3:00 AM. At some point in the night, I pulled my T-shirt back on, and Daniel put on his sweats.

My smartwatch vibrating where it lies near my head is what ultimately propels me from our lovely cocoon, telling me it's 9:30 and if I don't get moving, I'll be late to practice. It doesn't officially start until noon, but I'm expected for pre-workout and stretching by 10:30. I could skip it, but answering questions about my relationship with Daniel is the last thing I want. We're still technically fake dating for my teammates, and real dating—but only for the first time—to Jadea. Explaining all of that so early does not seem wise.

Daniel looks so unassuming, lying in a wild mess of pastel blankets and pillows. Some sunlight is starting to bleed through my living room curtains, though I try to draw them closed so he can sleep as long as he wants. I hum through my shower and my breakfast of avocado toast. It's either the sunlight or my good mood that stirs Daniel. "Annie?" He rubs his eyes adorably. "What time is it?"

I look at the clock. "Just after ten. I'll have to leave soon."

He somehow unearths himself from the blankets and heads my way. I'm sure I look thoroughly sexy in my towel turban and hot pink bathrobe. Daniel leans in to kiss me, and I have to hastily drop my toast. "Daniel!" I start giggling as he kisses down my neck, pulling me closer. "We're going to be late."

He leans back enough to raise a brow. "Late?"

"I need to be in the cardio room in less than half an hour." I look at the clock pointedly. "You can join me if you want, run on the treadmill." Daniel has already made use of our cardio room several times. But he's hardly paying attention to me, coiling the robe's tie around his finger. "Come on," I wheedle, "what's more tempting: sex or the runner's high?"

Daniel shakes his head in disgust. "You play dirty, Ms. Larger."

I laugh and press a lingering kiss to his mouth. "I know. Now, hurry up and get ready." I manage to half-heartedly pull away so he can get dressed and brush his teeth with one of my spare toothbrushes.

He's about to walk away, just barely holding on to my hand, when he pulls me back in. I bump into his chest in surprise. "One more thing," he says, real low. "And it's really important. Annie, there is nothing better in life than waking up next to you. Will you please be my girlfriend again?"

I shouldn't be surprised he asked, but I am. I try to hide the depth of my emotion behind a delighted smile. "I think I will." My voice is lower too, as though I can't just laugh this off.

We stare at each other like happy idiots, until I finally regain my senses and push him towards the bathroom.

"We're going to be late!" I look at the clock in alarm. "I hate being late!"

Daniel releases a long-suffering sigh. "*My girlfriend* is so punctual." He emphasizes the first two words as he heads into my bathroom.

"My boyfriend is, too!" I yell back cheerfully.

That feeling in my chest is too bright to ignore. Happiness suffuses through me. Why did I deny Daniel for so long?

Chapter 17

I wonder how love-struck Daniel and I look as we enter the cardio room before practice. The whole morning has had a very strange, rosy quality to it. We squabbled good-naturedly over the music in the car—he's not a fan of my bubble-gum princess pop, and I could take or leave his addiction to R&B from the 90s. We made plans to go thrifting together and for me to show Daniel the sights in St. Louis. He even casually mentioned that I come to visit him in New York once he finishes the story here.

I have this reel playing in my head that feels eerily similar to when we went out before—going to family dinners, shopping together, supporting each other at his shows or my games, running together. There is a moment where that reel abruptly ends, just like it did when he abandoned me at the hospital. But now that I know what was really going on in his head, I wonder if that reel could keep going.

First test, running together.

The cardio room is deserted, which tells me just how late Daniel and his kisses have made me this morning.

"Only twenty minutes," I tell Daniel sternly, hopping onto my treadmill.

He does the same, punching in the intense settings he prefers. "Yes, boss!"

I roll my eyes, and we get started. We're running in front of the viewing glass, and I can see down into practice. Some of my teammates have started their individual workouts, and I spot some of Daniel's crew getting set up. Today's cardio warm-up will have to be short and sweet.

Out of the corner of my eye, I check out Daniel's gait. I don't want to be too obvious, but this is the first time I've seen him run at track-star levels. Our glow stick adorned charity run was much more casual, and I didn't see any of the effects of his accident then.

I can't say I see any of them now either. He definitely has a raised, pink scar on his thigh, which is visible due to his teeny-tiny track shorts. But otherwise, he runs at a very high level. He looks like one of those people at the gym that you're convinced are putting on a show to make you jealous. His legs move swiftly, but quietly. I can see that his speed is at level seven, while I jog at a chill level four. To be fair, this is his workout and my warm-up.

The more I look at Daniel, the more distracted I become. Despite our love-struck morning, Daniel is laser-focused on his run. He's wearing Bluetooth headphones and sweat begins to form on his brow. A bead runs down his neck. One pools in his collarbone. His calf muscles are popping, his arms pumping.

Is it getting hot in here, or is it just the literal warm-up?

I look at the time and realize we've only been running for eight minutes. I should not be this hot.

Another peek at Daniel, and I can fully admit to myself that I am *really* attracted to him. Into him. Obsessed with his face, body, spirit. Want to pull him off the treadmill, towards me, run my hands through his damp curls, lick the sweat dripping down his—

Paying little attention to my run, I step a bit off the moving belt. I stumble too close to the back of the treadmill, and my hand misses the handrail. I land hard behind the still moving treadmill, with a sore tailbone and the embarrassing realization that falling for my boyfriend caused me to literally *fall*.

Daniel immediately punches the stop button on his treadmill, taking out his headphones. "Annie!" He hops down and kneels next to me. I blush even more furiously. "What happened?" He double-checks my knees and elbows, but I'm not hurt, thank goodness. I wouldn't want to explain that injury to Coach Rembert or the training staff.

I try to look anywhere but his shining, beautiful face. The words are too silly to say aloud. Daniel wasn't having any trouble concentrating, was he? I refuse to admit how ridiculously hormonal my brain is when he's near. "I just tripped," I admit, trying not to look suspicious. "Stepped wrong."

Daniel glances at my treadmill, which is still going at the very casual pace of level four. "You stepped wrong?" He doesn't mean to sound skeptical, and it's actually sweet that he thinks I'm so athletic I wouldn't fall off a treadmill. He furrows a brow. "That doesn't sound right."

It's his worried, kind tone that does me in.

He's still kneeling next to me when I grab his dewy cheeks and pull him towards me for a soul-searching kiss. Our chests touch, his hand wraps under my knee, we seek the heat of each other, and it feels amazing. Like touching a live wire. Like standing in a perfect summer rain. Like running through the finish line ribbon.

All those love-struck feelings.

When we finally break away, we're both breathing harder than we had been on the treadmill. "Sorry," I say, breathless and still holding on to him. "You're just so distracting."

The smile that spreads across Daniel's face is my favorite one, almost blinding. He leans into me, so much so that I find my back on the ground, and he braces himself over me, a hand on the floor near my head. My heart skips a beat at the expression on his face.

"Annie." He pulls on one of the curls near my face. "I hope to distract you every day of your life. That's how it should be."

There's an almost promise brewing in his face. I can't answer in words, too afraid and too unsure, but I do pull him down for another kiss. The heat between us is sickening in a way, like we both have a fever. I forget about practice and the time, reveling in these few moments we have to ourselves. Moments that are offline and all real.

We wouldn't have done anything too exhibitionist, control freaks that we are, but who knows how long we would have made out next to the treadmills if it wasn't for one of the gym staff, Keisha, who walked in to clean equipment and put away some of the foam rollers. She was very surprised by what she found instead.

"Oh my God!" We don't hear her come in, but we do hear her surprised exclamation. "I'm so sorry—" She stumbles over her words.

Daniel and I spring apart, Daniel jumping to his feet and pulling me with him in one smooth motion. Keisha stands near the cardio room door, eyes wide. "We're fully clothed!" I blurt out, mortified. "We're leaving now! So sorry!"

I hurriedly gather my things, avoiding Keisha's newly sly expression now that she's taken full stock of the situation. Daniel follows behind me quietly, eyes on the ground.

As we head down the stairs, the fever between us fully diminished, I venture, "I think this kind of distraction is going to get me fired."

The embarrassment between us evaporates, and Daniel laughs. "Maybe no more running together," he says thoughtfully. "Too much sexual tension."

I shake my head woefully. "That's what all the boys say."

I reach up to smooth my hair, hoping I don't look too disheveled, and notice my left braid has completely fallen apart. I stop in the middle of the stairwell, struggling to fix it without a mirror. Daniel's gentle hand stops me. "Here. Let me." He steps behind me, quickly assessing the situation. "I'll just redo it."

"Redo it?" I ask curiously, trying to peer at him over my shoulder. Without answering, he deftly begins braiding my hair, hands sure and soft. I savor the comfortable quiet between us as he works. He ties off the end with the proffered hair tie once he finishes.

"There." He says, walking back around to face me. He smiles in satisfaction. "Now they match."

I run my hands over the left braid, and he's right, it feels just like it should. "Where did you learn to braid?"

He rubs a sheepish hand over the back of his neck. "In sixth grade, I asked my mom for money to buy my girlfriend a Valentine's Day gift, but she insisted that handmade was better. She taught me how to make a braided friendship bracelet." A little pink colors Daniel's cheeks. My heart swells. "While my girlfriend was less than impressed, I became a little obsessive about bracelet making. There are still a few dozen of them at my parents' house in New York." His expression brightens a bit. "But now I can braid your hair whenever you need it."

I take a few steps backward, heading down the stairs. I slowly shake my head at him. "I've got to run, Daniel."

He furrows his brow. "Run? Why?"

I turn down the stairs, tossing over my shoulder, "Because if you keep talking like that, I'm going to do something very exhibitionist to you in this stairwell!"

Daniel's laughter follows me long after I enter the locker room. It takes all the power within me not to stop and lean against the door, grinning and clutching my chest like a swooning idiot.

Either way, I can't stop smiling.

*

"Arrows!" Coach is leveling us with her most severe glare. "We have two more games to prove our worth. Currently, Indiana is tied with us for first, though we have the tiebreaker for beating them twice already this season. If they win their last two games, and we don't, they'll get the one seed and the bye. It would be helpful if they lost at least one, but we can't control their fate." Jadea and Lynn are nodding seriously as though Coach is giving a sermon. I hide a smile. "We need to control our own. Win our last two games so we can skip the first round of the playoffs. Do you understand me?"

Her eyes sweep across our huddle to make sure we understand. It might not sound like a big deal to be the number one seed in the playoffs, as opposed to the two seed, but with the current WNBA system, it is. The team with the number one seed in the Eastern Conference and the number one seed in the Western Conference receive a bye from the first round of the playoffs. The Western Conference is already locked down by the Las Vegas Aces. Now it's just up to us and the Fever for the East. The number one seeds skip the first round of the playoffs, which is a one-and-done series. You only get one game to prove you should move on, not a best-of-three or best-of-five scenario. Definitely something you want to skip if you can.

"Yes, coach!" we parrot back obediently. We all huddle around her and our other assistant coaches, sweaty and motivated. I don't know if it's the scandal surrounding Jack or just a fluke, but we should not be playing so poorly at the end of our regular season. If anything, this is when we should be playing our *best* basketball. If we lose these next two games and the Fever win just one of theirs, they get our seed. They get to sit and rest while we play for our lives in the first round. We have to win the game tomorrow night and another game Sunday afternoon. Playoffs start the following Wednesday.

Jadea bumps my shoulder, and I startle guiltily. "Do you want to stay and watch film? I want to go over some of our fast break plays before tomorrow. We play Seattle, and they're not as quick as we are. I'm hoping we can take advantage..." Jadea trails off of her shop talk, noticing my strange expression.

It's time to come clean to Jadea about Daniel and me. I've been lying to her so long that I can't keep everything straight. She's the main reason that we even reunited, that we talked through our feelings, that we got back together. I owe her.

In fact, this whole film session would be a great opportunity to talk it out in private. And hopefully she'll shout and ask aggressive questions and be disappointed and then hug me and then forgive me. That's the order I'm hoping for.

"That sounds great." I try to give her a genuine smile, but I think it's coming off a little intense. Her brow furrows, just like it did when Daniel and I did so well in our who knows who best video. "I just need to talk to Daniel for a minute. He had a question about the piece."

Not exactly a lie—Daniel and I have been poring over his narration for the upcoming piece. He even showed it to some of the team during our lunch today. He and Lynn talked about it for almost half an hour. In the end, she gave her pleased approval. I hurry away before Jadea can ask too many questions, sidling up to Daniel who is not-so-obviously waiting for me by the locker room tunnel. "Daniel!" I lower my voice a bit once I get close. "Can I get a raincheck?" I try to ignore how handsome he looks in his glasses and how much I just want to drag him into the laundry room so we can make out again. "I know you wanted to have dinner tonight, but I really need to talk to Jadea."

He raises a quizzical eyebrow. "Everything okay?"

I take a deep breath, trying to release all of my anxiety in the exhale. It works—kind of. "I'm going to come clean. Tell her we dated at Stanford. Explain that I've been lying to her. All of it."

Daniel lets out a little sigh, too. "Oh, good. I didn't want to push, but I feel like now is the time. If you let it go much longer, she might never forgive you."

I rub my brow. "Not exactly what I want to hear right now, Daniel."

He grabs my hand, squeezing in apology. "Sorry. It's not going to be easy, but Jadea is worth it. And you're worth it to her. I know you'll work it out."

I look up at him hopefully. "Really?"

He rubs a soothing thumb along the back of my hand, and it really shouldn't make my whole body tingle with affection, but it does. "Well, consider if the roles were reversed. If she kept a secret from you, would you forgive her?"

I pause, thinking it over. Best friends aren't supposed to keep secrets. That seems like one of the tenets we came up with when we met in elementary school. However, adult emotions and relationships are messy. Confusing. There have been exes of Jadea's that I didn't like or that she defended when she shouldn't have. It's a part of life. Hopefully, you grow together as best friends, as sisters, as teammates in life. I feel a relief-fueled smile cross my face. "You're right. I'd be hurt and confused, maybe even a little angry, but I'd forgive her. Sometimes you make decisions without fully thinking it through." That's how this secret began, a strange instinct I had senior year when Jadea FaceTimed and talked about her love life but never asked about mine. She didn't have any expectations that I could be with someone, so I just didn't correct her. It snowballed from there.

Daniel's face softens when he sees me smile. "I'll meet you at your place later tonight, if that's okay? You can tell me how it all went."

"Sure." My voice is pitifully love-struck, and we just stand there looking at each other for a shamefully long time. His curls. His half-dimple. Those starry, ink pool eyes. The mole on his chin. I love everything about him. Thank goodness our team thinks we're dating already, or we'd be giving ourselves away.

The moment is torn in two with Jadea's furious, "Holy shit!" Daniel lets go of my hand, and I wheel around, seeing her stand near our bench, holding her phone in one hand. At her exclamation, a few of the lingering coaches and players head her way—Coach Rembert, Coach Zak, Lynn, Olabisi, and Taherah.

As soon as I start walking towards them, I know it's about me. Every recently exclaimed expletive while watching a video has been about me. My whole body feels cold as I approach. Everyone is listening and watching a video, horror-struck. No one looks my way at first. I catch Jack's name and my own coming from the phone's tinny speaker. "Jadea." My voice is faraway, quiet. "Give me the phone."

Silence reigns, everyone staring at me with a myriad of emotions on their face. Sadness. Pity. Anger. Disappointment. I clutch Jadea's bright red iPhone in my hand, tilting the screen towards me. Daniel lingers over my left shoulder so he can watch too. I'm not prepared for what I see.

It's Trenton, my half-brother and owner of our team.

I turn the volume up all the way and restart the video. He's sitting in an armchair, across from ESPN reporter Jonathan Watson. He writes a sports column for *The Washington Post* and is the head anchor for ESPN's morning basketball talk show, *The Jump*. A shockingly high caliber sports journalist. The churning in my gut gets worse.

It's Jonathan who gets it started. "Trenton, you called this interview because you claim to have new information about your father's mismanagement case. The WNBA is currently in the middle of conducting an investigation. Do you believe this will help them in their decision-making?"

Trenton nods seriously, adjusting his monstrous silver watch. "Jonathan, I wasn't sure what to do with this information when I found it. My father has been distraught ever since the news broke, so I've been trying to help him step back and keep it all running. While going through his home computer, trying to make sense of some business accounts, I found several emails saved to his computer. They were all from Annie Larger Smith."

"Larger," I whisper, my fingers shaking. "Just Larger." Trenton's lying. I've never sent emails to Jack.

"From Annie Larger?" Jonathan asks, curious. "And these are in regard to the mismanagement allegations?"

Again, Trenton nods. He looks like a silver-spoon Ken doll, his tie perfectly pressed, his face perfectly symmetrical. "I've sent the emails to the WNBA investigative team to verify. These emails prove that Annie Larger was a part of my father's mismanagement. He didn't draft her randomly; she *begged* him to draft her to the Arrows after she found out who he was."

I physically stumble back a step or two, running into Daniel and stepping on his toes. He grabs my shoulders, holding me steady. Begging to be drafted? Demanding it after finding out my father's power? It's too horrifying to consider. It's cheating, at the worst level.

Jonathan doesn't even bother hiding his shock. "Annie Larger, an All-Star level player, begged her father to draft her? Demanded it?" He manages to shake off his surprise. "Annie's current statement is that she did not know about her father's identity until Misty presented her with the allegations."

Trenton gives a very small, very brief smile. It looks like victory to me. "These emails prove all of that to be false. Her mom told her about her father's identity upon her graduation from college. Annie had pretty low draft stock. She was on the bubble of not being drafted at all. It would make sense she'd ask for help from the powerful father she'd just found out about."

I can't believe Trenton would do this to me. We're blood. I'm his half-sister.

Jonathan mulls this over. "These are extremely serious allegations. If this is true, it would likely result in Annie's suspension from the WNBA, maybe worse. You've essentially just ruined her career, and I have to point this out; you're her brother. Why did you come forward?"

It's a great question, and Trenton's ready for it. "Jonathan, I didn't want to. I love my father, and I was just getting to know Annie. But this is unacceptable. I want the WNBA to thrive, and they're creating a toxic environment. We need both of them gone." He doesn't say the words with malice or anger. Rather, he sounds like an avenging angel. Like he truly believes I'm a cancer to my team. "Hopefully, in the next week or two, the WNBA will have the information they need to make a decision on their investigation. I'm not trying to ruin Annie's life, but she did something wrong. We can't have her on the Arrows, and I'm sure the league will agree."

I can't quite tell what Jonathan is thinking when he asks, "And you'll take over for your father if he is suspended or forced out of ownership?"

Trenton smiles that little smile again. "I am hopeful that by coming forward early and being accountable for my family's mistake, I won't be forced to turn over my ownership. Instead, we can start a new legacy."

I almost throw up as Jonathan and Trenton shake hands. When I minimize the video, I see it's the number one sports topic on Twitter. None of the comments are kind.

One brands itself into my brain, the words searing hot.

@NBALover: This is one of the worst scandals in modern sports history. Consider Annie Larger blacklisted from the league. She's done.

It begins to register that everyone is talking. Shouting actually. Jadea's voice is loudest, as usual, "It's a fucking lie! We all know Trenton is a fucking snake!"

Olabisi sounds just as furious, stepping closer to Jadea. She shoves her perfectly manicured finger in her face. "He says he has proof, Jadea. What the hell am I supposed to believe? These are all just *coincidences*?" I'm stepping away from the group numbly, Jadea's phone still clutched in my hand. Daniel is hovering near me, unsure if he should break up the chaos or glue himself to my side.

Coach Rembert pushes Jadea and Olabisi apart. "This solves nothing. Let's just hear what Annie has to say."

Olabisi scoffs. "Annie? Annie never has shit to say."

It's a cruel truth and one that feels like it punches clean through me. I must make a noise of pain because Olabisi and the team turn to look at me, hunched and small on the outskirts. I see a flicker of something on Olabisi's face, remorse maybe, or pity, but then it hardens.

Jadea keeps her eyes on me. "Tell them, Annie, tell them the truth! You didn't even know about Jack until Misty told you."

I feel suddenly out of breath, and I can't feel my fingertips, and everyone is looking at me. I know it's not true, I know it's a lie, but I can't open my mouth. I can't explain when Olabisi is looking at me so evenly, sure I have nothing to say, when Taherah looks afraid for me, when Jadea has every expectation that I'm just like her.

Finally, I choke out, "I'm sorry. So sorry. He's wrong, but I'm sorry." And before anyone can question me or I start crying embarrassingly, I turn on my heel and run.

Deja vu.

I can hear Daniel for a second, about to follow, but I don't look back. I throw out a hand, signaling him to stop. "Leave me alone. Please. I just need to process on my own."

And he does.

I can hear everyone still arguing as I stumble to the locker room. I grab everything that's mine in blind terror— my backpack, my ball, my jersey, my many basketball shoes, my name plate that says: Annie Larger 33; my name and number, next to our scarlet arrow symbol.

I take a step into the hallway, tears dripping down my face, and the first thing I think about is leaving. It's the easiest thing to do. It's what Largers do when they have a problem to face. It's what everyone expects.

So, I'm surprised when I start walking, all my gear awkwardly bundled in my arms, to the elevator. I pass one or two surprised security guards and other staff. I don't look at them; I don't wipe my face. I march up into the glass offices above, right up to the secretary who works the front desk. Jenna Green. "Is he here?" I demand.

I shouldn't take it out on Jenna, but she actually blinks like she has no idea who I'm talking about. "Who?"

My words are clipped. "Trenton. Is he here?"

Understanding floods her face, then embarrassment. Does she know that Trenton's words are a sham, or is she embarrassed to be seen with a cheater and a fake? "He just left," she says finally. "You might catch him in the garage, ground level. He's probably waiting by the valet stand."

I don't even thank her, I just start running, my nameplate and Jadea's phone clenched in my sweaty palms. The run seems endless, hallways and stairwells, but finally I'm at the valet stand. We sometimes use valet on game days, but certainly not for practice. Apparently, Trenton uses it all the time.

The valet is nowhere to be seen, but Trenton is leaning casually against the stand. This floor of the garage is private, with only a few cars parked down here. It won't be long before Trenton's car is swinging around the corner.

"Trenton." I don't even recognize my voice. It's gutted. Guttural. "How could you do that to me?"

He turns around slowly, tapping something out on his phone before finally facing me. "Do what, Annie? Tell the truth?"

There's a twisting to everything he says, like he's winking at me with each word. I hug my basketball gear to my chest, realizing I look ridiculous. I try to soldier on. "It's not the truth, Trenton. It's a lie that will *ruin my life.*"

Trenton takes a thoughtful step towards me, tapping his chin idly with his iPhone. "I thought you had ruined *my life*, Annie. When it came out, what my father did, the affair, the love child, I figured our family had finally hit rock bottom." A little guilt swirls at that, but I hold on to my anger. To the truth. "But I was wrong. Apparently, my father had been reconsidering his decision to hand the reins over to me. Even though I won a championship. Even though everyone loved the decision." He shakes his head in disgust. "He wanted back in. He wanted me to *wait my turn.* As if I hadn't already been waiting for decades to have some semblance of a say." I'm surprised by the bitterness, the anger creasing his smooth face. It must show on my face because he inhales and recalibrates. "So, your little scandal provided me the perfect opportunity to push him out. For good." He eyes me carefully, probably noticing my gear bundled haphazardly in my arms. "I also couldn't have you splitting up my inheritance, or God forbid, trying to be a part of the family business."

I open my mouth to respond, saying I want no part of his ridiculous family, but he shushes me. He's not at all worried about any of my defenses or so-called truths. "Annie, let me tell you how this will go. You'll bow your head and take the punishment. You'll leave this league and go play in some backwater Lithuanian league where you can lick your wounds." Every word is a barb in my chest. "My team of extremely high-power lawyers will provide validation for the emails you sent. The WNBA's investigation will prove that you and my father colluded so that you could be drafted early and other mismanagement to get you more playing time and attention. You will be suspended for at least a year, maybe more. Even if you were allowed to come back, no team would take you. Players will hate you for cheating and taking the spot of someone who deserved it. They'll imagine all the misdeeds you and my father planned together." He finally allows that small smile to spread fully. "And you will bow your head and. *Take. It.*

"If you try to say anything about the Smith family, even to prove your innocence, you will violate the NDA I had you sign. If you violate the NDA, my high-powered lawyers will sue you within an inch of your life. No matter how you look at it, Annie, you will be out of this league and thus my life, forever." This was his plan all along. From that fraught moment in his office, where I thought he might want to help me. Instead, this was just a power play, and I was an unwilling pawn about to be sacrificed.

Trenton is everything I'm not. Rich. Powerful. Backed by a team of lawyers and well-respected billionaire friends. Charismatic. Social. Power hungry. Dissatisfied. Cutthroat.

What am I?

Quiet. Exhausted. Hard-working. Avoiding my problems. Keeping secrets from my best friend. Running away from my boyfriend. Fighting with my mom. Betraying my team. Tricking the world with PR schemes.

How to fight against who we are?

The tears haven't stopped flowing. The valet turns the garage's corner, pulling an Archer and Arrows colored Tesla up next to us. "Your car is ready for you, sir." The young valet gets out of the driver side door, trying to hide his curiosity at our exchange.

Trenton slips him a twenty and turns to look at me one last time. "Are we done here, Annie?" He smiles sympathetically. As though he's sorry he bested me, but it's too late. His perfect plan is already in motion. "This isn't personal, it's business. At one point, I thought we could use you for sympathy and paint Dad as the villain. But, in the end, if you stay here, so does the scandal. My dad will keep trying to contact you. I needed to separate myself from you both, permanently. I'm sorry."

Sorry for what? Lying to the media? Manipulating me? Caring about business more than his family?

The last breath of my anger suffuses through me. "You want to take it all? My teammates? My friends? My game?" I'm choking on my tears. "Fine. Take it all."

And as he walks calmly away, taking the keys from the valet, I hurl all my things at him and his car. My basketball bounces off his tire and flings back at the valet, who sidesteps it. My jerseys only flutter in the air, catching wind and floating down like deflated parachutes. But it's my nameplate, hard plastic, that makes a connection. It glances off Trenton's shoulder and he startles a bit, looking at me with the first show of anger.

"Stay out of it, Annie. Or you'll be hearing from my lawyers." Gritting his teeth, Trenton gets in the car and speeds away.

I immediately slide to the ground in front of the valet stand, spent. I press my hands into my face, shakily swiping away my tears.

It's the young valet who finally, nervously, asks if he should go upstairs and get my car for me. I look up into his kind face—he can't be much older than eighteen or twenty—and nod.

I can't stay here another minute.

Chapter 18

Daniel finds me in my apartment. I've just finished zipping my suitcase when he uses the spare key to let himself in. He practically sags in relief when he sees me. "Annie!"

He reaches for me, and that scared, stupid part of me just curls into his chest. Fortunately, my tears dried sometime during the drive home. Now, Daniel only has a woman who is half there, numb and cold. He leans back to look at my face, smoothing my hair soothingly. I close my eyes for a moment, feeling a flicker of warmth.

Then, he steps back.

He begins to pace. First to the kitchen table, then back to where I stand, then back again. "Okay, so I've been thinking about what we should do. Obviously, Trenton's confidence tells us he had someone in the tech world doctor those emails. He seemed to think they'd pass the investigative team's inspection. So, we need to get someone even better to debunk them. I have some contacts at *The New York Times* that we can reach out to—"

"Daniel," I say quietly. Tiredly.

"And then we'll need to call Jermaine and craft a statement. You'll want to deny all allegations as soon as possible. Jermaine's been calling, but he said you've been declining every time. I know the NDA doesn't help matters, but surely we can get it thrown out later if we prove Trenton was just using it to back you into a corner."

"Daniel." I say it a little louder this time.

"And then, I think we should get you on *The Jump*. Talk to Jonathan Watson. Tell the full truth. Make a statement that scares Trenton, that shakes him up. Force the investigation to look into him, too."

"Daniel." His endless plans spin through my brain. "I'm leaving."

He finally stops pacing, looks at me. "Leaving? Where? Did you already talk to a reporter?"

Do these questions show he has faith in me? That he believes I can salvage the situation?

Or do they show how little he knows me? That he thinks I could go on national TV and explain my story coherently and "scare Trenton, shake him up"?

"I can't be here," I explain. "The girls only have two more games until the playoffs. I'll only be a distraction. You saw how they were all fighting back there."

Their faces flash in my mind. Jadea's unwavering, fierce support. Olabisi's scathing disbelief. Taherah's fear that it could all be true. Coach Rembert's stress-lined face trying not to take sides.

I should never have made the league. The team. I *should* be playing some small-time basketball in Lithuania. I'd be lucky to do so. While I didn't ask my father for help, he *did* help me. That part is true enough.

Daniel shakes his head vehemently. "You'll just look frightened if you leave. You need to stand up to him—"

I can't stand his calm, controlling tone anymore. "I *am* frightened, Daniel! We're similar in so many ways, but in this, we are different. I can't talk to people. I can't say what

I truly mean. I can't make myself appear confident, charming, vengeful, anything like that. If I go on TV, I'll just cry in front of some strangers in nice suits!" My knuckles are white around my suitcase handle. "I know you need control, and so you're suggesting what you would do. But I'm not like that." Anger grows hot in my chest, and I loose it on the only available target. "And neither are you, when it comes down to it! You haven't aired your piece about mental health in sports because you're afraid. How is what I'm doing any different?"

Daniel winces at the assessment but doggedly continues with his plan. "I get what you're saying, and that's why I've been working with Jadea. We decided that maybe if we wrote a speech beforehand, give you some time to practice it—"

I can't believe what I'm hearing. I narrow my eyes. "You and Jadea?"

He has the good grace to look nervous. "Yes, we talked the rest of practice and came up with a plan."

I want to scream *without me*, but I was the one who left, so I try to focus. "Didn't Jadea find it strange that my boyfriend of 24 hours wanted to stay and help me through this shitstorm?"

He winces a little. "Maybe she just thought I was a really good guy."

"*Daniel*," I grit out.

"I told her," he says, the words coming out in a rush. I take a step back, the betrayal stinging. "That we dated at Stanford. That we just got back together. She understood. She says we should focus on Trenton for now—"

I laugh, loud and bitter. "It seems like I'm not even needed for this plan. You two will decide what I need and write me a script. It's all been fake, right, Daniel? I'm just the bad actress trying to fumble through her lines."

I march past him, yanking my suitcase handle so that it unfurls. "I'm leaving." My voice cracks. "I'll be at a motel. Hopefully, I can step aside, and the team won't be hurt in the crossfire. You and Jadea can draw the game plan up, but I'll be riding the bench."

I open my apartment door, equal parts hot and cold. Daniel's voice is quiet behind me. "Please don't, Annie. It won't help, I promise."

I turn halfway to look at him. "It helped you, didn't it?" Cruel words. A low blow, but I don't care. He should understand the loss of a dream. The trapped feeling of knowing your future isn't what you thought it would be.

He should understand that I just need a break.

Daniel doesn't look away. His eyes sear into me. "If there were any chance, any possibility that I could compete, I would have done it. I would have begged on my knees. I would have sacrificed anything. Running is *everything* to me." I'm almost drawn in by his words, leaning ever so slightly toward him. "But my body was broken. It was the one obstacle I couldn't clear, and so I didn't just leave. I went towards help. Therapy. My family. I rebuilt my life."

His voice grows harder. "I shouldn't have left things that way between us—that was my *one* mistake. But don't think for one second that what you're doing is anything like what I did. You're not leaving, you're *hiding*."

The words ring in the space between us. Space that was nonexistent just last night, as we lay intertwined and laughing giddily.

I want so badly to run to Daniel, to beg him to fix my life, but I'm not like him. He and Jadea think they know me, but they don't.

So, I slam the door between us.

Chapter 19

The motel I wallow in is a very sad Motel 6 about twenty miles outside of St. Louis. I got into my car and drove blindly, hopping on the nearest highway. I didn't really have a plan, despite my bitter words to Daniel. I *did* want to hide. Somewhere away from the noise. Away from people telling me what to do and the moral dilemmas and arguing teammates.

The only call I answered was from my mom. We sat in silence, both sniffling the whole time. Finally, I said, "I just need a break. It will only be for a few days, I promise."

A lie, possibly. I had no plan of leaving or staying. Just being.

My mom was quiet for a moment. "What about your game against Seattle? Or the one Sunday against LA?" They're both home games. I could drive back and play for our number one spot. I could prove my worth on the court.

Except, is that what I would be doing? Or would it just be hissing, booing, Olabisi pushing me on the bench, Coach Rembert wondering if she knows who I truly am?

No, I won't be playing. Frauds and cheaters shouldn't be allowed to play.

I don't answer my mom, and she finally says, "Be safe, Annie. And call if you need me." I know she thinks I'll come to my senses. I haven't missed a game since my freshman year of college when I had mono. Even then, I tried to practice that week, but I fainted halfway through the warm-ups. It's unthinkable that I'd miss a game willingly. Contractually, I have no idea what it means. I'm under investigation, so does it even matter when I'll likely be suspended soon anyway? It will just be more money down the drain, maybe a fine for missing the game. I could ask Jermaine, but I've been avoiding his calls too.

The Motel 6 is exactly what you'd expect. Tiny, weird, full of truckers and other people with furtive glances. There are a dozen rooms and not even half of them are full. I mumble to the front desk lady, a strangely perky woman named Wendy, that I'll pay on a "day-by-day" basis. The room I'm in is bare. The bed is old, but clean enough. There's an end table with chipped corners and a tiny little TV sitting on a dresser. The shower does have some hair in the drain but is otherwise doable. Nobody will find me here, not even the genius duo of Jadea and Daniel.

The first thing I do is take off my shoes. Throw my bag in a corner. Turn off the lights.

I toss and turn fitfully. And even when I do sleep, I don't feel rested. Like my body knows my brain is still awake.

Hating me. Hating Daniel and Jadea for trying to run my life. Hating Trenton. Hating Jack.

I've never been so angry.

I stew in the dark.

*

My instant oatmeal rotates in the microwave, something they had in the vending machine a few doors down from my room. I watch it disinterestedly, like I've done everything today. Our game against Seattle starts in ten minutes.

And I'm not there.

My phone has been off all day, but I know what I would see if it were on. Missed calls from Jadea, Coach Rembert, Jermaine. Maybe my mom. That would be the group begging me not to quit. To not give up. Jadea might even give me some bullshit speech about how badass I am if I just truly believe in myself.

And then, on the flip side, there would be hundreds of tweets mentioning what a monster I am. Analyzing the scandal. Monitoring the investigation. Currently, I can still play. It isn't until the investigation is complete that the WNBA would hand out the punishment. But to play now, with Trenton watching and my teammates hating me seems impossible. People believe I'm a cheater. How to convince them that I'm not? It appears that Jack did manipulate things in my favor, and the only thing I had going for me was that I never knew. Now it looks like I not only knew about it, I *asked* for it.

My oatmeal tastes terrible, like ash in my mouth. It's difficult to tell if that's because of its low quality or because of me. As the clock ticks closer and closer to tip-off, I itch to turn on the game. I've never seen us play on TV before. I think we're on a local channel, like The U or something, so who knows if I'd even be able to find it.

Instead, I watch the clock change numbers. I play solitaire with the deck of cards Wendy provided for me. I try to read the new Talia Hibbert book I bought on my Kindle. Nothing is working; nothing is distracting me. My skin is crawling, itching, buzzing.

I dig through my suitcase until I find a pair of leggings, a sports bra, my running shoes. And the neon pink tank top

I wore when I went on the date with Daniel. There's a flash in my brain, a memory of me encouraging Daniel to do what he needed, to take his time before he ran again. Why couldn't he see that I just needed time? A break?

Why did I push him back so hard? Was I looking for any excuse not to trust him, to accuse him of hurting me like he did before?

I shove the neon tank top back down to the bottom of the suitcase and grab a more nondescript one. The run helps that itchy feeling go away, at least partially. It's almost soothing to feel the repetitive nature of my footsteps, the pounding beat of SZA's latest song in my ears. I run around the motel eight times. Nine times. Twelve times. I walk a few laps in between, but it feels too slow, like walking through syrup. I run again. It's my fifteenth lap before I finally have the courage to go back into the room.

A sadder, lower song has come on in my earbuds. "Let Us Die" by King Princess. My hand finds the remote. I flip through the channels, looking for a familiar court decked in red and white. Jadea dunking and a solid lead on the scoreboard.

Instead, just as King Princess sings, *"If the only way to love you is to let us die,"* I see the game is almost over. I ran longer than I thought. The burning in my lungs and calves makes sense now.

The clock ticks down from twenty, and Taherah is just standing at the top of the key, dribbling it out until the end.

It's because we lost. We lost by fifteen points.

The broadcast ends with an image of Jadea, hunched on the bench with a towel over her head. I slip off the edge of the bed, landing in a similar position. I press my palms into my eyes, trying to find clarity.

How do you know when you're doing the right thing? Who am I really protecting, the team or myself?

*

The Indiana Fever and the St. Louis Arrows both have their final game on Sunday.

The Fever won theirs. We lost ours by six points.

We don't get the number one seed.

I'm still in the motel, feeling disconnected from everything. It's isolating at the motel. Most people are in and out, and no one bothers you. I wave to Wendy once a day, and that's it. My phone is long neglected. My friends and family held at arm's length. The only connection I have to the outside world is when I watch our games.

I convinced myself that the Seattle game was a fluke. Seattle is always good, and even if I was there, in my normal capacity, we still could have lost. Today, we played the Connecticut Sun, whose season has been incredibly up and down. We've already beaten them twice this year. It should have been an easy win. Instead, we had sixteen turnovers and shot 33 percent from the field. It was ugly, and it was my fault.

If I was there, I could have helped.

If I truly loved the sport, I would be better at ignoring the noise. I would take it one step at a time. I wouldn't be so hurt by Trenton's betrayal. I wouldn't curse Jack every breath I take. I would just play.

But I'm not strong enough.

After the buzzer sounds for the end of the game, I immediately turn the TV off. I cannot bear to see Jadea hurting. Olabisi furious. Everyone beat down. We lost our number one seed. We have to play in the one-and-done first round of the playoffs. The WNBA has sixteen teams, two conferences of eight. The top five teams make it in each

242

conference. Last I checked, the NY Liberty were the five seed in the east. It's a tougher match-up than you'd expect out of a five seed. The Liberty have all the talent in the world, but their superstar, Breanna Stewart, has been riddled with injuries all season. She's still not back in playing shape. On the other hand, Sabrina Ionescu was league MVP two years ago, before Jadea, and she's one of the best athletes I've ever seen. Jonquel Jones has great length and is great around the basket. They would likely have a higher seed without the injuries.

What's the right call?

I *want* to stay here. To curl up and go to bed early. To woodenly play solitaire. To hide in books and the bad soap operas that are on early in the afternoon.

I also want to go back. To apologize to Daniel and tell him I miss him. To clear the air with Jadea who sided with me even when she knew I had lied to her about Daniel. To play with my girls and stomp on the New York Liberty, win our first-round game and keep our campaign for a championship going.

If only there was an easy answer. Do I hurt them if I play? Will the crowd become distracting if I'm there? Will hurt feelings boil over? Is there any way to outsmart Trenton? Do I hurt them if I stay here?

I don't know the right answer, but something propels me to my feet. I grab my keys, phone, and wallet, more out of habit than anything. I'm wearing a stained Stanford sweatshirt that used to be Jadea's, rainbow tie-dye running shorts, and my sneakers. I head automatically to my car and just start driving.

I head further away from St. Louis and the motel, taking one of the first exits I see. I should be reading the street signs, but I figure if I get too desperate, I can always turn on my phone just for the GPS. I soon realize I'm entering suburbia. It must be one of the suburbs about an hour or so outside of St. Louis. The houses are nice, mid-sized and cookie cutter. I soon pass by a high school: Central High School with the damning colors of scarlet and white. They follow me everywhere.

Outside of the school is a football field, baseball field, tennis courts, and, to my surprise, outdoor basketball courts. It's a week or two before school officially starts and very early for any high school basketball team to be worrying about their seasons. But I'm surprised to see one girl standing on one of the courts, shooting. She looks young, maybe a freshman or sophomore.

I pull over into the school's nearly empty parking lot. I watch her raptly. She reminds me of Jadea a little bit, flying as she hurtles towards the basket, braids whipping around her in a halo. She runs a few shooting drills but gets stuck on her three-point shot.

Before I know what I'm doing, I'm out of the car. I walk across the grass until I'm standing on the edge of the blacktop. "I had trouble with that shot, too," I say evenly, surprising the girl enough that she almost drops the ball. She wheels around to face me, knees slightly bent as though on defense. "I still do, to be honest."

I'm so used to the anonymity of being a female athlete that I'm surprised when she says, "Annie Larger?" She sounds dubious, as though it would be impossible for me to be here.

I suppose it is almost impossible; I should have been playing in the loss today. "How many threes do you take a day?" I ask conversationally. I join her on the court, staring up at the slightly tattered hoop.

The girl shrugs. "Not that many. I hate missing."

Not only does she play like Jadea, she sounds like her, too. I have to smile then. "Everyone hates missing, at least a little bit. But my three didn't even become passable until I made at least a hundred of them a day."

The girl rolls her eyes like I'm a well-meaning, bothersome coach. "I know, I know." She dribbles the ball a bit, narrowing her eyes at me. "Aren't you going out with Daniel Chan?"

I have to bark a laugh at the non-basketball related question. Our fake relationship really was the talk of the town. "I was, I guess. It's hard to explain."

She takes a few steps back and throws up a three-pointer. It clangs off the rim. I rebound it for her, passing it back so she can try again from the same spot. She misses again and then says, "What about the team? Why didn't you show up to your games? Is *that* hard to explain?" She sounds a little sharper, pushy. I wonder if she's a fan and heard that I cheated to get on the team. I wonder if she's disappointed I didn't play in our last two games of the season.

She rolls up the sleeves on her gray Central High School hoodie and throws up another three. This one is better, her form falling closer to in rhythm, and the ball just barely rims out of the hoop. I keep my gaze on the hoop and rebounding the ball. Finally, I say to her, "You saw that, huh?"

She rolls her eyes. "If you have any interest in basketball at all, you've seen the video about you. They've talked about it every morning this week on *The Jump*, and my favorite sports podcaster is doing a whole week of content on it."

I sigh. "It's complicated."

The girl dribbles again and shoots another three. Swish. I smile a little and see one pulling at her lips, too. "It doesn't seem that complicated to me," she says, taking another pass from me. "There are only two things you need to think about."

Jadea's confidence, too.

"And what's that?" I humor her. It's nice to talk to someone impartial, even if she is just a kid.

"One: Did you cheat? Did you do what your brother said you did?"

I probably shouldn't answer a stranger so honestly, but I also don't feel the impulse to lie or duck the question. I keep my eyes on the hoop. "I didn't ask my father for anything. I didn't even know who he was." She gives me a look like, *see*. I continue, undeterred, "But I might have unknowingly benefited from bad things my father did. He manipulated the draft for me, I just didn't know he was doing it."

I expect her to nod thoughtfully, act like this really is complicated, but she just shrugs and says, "Details." Another shot, another swish.

I watch her make two more before I ask, "And what's the other thing? The second thing?"

I pass the ball back to her, and she actually pauses, turns to me fully. "Do you love the game?" Before I can answer, she says, "I'll play as long as anyone will let me, and I'm not nearly as good as you are. I probably never will be. So, are you going to quit what you love, or did you never love it in the first place?"

I grimace, wondering if it really is that simple. "How old are you? Who are you?" I try to make it a joke, but we look at each other seriously.

"Jordan Davis. I'm a junior at Central High School and the backup small forward for our girls' basketball team." She rattles it off like I'm a college scout.

I smile at her. "I think you're going places, Jordan Davis."

She smiles a little, too, then glances at her smartwatch. "Don't you want to head home?"

"What?" I ask confusedly. If she's referring to the game, it was at 2 PM and is long over.

"Aren't you going to watch your boyfriend's show?" I had been driving longer than I imagined if it was nearing 7 PM, when *Our World Through Sports* airs on HBO. She shows me her watch, "It's almost six fifteen."

I wave a hand. "I don't watch every episode." At least, I don't want to watch this one. I don't want to analyze every move Daniel makes, if he misses me, if he's still angry with me, if he's already moving on.

She looks at me like I have two heads. "Seems a little weird, considering the episode is about you."

"What?" I practically shout, fumbling a pass from her. I try to tone it down and take a deep breath. "Our piece isn't even close to being finished. It's supposed to air like a month from now." He would have had to rush the entire thing, which is not Daniel's style. I can't imagine him putting his production team through that.

She shrugs like any teenager would. "Maybe he rearranged things. He put it all over his socials. The Arrows' piece is definitely on tonight."

I'm already backing off the court, heading to my car. "Thank you, Jordan!" I shout at her, waving earnestly.

Just as I'm shutting the car door, I hear her shout back, "I better see you playing in Wednesday's playoff game, Annie Larger!"

Chapter 20

The drive back to the motel is a blur, but I'm feeling something for the first time in days. There's a little spark skittering across my skin, raising my hair, marking me with urgency. Why would Daniel push the piece? He can't be responding to the scandal; he wouldn't have the time to totally restructure the piece. What could he even say? While Daniel might believe in me, he has no proof. He doesn't even have me.

Of course my motel TV doesn't have HBO, but I manage to rig my TV with the help of an HDMI cord from Wendy and my laptop. It's a silly exercise anyway, considering the TV only has a few inches on my laptop screen. I wait with strangely bated breath for Daniel's show to begin.

When I first see him on the screen, I can't believe how serious he looks. He tends to walk the line between important social justice topics and inspirational stories. Normally, if he's serious, it only takes a moment before he's joking or smiling or throwing it gamely to Iris behind the camera. Daniel's delivery is part of what makes his show great. Today, he looks like an executioner. An assassin. A doctor about to give a grave diagnosis.

I wait for him to introduce himself, start the speech he prepared in my apartment that fateful night. I can almost feel his phantom hands on my hips, him reaching up to brush a hair out of my eyes. Daniel and Jadea were trying to make my decisions for me and that hurt. Like they didn't trust me to handle my own life, like the way I process things is so wrong. That my entire personality is *wrong*.

But, also, weren't they right? I haven't exactly been brave. I haven't exactly processed much of anything, up until now. At what point do you accept yourself as you are?

With that thought already lingering guiltily in my mind, I'm even more surprised when Daniel begins.

He's looking dead at the camera, no movie-star smile, no starry eyes. A small part of me thinks he's about to profess his love for me across the HBO airwaves, but I realize that would be a useless action. No one will take me seriously if my Emmy-award winning, extremely powerful boyfriend just sits there talking about how much he loves me.

So, why push the piece forward and air it tonight? Just because the team is getting so much press right now?

I freeze when he begins with, "I know what many of you expect out of this episode, and I intend to use those expectations to my benefit. The majority of tonight's audience thinks that I will defend my girlfriend, Annie Larger, in the wake of the WNBA's worst scandal. Potentially one of the worst sports scandals in history. The rest of you, who aren't in the loop, might be expecting an inspirational piece about the WNBA's most exciting team, the St. Louis Arrows."

He leans forward a bit. The camera is pulling him. The screen is doing the same to me; I almost lean off the edge of the bed. "I'm here to disappoint both groups." Daniel does smile a bit, but it looks razor-edged. There's some of the old

Daniel in his expression, addicted to track and competition. Addicted to winning.

"Tonight, I will be talking about the St. Louis Arrows' minority owner, Trenton Smith." A fissure of something, fear or excitement, slithers down my spine. I remember screaming and throwing my equipment at Trenton's car. I remember him standing coldly as I begged him to tell the truth. I remember losing my good reputation and standing as an athlete because of a selfish half-brother who worries I'll steal his toys.

Daniel continues, undeterred by what is basically everyone's favorite shock-talk topic of the week. Not something he'd usually address on his show, which follows more of the *60 Minutes* format than a weekly news report. "As many of you know, Annie Larger has essentially been blacklisted from the WNBA for alleged email communications between her and her father. She has not played in the Arrows' last two games of the season, with her agent releasing a statement about a withdrawal due to 'personal reasons'." Daniel levels a dry look at the camera. "I think we all know what personal reasons Annie is referring to. It could be because most of the sports world believes her to be a cheater, roster spot stealer, silver-spoon nepo baby. It could be because as soon as her teammates heard the news, they immediately broke out into a fight."

It's almost an out-of-body experience hearing Daniel talk about me this way. It's twofold, his strategy. One, he has to keep it professional, or no one will give any merit to his opinions on me. Second, he hasn't talked to me in days, and when we last spoke, we were fighting. He's truly speculating on my thoughts and motives. And he's not wrong.

Daniel continues, spreading his hands on his desk. "And I'm not here to do what everyone else is doing. Analyze Annie's life, question her quiet personality, debate whether she's helping or hurting her team by sitting out. In my mind, this has nothing to do with Annie. This has everything to do with a brilliant, egotistical man named Trenton Smith."

My breath catches in my throat. Daniel is a shark, circling and circling. "Let's set the stage, shall we? Trenton Smith is the only child of inherited wealth billionaires Jack and Tiffany Smith. After attending Dartmouth's business school, Trenton begins working with his father on creating two new teams in their hometown of St. Louis: The NBA's Archers and WNBA's Arrows. For many years, he's just a shadow to his father. Jack Smith is everything you could want in an owner; he's intensely focused and extremely enthusiastic about his teams. He even gives some credit to the Arrows. We can't say the same of his son, who had a small interview about the team when they were first founded nearly six years ago."

Daniel waves his hand to a video clip, which takes over the screen. As Trenton leaves the inaugural team celebration, a local reporter shoves a mic in his face and asks, "How important do you think a team like the Arrows is for the youth of St. Louis?"

Trenton, just as polished as he is in the present, responds with derision, "It's the St. Louis *Archers*." The clip ends with Trenton rolling his eyes.

There are a few titters from Daniel's live audience, and I almost pump my fist. "We had to dig around to find this clip, as no one has ever really cared what Trenton thinks,"—there are a few whistles at this bristling opinion from Daniel—"but his feelings here are clear. He doesn't even remember that he owns the Arrows. That women's sports even *exist*." He frowns at the camera. "Now, I can hear you saying: Daniel, this was early on, maybe he grew to become more involved with the team? In answer, I ask you to take a look at this. This picture is from last year."

The image on the screen shows Trenton sitting with his mother and father in their VIP box at an Arrows game. Jack has jumped up, grinning. Tiffany is clapping animatedly, sporting a very cute and sparkly St. Louis Arrows shirt. And where's Trenton? Sitting in a chair right beside them, reading a copy of Ayn Rand's *The Fountainhead*.

Daniel's studio audience full-on laughs at the image. I crack a smile, too. I remember my teammates sharing that picture in our group chat last year, memeifying it to holy hell. Daniel has a similar reaction. "This is a team you own, a team that made its way to the championship, and you're reading a book at the game? And it's Ayn Rand's *The Fountainhead*?" More laughter and a smirk from Daniel. "It had to be for fucking show, honestly. It looks brand new."

Daniel takes on that devil's advocate perspective again. "Maybe he's in it purely for the business. Maybe basketball isn't the part of ownership he enjoys." He gestures at a new screen that pops up next to his head. "Oh, he's in it for the business, alright." Daniel's voice grows dark.

The graphic is a tweet from Malika Andrews. *BREAKING: Jadea Jones announces she will no longer be performing her dunk show before Arrows' home games. She includes in her statement that this was a performative measure forced on her by Arrows' owner, Trenton Smith, in order to sell tickets. Interesting that Trenton didn't ask any Archers' players to put on the same show before NBA games, isn't it?*

I choke up a little then, the tears forming and glimmering in my lashes. Jadea did her part. She stood up for herself, and it's a signal that I still can, too. Even when we feel like we're letting some people down, we have to stand up for ourselves and what we deserve.

Daniel is growing more passionate in his speech, as though this story is building to some incredible climax. I wish I could be there with him, cheering him on. He can't compete anymore, but this feels like his comeback.

"Jadea Jones, the league MVP who you've seen in Gatorade advertisements and State Farm commercials, reduced to jumping on a trampoline before games because Trenton Smith tells her the team will suffer without her. Jadea Jones!" Daniel slams a hand on the table, and a few of his audience members cheer.

"So, we've established that Trenton Smith probably doesn't have a passion for women's sports. That he doesn't pay that much attention to the Arrows, unless he's demoralizing them in order to increase sales. For which, I'll challenge you out there, don't let him be right. You better show up to watch Jadea do her thing, with or without that trampoline." A tear wiggles down my cheek because isn't it any girl's dream to see her boyfriend hyping up her best friend? Defending her. Cheering her on.

I love Daniel. I fucking love him.

I think I always have.

Daniel shuffles his papers, and it reminds me of when he used to round the track, knowing he was steps from the finish, from the win. I'd be screaming, voice hoarse, praying he'd succeed. Now, I do the same, silently crying and smiling. "Now, let's get to the good stuff. The scandal itself. The emails. Jack and Annie." I swear my heart skips a beat when he says my name. "The original accusation leveled a few weeks ago was that Jack Smith had possibly manipulated the draft, demanding his biological daughter,

Annie Larger, be drafted to his team. There were also accusations that he paid reporters to write about her at Stanford. Annie Larger was famously ambushed after a game with that news, as well as her father's identity."

There's a clip of me getting red-faced and choked up as Misty holds the mic towards me. I can barely get any words out before Coach Rembert and Jadea break up the interview.

There's silence after the clip, and Daniel taps his chin. "If Annie knew about her father, if she sent those emails, that means she's an *incredible* actress."

Again a few titters and Daniel holds up his hands in appeasement. "But let's put that aside for a bit. After hearing this, the WNBA had no choice but to open an investigation based on the unknown source's accusations. And even without the anonymous source, Jack's mismanagement was corroborated by a wave of ashamed colleagues, including former GMs and other board members. Annie, after talking with her mother, is not denying that Jack is her biological father. And yes, it's plausible that some misguided parental guilt caused him to demand she play for his team. Or maybe some egotistical pride that he had a daughter in the league. Either way, both Annie and Jack are being investigated."

I'm rapt, even though I already know everything he's saying. Daniel grins. "But, because of Annie's incredible play and an increased social media presence, things don't go too badly for her initially. People seemed to think that Jack would get suspended or pushed out of his ownership, whereas Annie was a bystander, a victim of Jack's."

Daniel grows serious again, huffing out a breath. "But then came Trenton's video. He claims he just wants to play fair, but I want to be fair to Annie by giving this story its due diligence. So that's what I did." He lifts a finger. "First issue: timing. Why now? And how? Trenton claims that he found these emails helping his father on a personal computer, but I guarantee that the WNBA would have claimed any devices in their investigation. And even if this device was truly so personal that the WNBA had no claim on it, why would Trenton betray his father by making the situation worse? Jack had already given his son control of day-to-day operations. He likely would be suspended or forced to sell his shares. So, who exactly did Trenton make this worse for? Annie."

There's no response from the audience. I wipe my eyes, trying to figure out where Daniel is going with this. "It looked like Jack had acted alone when he demanded Annie be drafted, so she would be allowed to play and not suffer any consequences other than being related to a scumbag. Now, with these new emails, Annie looks to be just as complicit as Jack in the scheme, maybe more so."

Daniel's not wrong. If I felt some tension between Trenton and his father, he really turned that tension and hatred towards me. "And wouldn't it make sense if Trenton had it out for his younger half-sister? After all, he just found out his father betrayed him and his mother, and that his inheritance could be lessened quite severely. It would be in his best interest if Annie could never even get close to his family. Specifically, that she had no real claim to the family business or money."

Daniel waves a hand. "Let's take a look at one of these emails Trenton claims to have uncovered, shall we?" An email appears on the screen. It reads:

Dear Jack,

My mom recently informed me that you are my biological father. I couldn't be happier. With your connections to the league, I'm a sure thing. I can even play for my hometown team, assuming you can make that happen? I know you will, since you owe me so much.

Thanks,
Annie Larger Smith

I hadn't read the emails yet, and I'm astounded at how ridiculous it is. I sound like a fifteen-year-old with a hare-brained scheme and spoiled princess tone.

Daniel raises his hands as if to say, *see*. His audience laughs again. "Shy, and sometimes surly, Annie Larger is going to write 'Hey Daddy, I'm so happy to meet you. Can you please, pretty please, put me on the Arrows?'" There's more laughter from the audience, and I have to smile. It feels good on my face. "It's ridiculous! Obviously!"

Daniel has his audience now, and he can feel it. Trenton is turning into a joke in front of my very eyes. "Let's compare it to a quote from Annie's honors dissertation about sustainable fashion trends in a capitalist society." There's laughter even before he quotes, "Ultimately, the capitalist economic system doggedly beats down every business' attempt at sustainable practices. This laissez-faire economic model ensures businesses cannot deviate from their profit-pushing schemes and billionaire building schematics."

The studio dissolves into laughter. "That email was *clearly* not written by Annie Larger!" Daniel grins, and I want to swoon. "But, again, it's hard to prove. Trenton seems extremely confident that the WNBA investigative team will never discover that the emails are fake. I suspect he might feel that way because the outside investigator they hired a few weeks ago is someone he went to Dartmouth with." A few hisses emit from the audience, but Daniel is just pulling back for the knockout punch. "The investigator also occasionally works for the same law firm that Trenton Smith used when he created an NDA for Annie to sign saying she could never speak on their family business. The same law firm that handles Jack Smith's will and trusts."

The roar from the crowd is huge. I'm numb, eyes wide.

"These are the facts: the WNBA has hired an investigator, hopefully unknowingly, who is beholden to Trenton and Jack Smith. Trenton coerced Annie into signing an NDA a few days after the scandal broke, ensuring it would be very difficult for her to defend herself. And, before Trenton's bogus investigator plant could report back to the WNBA that the clearly fake emails are real, I sent them out to the very best in the business." There is an intake of breath from all of us. "*The New York Times* will be breaking the story as we speak. According to three different analysts, one being a cybersecurity expert, these emails are fake. We even procured Annie's laptop and verified that they couldn't have come from her account or IP address."

Fake, fake, fake. It's been verified that they're not real. I'm crying again, really blubbering now. Daniel is the best competitor I've ever seen, and Trenton is falling behind in this race. He's been beaten.

Daniel speaks over the passionate murmuring of his audience. He sounds deceptively casual, leaning back in his chair. "And if that isn't the nail in Trenton's coffin, here's Misty Haverford, local reporter for the St. Louis Arrows."

My brow furrows when I see Misty pop up on the screen. "Hello, everyone." She sounds strangely shy. "Hello, Daniel!"

He responds, polished and smooth, "Good evening, Misty. What do you have for us?"

She runs a hand through her hair. "While this goes against every journalist instinct I have, I'm going to reveal the anonymous source that told me Jack Smith was Annie's father." She takes a deep breath. "It was Trenton Smith."

The audience goes wild. My mouth falls open. This wasn't an opportunity Trenton seized? This was *planned*? He exposed his father on purpose. Trenton would have likely been there when Jack forced the board to draft me. Did something about it tip him off? Did he investigate and find out that he had a half-sister? And when the first attack didn't take me down along with Jack, he added a second act to bring us both down?

All because he wanted total control of the Archers.

Daniel grins, wild and victorious. "Well, there you have it, folks. Jack Smith is not an honorable man. Despite Trenton's lies, he was right when he said his father manipulated the draft. Too many other people corroborated his story for that to be a lie. But even worse than Jack is his son. A man who lied to the press, who set this whole story up, who was going to get his half-sister kicked out of the league she loved and leave her reputation in tatters. If there's anyone who should be punished, it's him. Leave Annie out of it."

I clutch my heart, feeling its frantic pace. Even when I yelled, ran, and hid, Daniel didn't give up on me. And not just me, my team. The truth. Stopping a corrupt man like Trenton.

Daniel looks directly at the camera. "One last thing, and it's finally about what you all wanted: Annie. Annie Larger is just like anyone else. Just like me." His voice grows quiet. "We fear our failure. We fear losing what we love. I felt that way too once, and I know how hard it is to keep going. And while our situations weren't exactly the same, I know how Annie feels."

The audience has grown quiet, but every part of me feels loud. What the hell am I doing in this motel room? How could I hide from the people who loved me? Daniel's voice is quiet too, but it rings with sincerity. "That's what I should have said, Annie. I shouldn't have talked shop, gone behind your back, planned your life for you. I should have told you I understand. That it's so hard to get back up and fight." His voice breaks a little at that last sentence, and I wipe away what feels like endless tears.

But these are at least the good kind. The hopeful kind.

"But you have to," he says, earnest and kind and the hottest thing I've ever seen. "If you were down, I've pulled you back up. But you need to get back out there and *run*."

Silence follows and then whistling and cheering and even a few moments of them chanting, "Annie! Annie! Annie!"

The show ends, and the credits roll.

Wiping away tears, I dial the only phone number I can think of.

Chapter 21

Of course, Jadea answers immediately and says she's on her way. I use one of my shoes to prop the door open so she can come right in. It feels right, considering she's not used to knocking.

I gave Jadea my room number, and when she arrives, I'm sitting on the floor, leaning against the bed. The tears have dried and crusted my cheeks. My thoughts keep cycling, imagining all the places I've gone wrong. All the mistakes I made in the name of fear.

How do Largers face a problem?

They don't.

I peek up at her from the corner of my eye as she comes in. She looks run-down. Her braids are pulled into a halfhearted top knot, and she's wearing sweatpants and slides. She doesn't say anything, just closes the door behind her, tosses my sneaker aside, and slides down the bed to sit next to me.

There're a few heartbeats of silence.

Jadea breaks it, like she always does. "How could you do that to us, Annie? We needed you." Her words are laced with hurt, accusation.

The gut reaction is to say we might have lost those games either way, but I push it down. Either way, I ran away from my best friend without a word. "I'm so sorry. I thought I was protecting the team," I find the courage to say, guilt almost choking me. "I saw how you were all fighting when the news broke. If my girls doubted me, how could we play together? How could we play normally if you all thought I was a cheater? What if we lost *because of me*?"

Jadea is quiet for a moment, looking around the room. Abruptly, she turns to face me, swiveling her whole body. "In the end, Annie, you've been thinking about this all wrong."

I flinch a little. "I know, I know. I probably don't have as much of an impact as I think—"

Jadea cuts me off. "No, listen! You will *always* have an impact. When it comes to those games, we'll never know. Maybe your impact would have been bad, like you imagined. Maybe your impact would have been great, like *I* imagined." I crack a smile at that. "The truth is: you've inherited a family. You might not claim the Smiths, and Trenton sure tried hard not to claim you, but you'll be associated with that family of billionaires forever."

I cringe away from her brutal honesty. She notices and soldiers on enthusiastically. "That's what I mean: you're thinking about this all wrong. *We've* been thinking about this all wrong. All the press about you and the WNBA, we should use it to our advantage. Your name is now associated with money, privilege, and power. Journalists, social media influencers, even old-fashioned newspapers will want to hear from you. *People* will want to hear from you." I cock my head, considering. She sees she has my attention, gesturing wildly with her hands. "You don't have to just talk about your family. You can help the league, help women athletes, help anyone you want. You've always had a voice in this league, more than some of us do, so use it!"

She deflates a little after the rush of energy, waiting for me to respond.

I let what she said really sink in before slowly nodding in agreement. "I know you're right. If I could let go of my fear and self-doubt, I could help change this league for the better. Maybe the Smith family name can even help me do that." I shudder a little at the idea, but admit, "I really want to be braver. Just like you are every day." She grabs my hand and squeezes it gently. I squeeze back.

I remember sitting in Trenton's office, genuinely excited by the idea of him setting up a fund for young women and non-binary athletes. He won't be keeping that promise to me, but could I do something similar? To help women athletes myself? Will I ever see any of the Smith money? Do I even want it?

Jadea breaks through my swirling thoughts. "We have to talk about Daniel now."

It's an unavoidable conversation, but an important one. I nod at her to keep going.

The words come tumbling out in a rush. "The games, the scandal, I might understand. Trenton was ruining your life and disrupting the team. Maybe it would have distracted everyone even more if you had played. I don't know." Impossible situation after impossible situation. "But, Daniel..." I'm shocked to hear the hurt in Jadea's voice. The hush that falls over her, the way she avoids my eyes, lets go of my hand. "How could you not tell me? Then or now? What did I do wrong?"

I take a deep breath, trying to focus. Finding the right words should be easy, but that's never been my strength. I turn to look her in the eye. "I wanted to tell you, deep down. Something incredible was happening in my life, and it killed me that I wasn't saying anything. That I was lying by omission."

It's true. All of it. Every day, I'd end our FaceTime call and wonder why I couldn't just spit it out. Why did I feel tongue-tied? Awkward?

I hold her gaze, forcing myself to continue. "Jadea, you're my best friend in the world. You're loud, funny, compassionate, a natural-born leader. I want you on the court with me, I want you shopping with me and forcing me to try on a fuzzy bucket hat, I want you going to dinner with me and our moms. When you moved to St. Louis, to my school, I felt saved. By you *and* basketball. Suddenly, we were a duo. The Jadea and Annie show. You spoke for both of us, and I liked it that way. We agreed on most things anyway; we understood each other." I take a deep breath. "But when you left Stanford, I had to adjust. I suddenly had all this space in my life that I didn't know what to do with." I'm relieved to find Jadea watching me, actually listening. "I had to be the leader of our basketball team, facing a serious letdown in expectation and enthusiasm since you graduated. I had to listen to you talk about Nike shoe deals and *TIME Magazine* spreads, all while I was feeling anxious about going to a simple college party. And so, when Daniel and I got together...I kept it to myself. I was used to you setting me up on blind dates or calling me up to the karaoke stage or slipping people my number, and I guess I was worried what you would think. What if you hated Daniel? What if the one time I tried on my own, I chose wrong? What if you wanted me to be your single best friend and nothing more?"

The words are just as hard as I expected. When you love someone, it's hard to say anything critical. But the truth was that Jadea sometimes eclipsed me.

And it was my fault for letting her.

I'm not surprised to see Jadea's expression grow furious, but what she says *does* surprise me. "Annie, you're not the only one who struggled that year apart. I may have achieved a lot of my dreams, but I was also away from my best friend in the world. I was being followed by paparazzi. People on social media were commenting racist or homophobic things on my posts. Commentators were constantly analyzing whether I was 'worth the hype. '" Furious tears waver in her eyes, but she doesn't let them fall. She hates crying. "I should have asked you about your love life, but I never did, and it's not because I wanted you to be *just* my best friend. It's because I wanted the Stanford years to stay perfect in my memory, to never change. I didn't ask what had changed in your life because I didn't want those memories of us playing together to be tarnished. And when you finally graduated, all I wanted was for you to come to St. Louis so we could start our life together. I thought I might feel that same joy and comfort if we were together again. And I did. That's all that mattered to me. I'm sorry I wasn't thinking about how hard it was for you to be left behind."

I remember those conversations about me moving to St. Louis to work with Jadea, even if I wasn't drafted. How she seemed excited about slotting me into her new life. Now, I can see she was just anxious for a familiar face. For something in her life not to be catapulted into the public arena.

I scoot closer to her, pulling her into a fierce hug. I press our cheeks together, wrap my arms around her shoulders, squeeze her tightly. "I'm sorry, too. I guess we were both afraid of change." I pull away, gesturing to the room.

"That's how I ended up in this motel room. I couldn't adapt. I couldn't figure out what I wanted, so I just froze."

"And now?" Jadea watches my face. "Did you figure it out?"

I smile for her. It feels freeing. "I know what I want to say, Jadea, *finally*. I can't be afraid to talk to the people I love. I can't be afraid to stand up for myself. Trenton is basically ruined after Daniel's show. It's time for me to tell my side and stop worrying if I say the right thing. In fact, I might say exactly the wrong thing, but that's okay. I need to try." I nudge her shoulder playfully. "But I'm not some new person. You can still do most of the talking at press conferences. I hate those things."

She laughs, wiping at her eyes. "Some things never change. But some changes are good." She regards me seriously, her brown gaze holding mine. "Daniel is one of the good ones. He's not perfect, but he's good. And that's what matters."

I'm sniffling a little now, too. "I ruined things between us, Jadea. I accused him of trying to control my life after he told you about our relationship. He had all these plans for me, and I was so overwhelmed, I snapped. But he was just trying to help."

Jadea laughs a little. "Daniel and I thought we were so smart, coming up with all these ideas to help you, but we pushed you over the edge. We didn't stop and listen to you."

I nod. "Maybe you weren't listening, but Olabisi was right. I hardly ever say shit. Even when I should. Even when it really matters."

Jadea rolls her eyes, dabbing her wet cheeks with her sweatshirt cuff. "Olabisi was such a pain this week. Her inner bitch was fully out."

I laugh a little, thinking of Jadea and Olabisi every practice, debating and arguing over the plays. "But we love her. We're a team."

Jadea gets to her feet. "We're *the* team, Annie. We have a game to win Wednesday. You coming?" She holds out a hand.

I clasp it, letting her pull me up. "Yes, I am. And I think we're going to win a championship."

I may still be teary-eyed, but Jadea lets out a delighted whoop. I scurry around the room, gathering my things, but stop when Jadea checks her watch. "Shit! I promised Daniel I'd only be ten minutes."

I freeze, only one sneaker on, the other shoe in my hand. "Daniel?"

Jadea rolls her eyes again. "You think he'd let me come here alone?" But I'm already moving, running out the door and into the parking lot. It's dark out here, but we're far enough from the city that a few stars sparkle in the velvet above.

I stop at the edge of the sidewalk, still with only one shoe on, and just stare at Daniel. The car is on, as though they were planning on kidnapping me and making a run for it if I refused to leave, but Daniel is pacing impatiently in front of it, his beautiful curls and lean figure haloed by the headlights.

"Daniel," I choke out, bawling like a baby again.

His head snaps up, and there's a flash of his half-dimple, his mole, those starry, starry eyes. His whole body is lined in light. "Annie." He sounds like he wasn't sure he'd ever see me again. As though he's ravenous at the sight of me and my one shoe. "I'm so sorry." He stays a few paces away. "About planning with Jadea behind your back. And..." he swallows nervously, "and the show, too. I wanted everyone to see Trenton as he was, and I wanted your approval to do the piece, but you weren't answering your phone, and maybe you think I was trying to control your life again, which I'd never want you to fee—"

"Daniel." My voice is soft, hoarse. "Stop, please."

He stops and looks at me, shining and brilliant and angelic. "You didn't make a mistake." I take another step towards him, off the curb. "I did, by running away. You were right; I *was* hiding. I'm so sorry for shutting you out. I realize now that I've been focusing on all the things that have gone wrong rather than accepting the gifts that life has given me. Basketball. Jadea. My mom. And you." I smile at him. "Daniel, you were the best gift I could have asked for." I try to sound like a warrior, but there's a little crack in my voice when I say his name.

I want Daniel to know that what he did for me was amazing. But now I have to come out of hiding and do amazing things, too. And I want him by my side if he's willing to be.

He's still staring at me like I'm an apparition, so I say, "Will you help me? Will you be...on my team?" The phrasing is awkward, but Daniel seems to understand.

He smiles slowly, the joy spreading to his dimple and eyes. "That's all I want, Annie. You're the only part of my dream that I'm missing."

My eyes are watering again, and I drop the shoe.

Abruptly, we're running at each other.

The collision is straight serotonin to my system. The inhalation of mint, the pleasure of my hands in his hair, the joy bubbling up as he lifts me and spins me around. "Daniel." I'm cry-laughing as he sets me down. "I missed you."

Daniel looks at me seriously, pulling my face into his hands, wiping away my tears with his thumbs. "Annie, now that you've been back in my life, I never want you to leave it again. We need to stop leaving each other."

As he's speaking, he rummages in his jacket pocket, finally unearthing a packet of tissues. He passes them to me, and all the love I have in me seems about ready to explode out of my pores.

I smile at him, hoping it's Hollywood-worthy. "Daniel?"

He looks away from the beloved tissues, back to my face. "What?"

I let all my bottled-up feelings loose, hoping they'll make me brave. "I love you. So much." The words come out triumphant.

The smile that unfurls on his face makes me blush. "Annie Larger. My love for you is larger than fucking life."

We're both laughing and delirious, and we start kissing like we're making up for lost time. We're staggering, spinning, and leaning on each other, silhouetted by the headlights. Daniel tastes like every word I've never said, like every opportunity I've been too afraid to take, every thought I've ever had that downplays my strengths. He tastes like redemption.

"Hey!" Jadea interrupts us, as usual. This time, I don't mind. "What's the plan now, lovebirds?"

We break apart, still looking at each other. Daniel's voice whispers across my cheeks. "Yeah, what's the plan, Annie?"

I step back from him so I can articulate myself clearly. "The Arrows are going to win on Wednesday. We're going to survive our one-and-done playoff game." Jadea pumps her fist in support. I smile at her, then look back at Daniel. "Then I need a slot on your show. Next Sunday."

I've surprised them both. National TV? Fear skitters down my spine. "I have a few ideas that will put this whole scandal to bed."

The words feel powerful and surer than any I've spoken in weeks.

Chapter 22

Everyone is quiet when I show up to warm-ups on Wednesday. The past two days have been a whirlwind, one that was rewarding but ultimately exhausting. I only went to a few individual workouts, missing many of my teammates in the process.

Jermaine, Daniel, and I have been working with a single-minded focus. I've been on ESPN's *The Jump*, *Good Morning America*, and various podcasts. Through each interview I have sweat and stammered. I wasn't perfect. I wasn't Jadea, witty and sparkling. I wasn't Daniel, polished and easy. But I was myself.

I talked about my fears, why I didn't play the last two games of the season. I explained my anxiety and using avoidance as a coping skill. I talked about how the team suffered under Trenton and how he twisted my words. I talked about women's sports, as best as I could. I missed things. I offended a few people. But I got through it. I showed people that I wasn't a ghost in this scandal, I was a living, breathing person. I had feelings, and maybe they were wrong, but I would put a voice to them.

I didn't mention my mom or Daniel, as it felt too personal. I didn't mention that I had already texted my therapist to restart weekly appointments. I tried not to let any anger or bitterness bleed into my words. Overall, I just tried.

So far, the response has been mostly positive. Some mixed reviews about my crocodile tears or the timing of these interviews, but I try to tune them out. This way, I'm not avoiding my problems. I'm not dodging my fears.

Daniel posts several inspiring, heartwarming, and somewhat sappy posts about me. Those bring in the best press, and it's even more infuriating because he means them. Every word. He's also started working in earnest on his mental health in sports piece, saying my bravery inspired his own.

He's a larger-than-life boyfriend.

When Wednesday arrives, I feel more nervous than all the interviews combined. It's my girls that I've been avoiding. We've always been a team, and I threw some doubt into that definition. Maybe it wasn't my fault we lost, maybe it was. We'll never know, and I have to live with that.

We're all getting ready, tying our shoes and tying back our hair. So far, everyone's been pleasant, but distant. Even Olabisi is avoiding my gaze, not one to usually shy away from a confrontation. Coach Rembert is busy talking with her assistants, so Jadea nudges me.

I take another one of those calming breaths. "Arrows!" I call them to attention, just like Jadea would. "I need to say a few things." Immediately, the room quiets. Coach Rembert turns my way, and the kindness in her gaze is not surprising. Nor is the eagerness in Taherah's. Or the knowing smile on Lynn's face. "I'm sorry," I say earnestly. I try to meet everyone's gaze head-on. "For leaving and not playing with you the last two games of the season. I don't know if I could have changed the outcome, but at least I would have been there. I thought if I played, everyone would be focused on the scandal, and we would be distracted. I should have known we would have been distracted either way. I was just too afraid to speak up for myself, to speak up against Trenton." I take another deep breath. "I'm trying to be better."

"It's okay," Taherah offers immediately. "I'm scared all the time." It's a kind and easy response, one that I expected. Taherah doesn't have a mean bone in her body, unless she's trying to catch a screen and shoot her shot.

Allyson rolls her eyes. "It's not your fault your family is full of assholes, Annie. Just talk to us next time."

I bark out a laugh. "Too true, thank you, Allyson." We're all laughing a little then, in relief.

That cuts off when Olabisi stands up. Her dark eyes meet mine, serious. "I'm sorry too, Annie. I should have believed you first. I should have considered your side. I'm sorry."

It's not a bleeding-heart apology. It's not wavering or tear-stained. But that's Olabisi. And if I want people to accept my watery eyes and stammered words, I have to accept her steely demeanor, her cutting gaze.

I walk over and give her a hug. She squeezes me hard, and I know she cares. The room hollers and applauds, and Olabisi flips them the bird as we pull apart.

I'm still grinning when Coach Rembert raises a brow at us all. "Are you ready to play now, Arrows?"

More cheering and Coach Rembert cracks a small smile. Coach Zak passes her a clipboard and whiteboard marker. "New York is a trickier match-up for us," she says honestly, uncapping the marker. "Sabrina Ionescu was MVP the year before Jadea. She's everything Jadea isn't: she's smaller, a better ball handler, and can shoot from everywhere. Annie, you'll have to handle her, and we'll put

Olabisi on Natasha Cloud." Coach Rembert shoots me a steely gaze, and I swallow. Sabrina is no joke, on and off the court. I've seen her in multiple commercials this year, including the coveted Nike spot. She's one of the league's biggest stars, and she *never* quits.

"On the flip side, they have two star centers, though Stewart is still hurt. Jonquel Jones is about the same height as you, Jadea. She's pretty quick for her size and has good touch around the basket. We need to keep the rebounds out of her hands. Natasha Cloud, Betnijah Laney, and Marine Johannes will also be in the mix. Ionescu and Johannes can shoot from anywhere, and Cloud can drive to the basket from anywhere, so defense will be tough tonight. Do not ease up."

Coach has named names before, especially during film. We played and won against the Liberty three times this season. They're a lower seed, and we *should* beat them. But our team's been off-kilter, and you can never count Sabrina Ionescu out. Or Jonquel Jones. Or Natasha Cloud.

You get the picture.

Coach stops scribbling plays and puts the whiteboard down. She sticks her hand out, and we follow suit, piling on top. Her gaze travels across each of us in turn. "This is our one shot, Arrows. We have one game left to prove our worth. If we lose this, there's no next game. No next round. It's one and done. Don't forget it."

I can feel the adrenaline pounding through my veins, making me almost dizzy with determination. I exchange fierce looks with Jadea. Coach nods at her. And Jadea, fully herself, shines as she shouts, "Arrows on three!"

"1...2...3...ARROWS!"

*

We warm-up, and it feels good. The ball swishes more than it rattles off the rim, and my lack of practice doesn't seem to be affecting me too negatively. I wave to my mom in the stands, sitting next to Jadea's mom as usual. I blow a kiss to Daniel, who is wearing my jersey and sitting courtside. No camera crew tonight, just him. He grins at me, full movie-star.

I notice that the owner's box looks empty tonight. No Jack or Trenton. There are rumors that the WNBA's investigation will be over soon, and the league will be considering possible punishments. That brings all the mixed feelings you'd expect, so I try to focus. Feel the ball between my fingers. Feel the space as I jump and shoot. Feel Jadea running on my right.

Warm-ups end and the crowd already feels electric. We're the higher seed, so we're fortunate to play at home. The crowd is a sea of scarlet, every seat full for once. If my strange press circuit brought any new fans here, I'm glad. We need all the help we can get. I see one sign that says, "Annie Cheater for Life!" and my heart skips a beat. I breathe through it and count three other signs that say, "Larger than Life". There's even one with an explosion of glitter on it, which I vow to hunt down later so I can take a picture with the owner. I don't have to be afraid to be called a cheater—because I'm not one.

Jadea and Jonquel Jones go up for the jump ball, and Jadea tips it my way. I don't even question it; I just sprint towards our basket. Jadea is fast, the fastest player out there, so she's usually out ahead enough to make our triple deceit play work. This time, though, I see out of the corner of my eye that Jadea has gotten tangled with Betnijah Laney. I have a split second to decide to pass the ball away or take my momentum and lay the ball up. Sabrina is a half-step behind me.

I'm hardly breathing when the ball kisses off the backboard. Swish.

2-0.

Jadea pushes off of Laney, grinning at me. Sabrina gets the ball, trying to slow down and control the tempo. We press her hard, jumping the passing lanes and keeping close. I'm only inches from Sabrina's face, arms and legs wide. Right before the shot clock is about to expire, thus turning the ball over to us, Sabrina passes it off to Johannes. We lose her in the shuffle, and she shoots a three as time expires.

Swish.

3-2.

The first half passes the same way. For every amazing shot we score, they score one better. We switch leads too many times to count. I foul Sabrina three times, which is too many for the first half. It only takes six to get me on the bench permanently. Surprisingly, Coach doesn't ream me out. "You're slowing her down, Larger," she says during a timeout as I guzzle water. "Just a little, but it's all we need."

Sabrina is fighting just as hard for her team as I am. The New York Liberty have been on the cusp of greatness for a couple of seasons now, but after winning a championship, they are officially a super team, even with one of their superstars cheering from the bench. I'm sure to Sabrina this is the opportunity she's been waiting for to win another championship. I understand her drive, but I have the same feeling pulsing through me. It's sort of a kinship we share—that we want to beat each other. We bang hips, slam shoulders, step into each other's space. It's a battle, and we're both snarling. I can feel the bruises forming already.

There's only a minute or so left in the first half when it happens. We're up by four points, a slim lead that we could easily lose. Everyone knows that momentum going into halftime is key, so I push Sabrina even harder. Nothing dirty, nothing painful, I just don't let her breathe. I wave my arms, I slap at the ball, I stay low until my thighs are screaming.

The shot clock is ticking dangerously, and Sabrina is stuck at the top of the key with me. She's swiveling, trying to find someone to pass to. Just as she does, Jonquel Jones moves up the right, and she swivels, and her elbow slams into my eye. It wasn't purposeful, but it was frantic. Strong.

The whistle blares, calling Sabrina for the foul. I stumble back a few steps, holding my eye. She caught the top of my brow bone, and the pain is splitting.

Jadea and my teammates hurry over. "Shit," I mumble, feeling the first trickles of blood running between my fingers. One drips onto my white jersey.

Olabisi calls over to the bench, and our trainer comes out with a towel. Head wounds bleed ridiculously, so I'm hoping it looks worse than it is. Her elbow couldn't give me a concussion, could it? Blood is trickling into my eye now, and our trainer, Mimi, presses down harder, shoving me into a bench chair.

"I'm fine." I wave away Coach's concern. "I can shoot free throws." Ionescu was called for the foul, and I intend to get those points.

Coach crosses her arms, or at least that's what it looks like through my good eye. "Larger, you've got blood running down your face. You can't even see the hoop."

I try to grab the towel, but Mimi slaps my hands away. "It will stop in a minute." I hope so, anyway.

Coach waves me away. "I'll have Olabisi shoot them. The refs can't expect you to do it. You need to go to the locker room to get checked for a concussion."

Before I can protest vehemently, Mimi and a few other staff members are leading me back into the locker room. My brow is pulsing, but I walk steadily. "I can't have a concussion, Mimi," I say desperately as she deposits me on the bench. "We still have another half to go."

Mimi narrows her eyes. "Basketball is not more important than your health."

It's hard to argue with that, though I'm tempted. How to explain that this game feels like life to me? I can hear the fans cheering through the last minute, but not at anything specific. The team tromps in eventually, and I almost stand up in the middle of Mimi's thorough examination.

Jadea heads my way immediately. "Are you okay?"

I nod, and the motion does twinge a bit. I hide the wince. "Mimi says it's worse than it looks, right, Mimi?" I try to give the trainer my best smile.

"Hmph," is all she says.

"What's the score?" I ask Jadea, like an addict who's going through withdrawal.

"We're up by two. As soon as you left, Ionescu went to work, scored two quick baskets. 59–57."

High-scoring game. We need to tighten up our defense, though theirs isn't doing much better.

Coach goes through our half piece by piece, laying into us just as much as she encourages us that the win is possible. We need to be more dynamic, play as quickly as we can. We need to get more steals, more possessions. I try to listen even as Mimi quizzes me.

Finally, Mimi says, "No concussion," switching out the bloody towel for a clean one. "But you should probably get stitches."

"Stitches?" If I get stitches, I won't be able to finish the second half. "What about a butterfly bandage?"

Mimi looks at my face, perhaps weighing my eagerness with my general safety. "Maybe. But if you get hit again, the thing will just bleed and bleed."

I nod excitedly. "I promise I'll be careful!"

Mimi shakes her head at me but ultimately pinches the wound together with two butterfly bandages. It hurts, pulsing too much, but it's bearable. I hope things don't get too messy.

Coach finishes up her message when I emerge from the bathroom, most of the blood cleaned off me. My face was easy enough, but my jersey still sports a few spots. Luckily, I have another I can change into, as players can't play with blood on their clothes. When we head back out to the court, I hear some people shout my name and then cheer when it's clear I'll be playing in the second half. Daniel mouths, "OK?"

I smile and give him a thumbs-up.

The second half is just as brutal, though I manage not to bleed on anyone. It's like New York didn't even need the fifteen-minute rest. If we're playing fast, they're playing even faster. Sabrina is trying to drive to the basket every few plays, and my lungs and cut ache from chasing her down. Jonquel Jones is on fire in the second half, and her extremely long reach snatches up offensive rebound after offensive rebound. They're beating us in the paint, something that should be impossible with the Jadea Jones dunk show.

We keep up well enough, with Taherah's threes, Olabisi's sneaky jumpers, and a few Jadea dunks. I only have eight points, but I also have eight assists. I've hardly sat for more than a few minutes, focused on stalling Sabrina's play.

As we hit the final three minutes of the game, New York is up six points, 108–102. I'm reaching for the ball, thinking I can take it from Sabrina, a clean strip, but at the last second, she whirls, and my outstretched hand smacks her arm. The whistle blows, and I mentally count my fouls. This is my fifth. One more and I'm riding the bench.

I'm practically vibrating with nerves as Ionescu shoots her flawless free throws. 110–102. We need a score here to keep the pressure on. My thoughts are racing, trying to think of something unexpected. Just as Jadea turns to jog down the court, waiting for me to dribble it her way, I catch her eye.

You. I tell her. *I'm going to you.*

She nods once, grim. Her 21 points are probably frustrating her. She'll argue she needs 40.

Then, instead of dribbling it calmly and surveying the court, as a good point guard should, I just run. I sprint down the court, face throbbing, and look only at the basket. I run right past Sabrina, who is surprised by my reckless play. It looks like I'm going to shove myself into the lane, that I'm scared we're about to lose this game.

Instead, it's a misdirect.

Just as I'm inches from the basket, pushing my way through New York defenders, I stop. Full tilt. Ionescu is on my tail, and Betnijah Laney is rushing over to my side, trying to help. Everyone is crashing the lane, right under the basket.

In the commotion, Jadea, who hardly ever shoots from outside the three-point line, has snuck to the corner. Without looking her way, I flick the pass overhead. I can almost imagine everyone's head turning, shocked Jadea ventured out so far. She doesn't need a good three-point shot; she can *fly*.

Jadea only shoots from three when she has to.

But she never misses.

The ball swishes through, and I swear the crowd is stomping their feet. 110–105 with 1:50 left in the game.

New York tries to push us around on offense, but we push back. I slow Sabrina at the top of the key, and she gives it away. Lynn jumps into the lane and steals the pass, running back down the court for an easy lay-up. The crowd loves the veteran presence, and Lynn raises her hands up, egging them on.

110–107.

1:34 left in the game.

New York isn't a quitter and when they bring it back down, they run a multiple screen play under the basket. Our defense gets lost in the shuffle, and Jonquel Jones catches and shoots an easy two a few feet from the basket.

112–107.

1:17 left in the game.

Coach decides to put Taherah in with me, even though she's typically my backup. It's a wise choice, because her fresh legs and excellent form provide us with an easy three from the top of the key.

112–110.

0:50 left in the game.

Coach calls a timeout, and everything in me is buzzing. When I look at the beloved faces of my teammates, I know they feel the same way. This is our chance.

Our moment. We just have to take it.

Coach remains as grim-faced as usual. "Annie, you need to stay up on Ionescu, but if you foul her, you're out. Be careful. Nothing sloppy, Arrows."

I catch Coach Rembert's eye. "We can do it, Coach. We can get you all the way to the Championship." I don't know why I say it, but Coach Rembert looks like she needs it. And I believe it, I really do.

The next two possessions, one for us and one for New York, are a bust. After a lot of passing, Allyson fumbles one, and it bounces out of bounds. New York goes back the other way but has a shot clock violation.

Still 112–110, New York with the lead.

0:19 seconds left.

We run a screen, trying to get Taherah open. She's hot, and a three would be deadly to New York. Instead, she gets a bad look and the ball rebounds long off the rim. The able hands of Jonquel Jones grab it, passing it off to Sabrina.

My teammates and I race to get back on defense. We're quick enough that Sabrina is forced to slow down, to hesitate at the top of the key. The clock is winding down. What should I do? If I foul her, she'll shoot free throws, and we'll really be dead in the water. But if I ease up, she might score anyway.

0:08 seconds left.

Thankfully, New York looks just as confused, and their coach, Sandy Brondello, calls a timeout.

Coach Rembert opens her mouth, but Jadea beats her to it. "Annie, you have to steal the ball."

I rear back, surprised. "I haven't stolen it off Ionescu all night."

Jadea's face is scary intense. "Don't foul her, or you'll foul out and she'll make her free throws. You just need to steal the ball and go."

Coach Rembert huffs. "Jadea, that's a risky plan. We'll intentionally foul Sabrina, and it makes sense for Annie to do it. There are only eight seconds left. We have to hope that Sabrina only makes one of her free throws and we'll have a chance at a three-point shot."

Coach is right. That's the safe plan. But it also has a slim chance of success. We only have eight seconds left, and New York would happily whittle that away and win by two. They'll know the intentional foul is coming. And Sabrina has been a flawless eight out of eight at the free throw line. She could waste five seconds and make both free throws, leaving us an impossible four points behind.

The whistle blows, and I stare at the eight seconds on the clock with growing dread. Safe or risky? What's the right call?

Johannes stands on the sideline, preparing to throw in the ball. Ionescu is already looking at me suspiciously, ready to evade my intentional foul. Everything fades away as Johannes throws it in. Sabrina makes a sweeping arc, trying to run right into the pass and evade me on the way. She catches the ball, turning back to face the basket. I plant myself right in her way. She slows down, dribbling the ball back on her right hip.

The clock ticks and ticks behind me.

I reach in, and I don't even know what I'm going for, the intentional foul or the steal. It doesn't matter because my fingers graze the ball. Sabrina's grasp on it loosens just a touch, her dribble unsteady, and I see my chance. Praying I don't foul, I lunge for the ball, and I time it perfectly. The ball bounces right into my hands, without me even touching Sabrina.

I'm out in the free court, running towards our basket. The time must be close to expiring. Every step feels heavy; I'm slow.

Through the buzzing in my ears, I swear I hear, "RUN!" From Jadea, of course. The crowd is screaming. There's a flash of Daniel saying to me in the locker room, "Lightning in a bottle."

Sabrina is only a step behind me. She's trying to run around me, to block my path cleanly. She wants me to shoot free throws, to not even get close to the basket. I slam into her, pain blossoming above my eyebrow. I just manage to toss the ball up.

We crash down together, huddled under the basket, a tangle of limbs. I watch my ill-timed shot hit high on the glass and rattle the front rim. Bounce to the back.

And then, swish right through. The clock buzzer roars.

0:00 seconds left.

The crowd is shouting, and there are whistles from the officials. Foul on Sabrina; she didn't get set enough for a charge. She threw herself in front of me, thinking the shot would never go in. But it did.

I can't believe it.

112–112. Tie game.

As Jadea helps me up, I notice she doesn't look as happy as I expect. That's when I notice my face is wet, and for once, it's not tears. Blood, blood everywhere. Sabrina's desperate attempt split the wound back open. I hurry over to the free throw line, before the blood gets out of control. I'm surprised they haven't dragged me to the sideline already.

The ball feels perfect in my hands, despite my sticky face and sweat-soaked uniform. A very small part of me wishes it was Jadea up here, Jadea shooting the game-winning shot, Jadea taking the risk.

Then—she grins at me from across the lane. I look over at the sideline, and there's Daniel, his competition face on. He looks aglow with victory, as though I've already won it. I glance up, and there are the moms, throwing their pom-poms and worriedly gesturing to my face.

I turn to the basket. Dribble. Dribble. Breathe.

It rattles, but it makes it. I make it.

113–112.

The explosion of love from the crowd is the best sound I've ever heard. My girls run over, jumping on me and screaming. I'm crying now too, tears mixing with the blood. Jadea whips off her jersey, presses it to my cut, proudly showing off her six-pack abs and sports bra.

"We did it." I'm bawling and smiling at Jadea. "After everything."

Jadea bares her teeth. "On to the next."

It's a stark reminder that this journey isn't over. This was the first obstacle of many, and yet it feels important. It feels like I'm so close to being who I want to be. Sometimes a sidekick, sometimes a hero. That's life.

When Holly Rowe sticks the microphone out to me, I'm crying and holding Jadea's crumpled jersey to my forehead.

"That was incredible, Annie. How does it feel?" Holly gushes, and she seems genuinely excited to hear what I have to say.

I'm still not one for speeches, but I manage to gasp out, "This wouldn't have been possible without all the incredible women in the league. Sabrina Ionescu challenging me. My teammates supporting me. Jadea boosting me up. My mom growing with me. And Daniel for loving me. I'm lucky. So lucky."

The words are a broken mess, but Holly seems to understand. "And what about the scandal? You've finally opened up about it recently. Is there anything you'd like to add?"

I laugh a little. "Honestly, now isn't the time. This is for St. Louis. For our fans!" The crowd cheers. "I want to put the scandal behind me, but before I can, I have one last thing to say. Watch *Our World Through Sports* this Sunday. I promise you won't be disappointed."

Afterwards, I turn and run into Daniel's arms. I'm clutching his—actually *my*—jersey, and laughing into his neck as he swings me around and then worriedly cups my face. "You okay?" He lifts Jadea's wadded jersey up a bit, glancing at the cut. "It's definitely a bleeder. But it shouldn't need more than a few stitches."

He sounds relieved. I laugh again, giddy. "I can't even feel it." Too much adrenaline, too much joy.

Sabrina comes over, trying not to interrupt. She looks her usual fierce, MVP self, but also a bit nervous. It takes me a minute to remember that she accidentally caused my bleeder.

Before she can say anything, I blurt out, "That was the best game ever, don't you think?"

It's a ridiculous thing to say, because she lost. Her team lost. I try to backtrack and feel Daniel stifling a laugh behind me, but I'm surprised to see Sabrina crack a small smile. "Sorry about the elbow, Larger. I promise it wasn't intentional."

It might be the adrenaline, or the joy, but it goes to my head a little. I grin at Sabrina Ionescu and say, "This was a battle, Ionescu. We all have a few war wounds."

Sabrina laughs at that, and we hug briefly before she leaves to commiserate with her teammates. The moment of this win is about to slip through my fingertips, so I raise up Jadea's jersey to the crowd and hear them roar one more time.

One moment of bravery down, one to go.

Chapter 23

My father and I meet in the green room of HBO's New York studio. The Arrows have a few days off until our next playoff series against the Fever, so our Sunday meeting seemed wise.

Now, I wonder if I've made a huge mistake.

I feel like I've just grabbed the power back, speaking against Trenton and his lies. It was easy to decide how I should feel about him; he was doing terrible things to me and my team.

Jack feels different.

He also did terrible things. His WNBA investigation wrapped up two days ago. He officially has to turn over team management to the minority owners and sell his stake in the team. He and Trenton must step down from day-to-day management and will incur massive fines. It's a disaster for my biological family, but how exactly should I feel about it?

I've never even met Jack before. Besides the few times he tried to call after the scandal, and was seemingly blocked by Trenton, I've never talked to him. He might have drafted me with fatherly intentions, but he's not my father. It's difficult to confront something when you don't know exactly how to feel. I believe the WNBA punished him appropriately, but how to go forward with our relationship? Will we ever be father and daughter? Can he make up for the mistakes he made?

I have a few ideas, and now is the time to be brave. Again.

Why does bravery involve so much talking?

Daniel is prepping for the show in his dressing room, but I have my phone clutched in my hand, ready to text him 911 if needed. I'm sure he's on standby. I talked through my tentative plan with him, Jadea, and my mom. They all approved of it, and hopefully we'll be able to announce all the changes on Daniel's show today.

Another reason to be nervous. Me, on live television?

When Jack and his wife Tiffany enter the room, ushered in by a frazzled-looking PA, they look exactly as I remember. Tiffany is a bright blonde that is clearly fake but well-maintained. She has a few wrinkles that show her lovely smile lines and the startling blue eyes that Trenton shares. Jack is a little older, in his mid-seventies, but in great health. His white hair is neatly trimmed, and his hazel eyes are shrewd. They both sport Arrows' scarlet red. I don't know if it's calculated or not.

I nervously wipe my sweaty palms on my pants and stand up to greet them. Daniel assured me that I should dress however I wanted for the show, that just because he wore a suit, didn't mean I had to. However, I was inspired by his look and am wearing a long red blazer with matching wide-legged dress pants and studded black boots with a three-inch heel.

It gives me a strange sort of pleasure to see I have a few inches on Jack when I shake his and Tiffany's hands.

We all sit down, me in an armchair, them on the couch across from me.

It's clear that Jack expects to run this meeting, even though I'm the one who called it.

"Annie." He sounds extremely warm, shooting me a smile. "I'm so delighted to finally meet you. I know it's not under the best circumstances, but I intend to start fresh—"

I can't say I'm surprised. He sounds like a politician or anyone with lots of media training, not like a doting father. I cut him off. "Jack and Tiffany, I don't know if it's nice to meet you." I let those words fall heavily between us. Jack shuts up immediately, but Tiffany almost looks curious. "But it *is* necessary. I've been putting this meeting off as long as possible, and obviously, you know your son has been blocking a lot of our communications."

Jack immediately jumps in. "Yes, and I have been talking more with Trenton, and he's truly sorry—"

Tiffany shoots him a look. "What Jack means to say is that *we're* truly sorry. Trenton was terrible to you and blamed you for Jack's mistakes. You're a victim in this story, and I'm sorry many people have taken his mistakes out on you." There's a hint of viciousness in Tiffany's words that I appreciate. Maybe she hasn't totally forgiven her son and husband for everything they've done.

"Thank you." I smooth my pants nervously. "I don't agree with what you did, Jack. It was wrong. You put me in an impossible position, one I will have to grapple with for all my years in the league."

Jack opens his mouth, but I hold up a finger, and he relents. "But today, I have an idea for how we can change things for the better. It won't fix the damage you've done, but it will be a sign of faith in women's sports. And that's really important to me."

I lay out my idea, the financial schematics, which have already been checked by the other minority owners and team accountants, and explain what I need from the two of them. I show Jack the paperwork he would need to sign. It feels like a parallel universe, the memory of me signing damning documents from Trenton flashing through my mind.

Jack protests immediately. "Now, Annie, I know I've made mistakes, but they were all for you. I was trying to connect with you. Money won't solve any of those mistakes."

I raise a brow. "Spoken like a true-blue billionaire. This money is important. It's symbolic. It's equalizing. And you don't need it. Billionaires shouldn't even exist."

Jack looks nonplussed at my statement, and he reminds me a little too much of Trenton. On the other hand, Tiffany nods along at my words. Jack tries a new tactic. "We can be a family, Annie. I can give that money to you. You can inherit, be a true Smith." He leans forward, almost reaches to clasp my hand, but I inch mine away from him.

It's a strange epiphany, staring at my birth father. I know the journey isn't the same for everyone. Sometimes, meeting your biological father feels like a homecoming. Like a puzzle piece that fits. But, right now, I just feel like Jack is a stranger. He's someone I don't understand, and I don't really want to understand. I have everyone I need already. Just because we share DNA doesn't mean I have to make him *my dad*. Maybe what he did, demanding I be drafted and bribing reporters to bring me attention, maybe that was done with something akin to love or affection or misguided loyalty. And so, I'm not furious. I don't hate him.

But I don't really like him.

I sigh a little. "Jack." I try to infuse some kindness into the words. "I can't be the daughter you want. I'm never going to be a Smith. I'm already a Larger and a WNBA All-Star. I don't want your life." His brow wrinkles. "But you gave me the Arrows. You love St. Louis, just like I do. And for that, I'll always be grateful."

Jack smiles a little at that. The one thing we have in common. He looks back at the papers I gave him. His expression eases, and he says, "Do you have a pen?"

I hand him one and hope he doesn't notice my hand shaking. I can't believe he's agreed to it. This wouldn't work without his permission, sad as that may be. He signs, and we shake hands again. "Goodbye, Annie. If you don't mind, could we meet every few months to catch up?"

It's the first genuine thing he's said to me. "Fine," I relent, smiling a little. "We can give it a try."

He waves goodbye and immediately backs out of the room, already on the phone with one of his many lawyers. I straighten my suit, feeling the adrenaline leave my body. It's so strange to talk to my father and keep it impersonal. But it would be even stranger to pretend he's something he's not.

It only takes me a few beats to realize Tiffany is awkwardly hovering by the door. I clear my throat. "Yes?"

She takes a few steps back in the room. "Jack would prefer I not say this, but he and I are getting a divorce." My mouth must drop open, because she laughs bitterly. "It's been a long time coming. We separate every few years, then get back together because we don't want to deal with the trouble of divorcing. Well, after this whole debacle, I couldn't ignore how toxic my family has become. Unlike Jack and Trenton, I genuinely hope we can change."

I finally stutter out a response. "That's great. I hope you get everything you want."

There's another awkward pause. Tiffany looks unsure and strangely vulnerable. Should I say more? Does she want comfort? Before I can uncomfortably launch into a pep talk, Tiffany takes it in another direction. "We don't have a prenup, you know? I'm about to become one of the richest women in the world."

Even more surprises. "Congratulations?"

She laughs again, this time with more sincerity. "I'm only saying this because I genuinely love the Arrows. It's my favorite investment Jack's ever made. Those games are home to me. The arena is my favorite place. I know every play, every draft pick. I have a business degree." I'm trying to follow but failing. She senses it. "In college, I was on a D1 volleyball team. We were really good, and our stadium was packed. It felt like my life was volleyball, that's how much I loved it. But after five years of college, I got my master's degree, and then I was done. Volleyball doesn't have a professional league, despite its popularity as a college sport. This could be a homecoming of sorts. I want women's sports to grow, and I think I can help it along," she shifts uncomfortably, "with the Arrows. After my divorce, I want to put in a bid for majority ownership."

"Whoa." Tiffany suddenly appears to me in a new light. I don't know her well enough to say whether she'd be perfect, but I do remember that picture of Trenton reading Ayn Rand at a playoff game. Who was screaming and watching every second of the game? Tiffany. It might just work. "I have no authority over any part of that, but it would be great to have a true believer on our side." I smile at her and she grins back, relief showing on her face.

"I wanted to ask you first, to see if it made you uncomfortable. I wouldn't want you to think I was pushing into your life." It's a courteous attitude and one I wish her son and husband would employ.

There's a lump in my throat, and I swallow thickly. "Thanks, Tiffany. I hope things work out for you and your family." I mean it, even as I hate Trenton's games and Jack's arrogance. Tiffany's life was blown apart by this too. I want her to survive the damage, just like I have.

She nods and waves goodbye.

Only a few minutes later, there's a knock on my door. Daniel pokes his head in. "How'd it go? Are you crying?"

He waves a travel tissue pack, and I laugh. "No tears today, I promise."

He steps fully into the room, handsome in his navy suit and sexy glasses. "So, did you convince Jack? Are you going to be on the show?"

I nod and he fist pumps like a dork. I laugh and walk his way, winding my arms around his neck. "This is the finish line. Soon our lives will be normal again. Can you believe it?" Sometimes, staring up into his face, it all feels like a dream. Do I really get to keep it all? His love, the ghost of his fingers on my waist, the sweat dripping down my temple as I shoot the winning shot, is it all mine? It doesn't seem possible.

Daniel grows serious, looking at me thoughtfully. He reaches a finger to my cheek, tracing the bone and down my chin. I stifle a shiver. "Larger than life," he whispers and it feels like our version of *I love you*.

The moment is heavy with love and joy and everything deliciously gooey and it's the same PA that ushered Jack and Tiffany in who interrupts us. "Five minutes, Daniel." He shoots us a knowing look and closes the door again.

Daniel gives me a quick, scorching kiss and then backs away. "Show time." He must see the fear on my face because he says, "You don't have to do this if you don't want to, Annie."

Daniel understands debilitating anxiety because he's experienced it. He knows that sometimes you can't force yourself to feel better. But I know this isn't the same. If I tried to be a whole new person, someone who put herself out there all the time and was loud and enjoyed the spotlight—that wouldn't work. But this, this is a ten-minute segment talking about basketball and the scandal. This is well within my grasp.

"Show time," I say firmly, and he smiles. "And before you go, I have a gift for you."

He raises a brow. "A gift?"

I hurry over to the side table, pulling two shoe boxes from underneath. "I saw when we were at Fire Town that you still had those ratty Converse that I doodled on. I figured we deserved an upgrade."

I hand him his box first, carefully watching his face as he opens it. "Annie," he says with wonder, pulling out the first shoe. They're still high-tops, but the canvas is white. He pulls out the second one, his fingers tracing over the numerous doodles I've drawn onto them.

His fingers graze the Olympic rings. The St. Louis arch. A small caricature of his terrier, Dustin. A stethoscope for his mom's job as a doctor and a book for his father's job as a professor. Stanford's logo. A ballet slipper. A glow stick. The Arrows logo. LGL—larger than life—made of a font that looks like lightning bolts.

And lastly, on the heel, the original basketball and Daniel's track cleat.

He doesn't say anything, still turning the shoes round and round. I clear my throat nervously. "I know it's small, but I just wanted to show you how much you mean to me. You've done so much for me—"

Daniel cuts me off, finally looking up at me. I'm surprised to see his eyes are a little glassy. "They're perfect, Annie. You're perfect." And then he tears off his dress shoes in a frenzy, pulling on the sneakers.

"What are you doing?" I gesture wildly, trying to get his attention. "They don't go with your suit!"

He looks up at me, in the process of lacing them. "Of course they do. Do you have a pair too?"

I'm secretly delighted at this outcome. I pull mine out of the box. "They're the exact same, except they're—

"Pink." He smiles. "You have to wear yours, too."

Before I can answer, the same PA sticks their head in the room. "One minute, Daniel." This time, the look he levels at us is less endearing and more severe.

Daniel starts backing towards the door. Then he changes his mind, clutching me close and kissing the breath out of me. "Show time!" he says breathlessly, backing towards the door. He winks. "See you out there." He leaves, heading to his desk on stage. I smile when I hear the audience start clapping for him. He'll go through the first forty-five minutes of the show without me and then my interview will be at the end.

I immediately put on the pink Converse. Even if they weren't exactly what I envisioned with this outfit, they might bring me luck. Daniel and I are in a good place, and hopefully, with today's interview, the scandal will finally be resolved.

I look at the papers Jack signed, tucked partway into my purse. I breathe in deeply through my nose, trying to calm my fluttering heart. This is it, one small change that I can enact for good.

I hope.

*

When Daniel announces my name, it feels like I'm walking through a soundless tunnel, not out onto a stage. There are bright lights, my mic pack pressed against my spine, and an intimate studio audience. I wave and try to smile genuinely, which becomes easier when I notice Jadea and my mom cheering for me. I almost laugh out loud when I see they're both holding the scarlet and white pompoms usually reserved for games. Jadea and I hop on a plane as soon as the show's over so we can attend practice tomorrow morning in St. Louis. My mom wanted to come to the show too, but decided it was best to avoid Jack and sit with Jadea in the audience.

I'm so glad they're both here.

When I sit down at Daniel's desk, across from him, I feel his toe gently nudge mine. A reminder that he's in this, too. I relax a little and smile at him. "Hi, Annie." He greets me warmly, as if we're strangers, which makes the audience laugh. He turns to them a bit, mock outraged. "What's with the laughter? How else should I greet her?"

This prompts more laughter, then even more when I roll my eyes at his antics. "Daniel." His name is twisted by affection and exasperation. "Thanks for having me."

Daniel grins at me again. "It's hard to say no to you, Annie Larger. But, on to business. This is not your first official interview this week—you've actually broken your silence on your father's scandal several times already. Why the sudden change in strategy?"

This is a rehearsed question; they all are. I take a deep breath to settle my nerves and remember what we practiced. "Well, I've never liked interviews. Or speaking in public. Honestly, I'd rather do anything else." Daniel acts

296

affronted, and the crowd eats it up. I soften a little, appreciating that he's trying to make me feel comfortable. "Sorry, honey, but that's the truth." I refocus and even dart a look at the audience, which is almost impossible to make out with the lights. I spot a few curious expressions. "But, after the scandal and Trenton's false accusations, I realized that I needed to be brave and confront my problems head-on."

This prompts a small smattering of applause, and I duck my head. Daniel is looking at me proudly. "I imagine that must have been a difficult decision. So, this leads into my next question—why *Our World Through Sports*? You've already cleared your name and told your side of the story, most memorably on ESPN's *The Jump*."

Another rehearsed question and a segway that Daniel handles deftly. "First, it's because this show is important to me. I trust you." Not exactly the answer we rehearsed, but it needs to be said. The audience claps a little, and I blush. Daniel is looking at me like he's in love with me, and everyone is noticing. Before I jump over the desk and start making out with him, I regroup. "Second, I have an announcement for WNBA fans. Even though I was not involved in any of Jack's decisions, I did benefit from them. I made it into an extremely competitive league, and I achieved my childhood dream. That might have happened without Jack's interference—but we'll never know."

There are some murmurs from the audience, and I hope they appreciate my candor. There's no good hiding the truth. I can see Jadea nodding along in encouragement. "My biological father and brother are being forced out of ownership. They also face other consequences from the league. They won't touch the Arrows anymore." This prompts a giant whoop that sounds suspiciously like it comes from Jadea and surer applause from the audience. I take a little bravery from them and finish with the big secret that Jack just signed off on. "Jack was willing to give me a large inheritance as his newly legitimate daughter, but it didn't feel right to take it because I'm not a part of his family. That's not my life. My future." I fold and unfold my hands nervously. "So, after talking with him and Tiffany, we have agreed that each year the Smith Family will sponsor an in-season WNBA tournament intended to bridge the gap in pay disparity between male and female athletes. Besides the traditional playoffs, teams will also have a tournament partway through the season with a ten-million-dollar prize."

There's a gasp from the audience, and my heart is pounding so loud in my ears. I force myself to keep going, hoping no one can hear the nervous shaking in my voice. "The winning team will receive a six-million-dollar prize to be split between players and staff. The second place team will receive two million and the remaining seeds will have a tiered system of cash prizes as well." The room is silent now, listening to my plan. "This tournament will begin next year and has already been approved by the necessary WNBA stakeholders. While I know this does not make up for what has happened, I hope that this shows how much I believe in this league. In women's sports. I hope this shows you that I do not take living my dream for granted. That, in fact, none of the women in this league do."

There's a cheer from the audience, and I smile in relief. That was it. That was the main speech I had to make, and I got through it without stuttering, tearing up, or crawling under the desk. There are gaps in it, places I maybe should expand or questions left unanswered, but I made it. I spoke on live television and took one step towards fixing the many errors the Smith family has made.

Daniel is looking at me, and when our gazes meet, I can't help but sit up straighter. Everything is a little easier when you let love in. "Annie, this plan sounds wonderful. I hope it's everything you imagined."

"Me too," I agree. "I hope it's a domino effect. Women and LGBTQ+ athletes are frequently mistreated in the realm of sports. I hope this tiny, small, minuscule gesture shows we deserve to be taken seriously."

"I think it does." Daniel nods seriously. "And I think our audience does, too."

I look out at them and see them on their feet. I do the only thing I can think of, the only thing I know to get a crowd excited. "Let's go, Arrows!" I stand up from the desk and pump my fist. "Watch our next playoff game on Tuesday!"

The crowd cheers louder, and I hear Daniel laughing behind me.

"Well, folks, that seems like a perfect ending to another episode of *Our World Through Sports*. I'm Daniel Chan, and that's my fantastic girlfriend, Annie Larger. Good night!"

I blow him a kiss.

Sports give us something, no matter how small. I hope people watch our game this coming week.

And I hope we win.

Epilogue

About a year later...

I haven't seen Daniel in nearly ten days, largely due to our crazy schedules when I'm in season. The buzzer has just rung on our most recent regular season game, a win against the Atlanta Dream. After celebrating quickly with my teammates, I scan the crowd for Daniel. He was supposed to be here for the game, but I know he had some important meetings in New York this morning.

I have exciting news to share with him.

In the off season, Daniel and I settled into a routine. We basically moved into each other's apartments, splitting our time between St. Louis and New York. We try not to spend more than two weeks apart at a time, but it's not easy. Fortunately, the rest of our relationship is. His show is thriving, particularly since his vulnerable piece about mental health in sports went viral earlier this summer. He had other athletes on the show and shared his own experience after his accident. I had never seen him more obsessive over a piece before, but it came out beautifully. And he says he feels lighter since its premiere.

Jadea led the Arrows to an incredible Championship win last year. We almost couldn't make it past the Indiana Fever, but the series was thrilling in hindsight. We played the Las Vegas Aces for the championship and won in four games. We gifted Coach Rembert her new varsity jacket patch, and Jadea won Finals MVP. It ended up being a perfect season.

This year, the first annual Smith Tournament began. It wasn't without some difficulties, but between Tiffany and me, we made it happen. She isn't a majority owner yet, as she's still working through what's turned into a nasty divorce, but we've grown closer, and she's been consistently helpful. Jack, however, is not so consistent. I've kept my promise to meet with him occasionally for an update, but he forgets sometimes and isn't the best listener. At least he's trying.

I finally spot Daniel in the crowd, trying to work his way down to the court. It still gives me butterflies when I see him, even more so when he's in my jersey. Security lets him onto the court, and I run his way. He's surprised when I barrel into him, letting out a soft grunt. I give him a sweet kiss. "Hi." I smile at him.

"Hi." He smiles back. "I have news."

I'm practically vibrating with excitement. "Me too!"

At the exact same time, we say, "I'm going to the Olympics!"

"What?" We say again at the same time.

I shush him. "What do you mean you're going? To cover it?"

Daniel nods excitedly, his smile unfurling again as though against its will. "Yes! I pitched my idea about covering the Olympics from a geopolitical angle, and the producers loved it. We're going to be there the full two weeks!"

"That's amazing! It's your *dream*." I'm getting a little misty-eyed at his journey's conclusion, and Daniel notices immediately.

"It's alright, Annie. I'm excited to go in any capacity, but I'm especially proud to be bringing a new angle to the Olympics." He grips my arms then, suddenly remembering that we had the same news. "But what about you? They called?"

The summer Olympics happen in about a month, and there's been lots of speculation about who will be invited to be on this year's women's basketball team. Jadea was a shoo-in, as were many other superstars, while I was more a fringe member of the discussions. But I got the call this morning. If I accept, the official roster will be announced next week. Jadea and I screamed and screamed when we both got the calls.

Our first Olympics. Together. More dreams coming true.

"They called," I confirm. "And now we're all going to be together. Are your parents excited?"

"They already told me they're coming." He grins. "The whole big Larger-Chan clan. And Jadea and her mom, of course. It's going to be incredible."

The court is clearing out, and I grab his hand, tugging him so we can walk off. "Can you believe it? That we'll be together all these years later, achieving our Olympic dreams?" I wonder. "After how things went at Stanford? After we awkwardly met for the first time at that frat party?"

Daniel ponders the questions, swinging our hands between us. "I don't know about the party. But that game I saw you play—that 'lightning in a bottle' moment—that seemed like a good sign."

"There were lots of good signs," I agree. I remember all the times we pushed each other, him about the scandal and me about his piece on the accident. We weren't made for each other exactly. But we do bring out the best in each other.

We walk into the tunnel together, hands clasped.

Larger than Life. That's how it feels, even now.

Acknowledgements

Every writer (or athlete) needs an amazing team supporting them. Luckily for me, I had the very best team with me as I worked on *A Shot at Love*.

My parents are like the steady, helpful veterans on the team. They're so used to giving advice and inspiration, they do it without asking. Whenever I doubted myself or worried about this story, they were there to back me up. You can ask anyone, I've always been someone who listens to their parents. And that's been true during this writing journey, too. Thank you for being there through all the ups and downs. I couldn't have done this without you.

My two siblings are the bright, young rookies on the team. They might not have enough writing expertise to tell me how to fix a scene I'm struggling with, but they ultimately help me fix it myself by being positive and making me laugh. My sister, Zoe, is the person I spend the most time with, my built-in bestie. She loves romance novels, and I knew this book was ready to be published once I heard her gushing over it. My brother, Zack, loves the WNBA and is a proud feminist. He gave me some amazing tips about basketball and shared his own experience as an athlete. I'm so lucky to have you both in my corner.

Thank you to my grandparents, who asked about my writing every time I saw them. Thank you to my Aunt Mimi, for showing me what hard work can reap. Thank you to all my aunts, uncles, and cousins for creating a family environment where I felt like my dream could become a reality. No one ever doubted that it would happen, and I cannot tell you what confidence that gave me.

Thank you to Kris VanLoon, Dawn Bergland, and Kailey Moore. You are proof that having amazing girlfriends can change your life for the better. There are no better listeners in the world than you three. Thank you to my friends Tina, Marisa, Lauren B., Lauren K., Simi, Alexis, and Shana for never letting me quit and always being my cheerleaders.

Outside of writing, my other dream has always been to be a teacher. I'm delighted that that dream can live alongside my writing. Thank you to my coworkers who were pleasantly surprised when I said I was publishing my novel and then relentlessly excited every step along the way. I also want to shout out the teachers (basically my writing coaches!) who encouraged me to pursue my writing dreams. Keisha Rembert, Gillian Schneider, Kate Trtan, and Michael Rossi, I'm sorry you had to read so much of my writing during the early days. I hope I've improved!

My cover artist, Jessica Lynn (@jessicalynndraws), absolutely blew me away with her work and her amazing spirit. Thank you, Jessica, for helping bring Annie and Daniel to life. To my editor, Laura, you went above and beyond the call. I'm so glad there are people like you out there, trying to help us young indie authors succeed.

And most of all, thank you to my readers. Whether you know me in real life, know me through social media, or just happened to pick up this book randomly—thank you. I hope this book made you fall in love with fierce women athletes, soft, supportive love interests, and the WNBA.

Let's go, Chicago Sky!

Want to follow along with Taylor LaVonne for more? More updates? More books? More about the Women in Sports series? Join her monthly newsletter using the QR Code below!

Did Annie and Daniel's journey touch your heart? Let other readers know using the QR Code below! Reviews like yours help other readers discover these stories and find new fans for Women in Sports.